THE GUARDIANS OF EVERNOW

BOOK FOUR - THE KINGDOMS OF EVERNOW

HEIDI CATHERINE

SEQUEL HOUSE

For my father - my fiercest protector

BEFORE THE EVERNOW

"*Next! Step up. Next! Next! Next! Step up.*"

The women shuffled forward, their pace slow and measured, their heads held high. The navy tunics they wore had been neatly pressed and their blonde hair pulled back into braids, making them look like mirror-images of each other. As each woman reached the front of the line, she paused and waited for the King to make his assessment, aware he was selecting which of them would carry his bloodline into the future.

It would be an honor to be asked to step up. A privilege to make his shortlist. This group had been chosen for their purity and youth, but only a handful would make it to the next stage. And only one would make it to the end. But they were all grateful to have been given the chance.

For these were no ordinary women. These women were Guardians, protectors of the kingdom of The Bay of Laurel, bred for strength and trained to fight. Their bodies were lined with muscle, and their hearts coated with courage. The Guardians' duty was to their King. There could be no greater purpose than serving him. All the generations of Guardians before them felt the same, male and female alike.

However, they'd never been asked to step up in this way before.

There was one Guardian waiting patiently in line who was different from the others. She wasn't different on the outside, though. She walked in step with the rest, doing what they did, dressing as they dressed and saying what they said. She was the same impressive height as the others, had the same muscular build, and the same blue eyes and fair skin. Just like every one of these Guardians, she took her tonics as instructed, performed her daily exercises, and prepared to pair with a male Guardian to ensure the next generation was stronger and more courageous than ever before.

In fact, so similar was this Guardian on the outside that she didn't even know she was different. But there was no question about it. For this Guardian was destined to alter the course of the Kingdom. This Guardian was no ordinary Guardian at all.

"Next! Next! Next!" Small particles of roast potato mingling with saliva flew from the King's mouth as he shouted. This was a leader who liked to sample the produce of his kingdom and was rarely seen without a fork gripped tightly in his pudgy fingers, almost like it was a scepter.

The Guardian reached the front of the line and lowered her gaze so as not to make eye contact with the King unless asked to do so.

"Step up."

Her heart swelled to have made the shortlist.

"Ne—" The King set down his fork and wiped his mouth with the back of his hand. "No, wait. The last one. Step back."

She stepped back, disappointed at being returned to the pack of Guardians, but determined not to show it.

"No, not back to the pack," the King said. "Back here."

She stood in front of her master and waited.

"Look at me," he instructed.

Trying not to focus on the enormity of the King's girth, she locked eyes with him, feeling her life change with each moment that passed.

"Untie your hair," he instructed.

She pulled the tie from her glossy hair and let it fall across her shoulders, the blonde waves shimmering like moonlight.

"Yes! This one. Send the rest away."

She steadied her breathing and waited. She may not be able to see that she was different, but the King had.

"Send for my son immediately," he said, picking up his fork and banging it on the arm of his throne. "Tell him I've found him a bride."

RIVER

THE NOW

*R*iver took the small wooden cup, lifted it to her lips, and winced as the bitterness assaulted her tastebuds. She swallowed the first gulp down and imagined the goodness pooling in her stomach before her body got to work to draw strength from it.

She'd come to the tavern to take her daily tonic ever since she was weaned from her mother's breast. And given that her mother also drank them, she supposed really she'd been taking them for the full seventeen years of her life.

River took another sip and swished the liquid around her mouth, certain she could pick up on some of the separate ingredients as the liquid swirled across her tongue. She'd asked the herbalist about the tonics before and knew there was turmeric to prevent disease, flaxseed for a strong heart, and milk thistle to protect the liver against toxins. She'd forgotten what the rest of the ingredients were, though.

The herbalist worked from ancient recipes recorded by her ancestors in a large leather-bound book that River had seen in the kitchen adjoining the tavern. Her work took place in isolation, apart from the assistance she got from her son, Edison, who sadly seemed more interested in the Guardians themselves than the tonics they drank. River imagined this was a source of frustration for his mother, although she'd never heard the herbalist complain.

Soon, River would be taking her tonics in the palace, instead of here in the tavern. Did the Prince drink them, too? She didn't think so. He didn't look like it, although admittedly she'd only ever seen him from a distance. Perhaps he took another kind of tonic to make him wise and fair—fit to be King one day. He didn't need to be strong when he had an army of Guardians to protect him. Their current King was proof enough of that.

"Thank you, Edison." River slid the empty cup across the table to the herbalist's son, keen to leave the tavern and get back out into the sun where she could lift some weights to transfer the energy from the tonic into her muscles.

"I heard you got selected," said Edison, stilling her retreating steps.

She turned. It wasn't like Edison to engage her in conversation. He was usually too focused on her sister, Daphne, which suited her just fine. Not that it suited Daphne all that much. She was always trying to avoid him. Although, Daphne wasn't here right now to deflect the attention away from River.

"I did." River tried not to look as impatient as she felt.

"I'm not surprised he chose you." Edison let his pale blue eyes sweep over her, lingering on her chest far longer than necessary.

Resisting the urge to cross her arms, River flicked her blonde braid behind her back and held Edison's gaze, waiting for him to finish his assessment. She could crush this puny man's skull with one hand if she wanted to. If anyone should be intimidated, it should be him. He was shorter than her, thinner than her and most definitely weaker. She wasn't sure how smart he was, but she liked to think she was smarter than him, too.

"People think you all look the same." He lowered his voice and glanced at the other Guardians nearby. "But I can see the difference. You're not as pretty as your sister, but you're prettier than most. And you're not quite as tall as some of them, which is good. And you're not flat all over."

"Have you finished?" she asked, wishing she could make him flat all over…on the floor. But it wouldn't go down well with the King if she killed the herbalist's son. The man destined to take over and be the herbalist himself one day.

"I was giving you a compliment." Edison rolled his eyes as his boney fingers toyed with the braided hemp cord he wore around his neck. "Women never know how to deal with compliments. Not that Guardians are real women, of course."

"Thank you for the compliment." She pulled her lips tight as she ground down on her teeth. "But if you ever comment on my appearance again, I'll ram that cup straight down your throat."

"I like my women feisty." He let go of his necklace to stroke some wispy sprouts of hair on his chin that he seemed to think constituted a beard.

"And I like my men quiet," she hissed. "Not that you're a real man, of course."

She left the tavern, letting the door slam behind her.

"Ungrateful wench!" Edison called after her.

She paused, wondering how she'd never noticed just how insipid this creature was before now? When Daphne got better, she was going to have to ask her more about him. Hopefully, he hadn't harassed her like that. Certainly, River had never witnessed him doing anything quite so extreme, or she'd have flattened him for real.

They all had their jobs to do in the kingdom, and as the herbalist's son, Edison's was to feed the Guardians with tonics, not poison them with his words, or his lecherous gaze.

She'd thought her job was to protect the kingdom, but it seemed she had another job now. As a Princess. And one day as a Queen. The Bay of Laurel hadn't had one of those since River was a young girl. She could barely remember the King's wife now. The Guardians may have been able to stop the kingdom from being invaded, but they hadn't been able to prevent the premature death of their Queen. But did becoming a Princess mean that she was no longer a Guardian? Was it possible for her to be both?

River made her way out to the training fields and joined the group of Guardians lifting iron balls and raising them above their heads.

It was good to see everyone looking so healthy. Far too many Guardians had been falling ill and it was becoming a concern. Daphne was the latest victim, having gotten so bad she'd taken to her bed, recently. Her skin had turned yellow and looked a little like it was made from wax. She hadn't been well enough to attend the King's selection and River wondered if the outcome would've been different if she had. Edison had been right when he'd said Daphne was prettier than she was. Well, she had been, before she got so sick. And one day she would be again, which was perfectly fine with River, just as long as she got better.

The herbalist was working hard to adjust the Guardians' tonics to find a way to return them all to full health and River was confident Daphne would be okay. She had faith in the herbalist, who wasn't anything like her son, and not just because she was a woman. It was because she was kind. She'd never stop a Guardian to comment on their appearance.

River went to the end of the line of Guardians where the lighter of the iron balls were kept, but as she bent to pick one up, she changed her mind and moved further up the line.

Edison had hit a nerve when he'd *complimented* her size. She was a little shorter than most of the other Guardians, albeit still taller than any ordinary person. And she did have curves that refused to be tamed into flat lines of muscle. Was that why she was selected by the King? Because she was a Guardian, but also still resembled an ordinary woman at the same time?

She'd never thought of herself as different before, but perhaps she was. The King certainly seemed to think so. But was this difference a strength?

No, she refused to accept that. Being different was a weakness and weaknesses must be abolished. Guardians were strong. She was fearless.

She picked up an iron ball, far heavier than any she'd attempted to lift before and hefted it into the air. She could do this. She was no weakling.

"River!" her father called out from the other end of the line, a weight of his own in his hands. "What are you—"

Before he could get his question out, River had hoisted the ball to her chest and planting her feet on the soil, she lifted it over her head. Let the curves cling to her body after this.

It was only when her arms began to shake that she realized she'd made a dangerous error. Then her legs joined in and the shaking in her upper and lower limbs spread like a wave through her body, meeting up in her core.

She caught her father's startled gaze as he set down his weight and ran to her.

He plucked the ball from her hands as if it weighed nothing and placed it on the ground, motioning for her to follow him with a twitch of his head.

She drew in a breath to wash away the trembling of her body and followed him to a patch of grass away from the group.

"River," he said, when they were out of earshot of the others. "What was that about?"

She shrugged. "I want to increase my muscle."

"You could've injured yourself. How would we explain that to the King?" He ran a large hand through his finely cropped fair hair. It was no wonder he'd lifted the ball so easily with hands like that. The female Guardians were strong, but they'd never been able to get close to matching the strength of the males. As powerful as the tonics were, it seemed gender had far more influence.

"You're right," she said, not wanting to anger him further. "I'm sorry, Father."

"I don't think you should be training anymore. Your duty to the King has changed." These words seemed to pain him to say, almost as much as it did for her to hear them. He'd just answered the question that'd been plaguing her since her selection by the King. No, she couldn't be both a Princess and a Guardian at the same time.

"I can still train!" She grabbed at the front of his shirt, desperate for things to be different. "I'm still a Guardian. I'll always be a Guardian."

"You won't." He swallowed hard and looked away, as if the intensity of her gaze was hurting him. "You'll be a Princess soon. It'll no longer be your duty to protect the royal family. It'll be our duty to protect you."

"I can protect myself." She let go of her father and thought of Edison and how she'd stood up to him earlier. She knew how to look after herself.

"I don't think you're listening to me," her father said. "Do you realize what's happening to you? How your life's about to change?"

"Of course, I realize." Surely, he didn't think she was stupid? Just because she'd accepted her duty to her King, didn't mean she had no understanding of the gravity of what was happening to her.

"You're not acting like it." He shook his head and River thought she could see a glint of something other than frustration in his eyes. Concern? Was her father worried about her?

"Do you wish he didn't choose me?" she asked, wondering for the first time how he felt about it. She'd just assumed her parents were as honored as she'd been.

His eyes still refused to meet hers. "Your mother and I are very proud of you."

"I know you're proud of me." She stepped to the side to force his eyes on her. "But I asked if you wish he didn't choose me."

He looked at her for several long moments, a deep sadness pooling in his eyes as he let her question hang in the air.

"We live to serve the King." His voice cracked as his shoulders sagged. "It's an honor to serve him."

She nodded, not wanting to press him any further when she'd just been given an answer, even if he'd sidestepped her again. His eyes had spoken for him. No wonder he hadn't wanted to look at her.

It was hard to know what to do with this revelation. If her parents weren't happy with her selection, then should she be? She hadn't realized she had a choice in how to feel about any of this.

"I may not always be a Guardian." She pushed down a lump in her throat, trying to accept what she now knew was true. "But I'll always be your daughter."

He brushed some imaginary dirt from the sleeve of his tunic and took a step back from her in typical male Guardian style. Like his peers, her father wasn't known for his ability to express emotion.

"Go and do whatever it is that Princesses do," he said, turning away. "I don't want to see you at training again."

"Yes, Father." She watched him go back to the other Guardians, leaving her standing there with a new kind of panic washing over her than when she'd been stuck holding that iron ball.

She'd been raised to fear nothing, with her whole life mapped out for her. But now everything had changed. Her father had made it clear that she was no longer a Guardian. She was the Guarded.

It was no different to someone telling her she wasn't a female or her name wasn't River. Being a Guardian was who she was.

She sat down on the grass and put her head between her knees, drawing in a series of deep breaths. For the first time in her life, she knew what it felt like to be scared.

Instead of holding an iron ball, she was holding her whole future above her head, and it was heavier than any weight she'd ever dreamed of. And the only thing that seemed more impossible than continuing to hold it, was deciding to let it go.

TATE

THE NOW

*T*ate dashed through the cornfield, hoping to beat the farmers to the traps. He normally came before sun-up, but this morning he'd been delayed.

He picked up his pace, aware he was probably too late. The farmers had a lot of work to do. They wouldn't have slept until this late hour.

But he had to try.

A loud squeal pierced the air and he knew the early morning talk he'd had with his father had cost at least one life. Peeking through the corn, he could see a farmer holding a rabbit by its injured leg, the open trap lying on the ground beside them, wet and sticky with blood.

That poor rabbit had no hope now.

Tate winced as the farmer twisted its neck and hung it from a hook on his belt. It would be rabbit stew for dinner tonight.

The farmer reset the trap and headed south. So, Tate headed north, running down a row of corn until he reached the next trap, pausing only long enough to see that it was empty.

He heard a familiar sound nearby. It was the unmistakable crunching of a rabbit grinding its teeth, both in frustration and fear. He took a shortcut through the next row of stalks. There! He may not have been able to save the last rabbit, but this one was in luck. Hopefully, its injuries were only superficial.

It was a young rabbit with black fur. Its eyes widened as it tried to work out how frightened of Tate it should be.

"Hey, little guy." He crouched down and got to work on the trap to prize it open, pleased to see it was only the tip of one paw held inside the vice. The rest of the rabbit's body was doing its best to escape, digging up the dirt as it thrashed and scurried.

"It's okay, it's okay." Tate tried to lift his deep voice into a higher, less threatening pitch.

The trap opened and Tate quickly swabbed the rabbit's wound with an ointment the herbalist had made up for him. He set the rabbit on the ground and let go, watching as it took off, limping but still fast as it moved like a streak of black lightning across the cornfield and out of sight.

Tate smiled, removed a cloth from his pocket, wiped down the trap to remove the evidence, and reset it. Very carefully he jammed a small twig in the release mechanism in just the right spot that would ensure it would fail to operate the next time an innocent creature ambled into its jaws.

Then, just like the rabbit, he took off before he too was caught.

Knowing he'd never be able to check all the traps, he decided to only check the ones that were on his way back.

The next two were empty and he paused, wishing he could jam twigs in these ones too, but he never sabotaged more than two traps a day, fearful that if he did too many at once, the farmers would figure out it was more than just nature at work.

He paused at the final trap, almost missing the tuft of brown fur in his haste. This poor rabbit wasn't as lucky as the last one. The dirt around had been dug up as the poor creature had tried to release itself from the vice that was caught firmly around its middle.

Tate crouched down and reached out to touch the rabbit, expecting to find its body cold and stiff. He startled to realize it was warm. The faint sign of a heartbeat could be felt underneath his hand.

"Oh, you poor little guy," he soothed, knowing there was no hope. The farmer could take hours to find this one and put him out of his misery. It wasn't right to let a creature endure this kind of pain.

Acting quickly, Tate reached into the sack he carried on his back and took out a small shovel. Then, closing his eyes as he held the shovel over his head, he brought it down hard and fast, with just the right pressure to kill the rabbit without crushing its skull. A sour tang flooded his mouth. Never, would he enjoy taking a life, no matter how necessary it was.

He opened his eyes and put a hand on the rabbit's chest, feeling the life leach from its small body. It was done. He was only sorry the last night of that rabbit's life had been spent in agony.

"Hey! You there!" came a voice from the other end of the cornrow.

Tate leaped to his feet and ran, grateful the sun had yet to rise fully into the sky.

He couldn't afford to be recognized by the farmer. It was one thing for a man to sneak onto another's property and interfere with his farm, but it was another altogether for that man to be the Prince of The Bay of Laurel.

He thought about that as he put the necessary distance between himself and the farm.

What was a prince doing rescuing rabbits from a farmer's land? One day he'd be able to outlaw traps if he wanted to.

But that day wasn't now. And every day between now and then meant painful deaths of those beautiful creatures. It made his heart ache.

Rabbits didn't even really like corn, which meant the damage they made wasn't all that extensive. The farmer could make plenty of corn soup if his stomach was growling. There was an abundance of vegetables in this kingdom with their fertile soil.

If only he hadn't been delayed by his father this morning, he could have saved more than one life. But his father had wanted to talk to him about his nuptials. Not his wedding, for that implied love and promises.

Nuptials.

The ceremony was as ugly as the word itself.

Unable to run any further, he dropped his speed to a walk. The farmer hadn't followed him. Nor would he have realized who his visitor was. Still, he should be more careful next time.

His thoughts returned to the Guardian he had no interest in marrying, no matter how strong and beautiful his father said she was. He was certain she'd have no interest in marrying him, either.

She'd have grown up amongst Guardians who towered over ordinary men. What would she want with a man with Tate's lean frame? A man who'd rather run through a field in the early morning light releasing rabbits than train with the Guardians to lift weights above his head.

He wished he could remember which Guardian she was. But they all looked so similar. Blonde, blue-eyed giants, who his father said would help strengthen their bloodline.

As he approached the palace, he thought he could make out his sister, sitting at her window.

He squinted. Yes, that was Pip alright. Staring out her window at the very same world she shut herself away from.

It was no wonder their father wanted to strengthen the bloodline. He had a daughter who refused to leave her bedchamber and a son who was unable to harden his heart to the cruelties of the world.

But with a half Guardian grandchild, all that would change. The future would be secured.

He just wished he didn't have to be the one to grant his father this wish. He'd had hopes to marry for love one day. But just like that poor rabbit in the trap, sometimes life just didn't work out the way you expected.

He was trapped. And it was his father who stood beside him with his shovel in the air.

And just like the rabbits, Tate had a miserable choice. He could kick up the dirt and struggle, bringing more pain to his doomed life. Or he could accept his fate.

And it was for this reason alone that he headed back to the palace where he'd be taken directly to the throne room and his nuptials would begin.

Nuptials.

It really was an ugly word.

PIP

THE NOW

*P*ip watched Tate walk toward the palace. Where did he go each morning? She'd asked him plenty of times, but knew he never told her the truth. Once, he'd even told her he'd been in the cornfields rescuing rabbits! Was he meeting a girl? A commoner their father wouldn't approve of? Perhaps he was meeting a boy. Their father wouldn't approve of that, either. Although, she was fairly sure that wasn't the case.

Tate was to be married to a Guardian today. Father had asked Pip to attend, but she'd refused, despite her curiosity. Her fear of leaving her bedchamber far outweighed her desire to see the woman their father had selected for Tate.

Besides, she doubted she had a dress that would fit her. It'd been ages since she'd worn anything fancy, and she'd turned the palace seamstress away whenever she'd tried to visit to make her anything new. No doubt the Guardian girl would be wearing something fancy.

Pip was the Princess. It wouldn't be right for someone else to look better than she did, even if it was the Guardian girl's wedding.

Poor Tate. A Guardian for a wife! The match would be a disaster. And Pip didn't just mean because of the Guardian's strength. It was because Tate was too gentle, too kind to marry a Guardian. But yes, that was the whole point, she reminded herself. They had to breed out the weakness in their family and marrying a Guardian was the best way.

She knew she'd disappointed her father. She'd disappointed herself, sitting in her room, getting fatter with each rise of the sun.

Pip looked down at her middle and poked at her stomach with her index finger. Disgusting! That's what she was. It was no wonder her father hadn't arranged a wedding for her. Nobody would have her. A Guardian would only laugh if her father presented her as a bride. Although, having a husband would be nice in a lot of ways. Then she'd have someone to talk to. Someone who might actually talk back, unlike the walls or her collection of dolls.

Tate disappeared from view as he entered the palace and she wondered if he'd come to see her. Normally, he brought her breakfast after his morning mystery walk. Sometimes he had blood on his trousers. Maybe he secretly murdered people before the sun came up? She laughed at this idea. That was about as likely as her attending his wedding.

She sat at her table and waited, her stomach grumbling in anticipation of being fed.

A knock at her door a little while later told her Tate hadn't let her down. He never did. He may be a little later than usual but he'd never forget about her.

She went to the door and slid back the cover on the spy hole.

As expected, Tate was in the passageway, holding her breakfast tray with both hands.

"Hey, Pip." He held up the tray, knowing she'd be watching him.

She opened the door and held it for him.

"You're late," she said, wincing when she realized she sounded angry. He might stop visiting her if she greeted him like that. Then she really would have to start talking to the walls.

"Sorry, big day today." His tone was cheery, ignoring her rebuke. "You sure you won't come?"

She shook her head as a thickness settled in her throat. "I'm not feeling up to it."

"You're never feeling up to it, Pip." He put her tray on her table and stooped to kiss the top of her head. "Will you do it for me?"

"I have nothing to wear." She drew in the delicious aromas wafting up from her tray, planning what she was going to eat first. The warm porridge drizzled with honey? Or maybe the blueberry muffin, still steaming from the oven? Or perhaps she'd start with the strawberries dipped in cream? But her food was going to have to wait. She didn't want to eat in front of her brother. Or anybody, for that matter.

"You have lots of pretty dresses." Tate reached for a strawberry and she swiped his hand away. "Besides, who cares what you wear! Wear what you have on now."

"Father cares."

He nodded as he pulled up a chair and sat down, making another grab for a strawberry, grinning as he succeeded this time.

He was a good looking man, really. Tall for a regular man and lean, with long dark hair that he wore tied in a knot behind his neck. Strands of hair had escaped during his walk, which added a sort of rugged appeal. Any ordinary woman would probably find him handsome. But would a Guardian? It was doubtful.

"Eat," he said, pushing her tray closer. "Or I'll take another strawberry. They're so sweet."

She moved the strawberries away from Tate and picked up her spoon, pushing around her porridge and she blended in the honey. Her stomach groaned in anticipation of the sweetness on her tongue and the warmth in her belly. "It's still a little hot."

"Wonder who Father chose." Tate rubbed his chin and sat forward. "Think she'll like me?"

"Everybody likes you." She rolled her eyes.

"Except Father."

Her eyes stilled. He had a point there. Did Father like him? Or her? It didn't seem so.

"Well, here's your chance to turn that around." She smiled. "Father will love that you're going along with this."

"Like I have a choice." His hands clenched into tight balls. "Mother always told us to marry someone we love. How can I love someone I've never met?"

His dark eyes searched her own, looking for an answer she couldn't provide. What did she know about love? She'd only ever loved one boy and he'd let her down in the worst possible way.

"Well, Mother's not here, is she?" She put down her spoon and rubbed at her arms.

"Do you think she loved Father?" asked Tate. "Was that why she was so unhappy?"

"Of course she loved him," said Pip, automatically.

Tate sighed, not seeming to believe her answer any more than she did. Their delicate, pretty mother had married their oaf of a father for many reasons, but love was unlikely to have been one of them.

"So, where did you go just now?" she asked, trying to steer the conversation in a more comfortable direction.

"Had to see a man about a rabbit." He grinned and she was pleased to see his mood lift once more. It wasn't like Tate to be glum.

"Your wife might not like you sneaking out like that," she said.

He shrugged. "I'm sure there are plenty of things she won't like. Anyway, Father will only expect us to be married in name only. All he's interested in is a royal baby."

A laugh escaped Pip's lips. "Tate! You do know how babies are made, don't you?"

"I don't really want to think about that right now." He stood and brushed down his pants.

"I don't believe a lot of thinking's required." Pip's laughter continued, despite the stricken look on Tate's face.

"It's not funny, Pip! I don't want to do *that* if I don't love her."

"Oh, Tate." She pulled her face into a serious expression to match his. "You're so sweet. If you weren't my brother, I swear, I'd marry you myself."

"Come on, Pip, eat up." He shoved his hands into his pockets and coughed. "Your porridge has cooled off now."

"I will, I will. Off you go. Leave me and my breakfast alone." She waved her hands, but he didn't move.

"What do you think Mother would've made of this idea?" A frown crept across his brow. "The marriage I mean, not the other thing."

Pip stood and went to him. Could he talk of nothing but their mother today?

"I have no idea," she said. "You knew her better than me, don't forget. I was only young when she died."

"I can't remember her face." He blinked back a tear and Pip felt pain pool in her stomach, pushing away all thoughts of porridge.

"She was beautiful," said Pip.

"Like you." Tate put a hand on her shoulder. "I wish you could see how beautiful you are."

She lifted to her toes and gave him a quick kiss on his cheek. "Biased brother. Now, go and get married and come back later to tell me everything."

"You sure you won't come?"

"I'm sure." She felt her heart double in size, as it weighed down her chest. How could she miss an occasion as momentous as this? But how was it possible for her to attend? Even just the thought of leaving the safety of her room sent prickles down her spine. "Good luck."

He nodded, not seeming to trust himself to say more, and left the room.

Surely, he didn't really think she was beautiful? If that were the case, he was crazy as well as kind.

She went to the table and lifted her spoon once more, this time spearing it into her porridge and emptying the contents of the bowl into her mouth as quickly as she could. Then, lifting the bowl to her lips, she licked it, her tongue searching for a final hit of sweetness.

So hungry. She was so hungry. That porridge hadn't been nearly enough.

She smeared her muffin with lard and tore off pieces to stuff in her mouth, as if it were going to vanish if she didn't hurry. Washing it down with the strawberries, she licked her fingers and cleaned the plate of any remaining cream.

When everything had indeed vanished, she put her hand on her stomach and felt the roundness swelling underneath. She was disgusting, not beautiful.

Her brother was completely mad.

RIVER

THE NOW

*R*iver was greeted at the doors to the palace by a Guardian named Heath. She knew him, of course, having grown up beside him in the Guardians' village. When she was younger, she'd even had hopes that one day he might be her husband. But all of that had changed now. He wasn't here to greet her as a friend. He was on duty as a Guardian and she was a guest of the King. Soon to be a whole lot more than that. She was about to become the King's daughter by marriage.

She smiled warmly at Heath, grateful for the familiarity of his face at such an uncertain time. She'd never set foot in the palace before the selection day and was sure she wouldn't be able to find her way back to the King's throne room.

Heath provided her with a formal nod of his head in place of his usual smile.

"His Majesty is waiting for you," he said.

Was this how it was always going to be now, with the Guardians treating her like a stranger, instead of their peer?

"Come with me." Heath turned his back on her and headed down a passageway and up some stairs.

River looked around as she followed him, trying to take in her surroundings. The last time she'd been here, she'd been far too nervous and distracted to notice anything, but it was important she pay attention now that this was to become her home. It was so different from the small hut she'd grown up in in the Guardians' village, with walls of mud instead of stone.

The ceilings were so high in here and it was a strange sensation to walk up so many stairs, feeling the way it stretched the muscles in her legs. And the walls were all so far apart! It sort of felt like she was outside when in fact she was inside. There was nothing at all about this cold building that felt like a home.

Seeing that Heath was getting quite far ahead of her now, she picked up her feet and hurried after him, taking the stairs two at a time, then following him down another passageway. She had a wedding to go to.

The King hadn't called it a wedding when he'd selected her from the group of Guardians presented to him. He'd used another word she couldn't remember right now.

Not that it really mattered what word he'd used. It was all the same thing. She was being tied in name to Prince Tate today. And she was going to do her best to serve him well as his wife. The King wouldn't regret his choice.

She'd never heard of a Guardian marrying anyone other than another Guardian before. It was important they didn't mix their genes. How else could each generation of Guardians be stronger than the last if they were to marry ordinary people?

But Prince Tate wasn't an ordinary person. He was a royal. What did that mean for her future children? Would they have her strength or their father's weakness? Because he didn't look very strong. She doubted he could lift the lightest ball in the line of weights. Although, he did look fast. Perhaps their children would be able to run like rabbits.

Heath led her toward a handmaiden, who was smiling warmly at River as if she'd been expecting her. She was an older lady, short and plump, wearing something that looked more like a fancy nightgown than a dress. River hoped she wasn't going to be expected to wear anything like that in place of her tunic.

"I'll take her from here," the handmaiden said to Heath.

"I was told to go directly to the King," said River, her chest tightening. "Take me to him first."

"You can't go directly to him looking like that, can you?" said the handmaiden, causing Heath to break out in a smirk as he looked her up and down.

River ran her hands down her perfectly clean tunic, then locked her gaze on Heath, deciding she preferred it when he'd treated her with distant formality than this kind of wry amusement.

"There's nothing wrong with how I look," she said. "And may I remind you both that you're talking to your future Queen."

Heath's eyes darted to the floor as a flush spread up his cheeks, wiping away his smirk. Edison may have thought he could get away with making disparaging remarks about her in the tavern, but it was time the men of this kingdom learned how to treat her with respect.

"You look perfectly fine," said the handmaiden, sighing deeply. "For a Guardian. But we need to turn you into a bride. It's my job to prepare you for the nuptials."

Nuptials! That was the word the King had used.

"Of course," said River, turning to see Heath scurrying back down the passageway. How different her life would've been if her childhood hopes of marrying him had come true. Being his wife would be a life she understood. Although, hopefully now her life was about to get a whole lot better. She'd never seen Prince Tate smirk.

"Come now." The handmaiden took her by the arm and led her down an impossibly long corridor to a room with a sweeping view of the fields of the kingdom. With the Guardians' village firmly planted on the ground, she'd never been up this high before. It felt like she was standing on a cloud.

River went to the window and drank in the spectacular view with hungry eyes, taking in every detail. It was no wonder Princess Pip was seen so often, sitting at her window.

There were crops of corn, wheat, and barley, stretching all the way to the horizon. Closer to the palace were carefully groomed beds of vegetables. From where she stood, she could make out broccoli and carrots and something she was certain might be pumpkin seedlings.

River knew The Bay of Laurel had rich fertile soil, able to produce crops far superior to any of the other kingdoms, except perhaps Wintergreen. This was one of the reasons they were all so healthy and strong. There was no shortage of food for any man, no matter how rich or poor.

"Looking at your kingdom, are you?" asked the handmaiden, as she fussed about the room, picking up various strange-looking items and setting them down again.

"My kingdom?" River asked, tearing her eyes away.

"But, of course. As you just reminded us, you'll be our Queen one day. That is, if I ever get you ready on time."

She went to River and began tugging at the cords that fastened her tunic together.

River tensed, not used to anybody dressing her. Or undressing her, for that matter.

"I can do that." She brushed away the handmaiden's hands, unlaced the leather bodice of her vest and handed it over.

"Thank you." The handmaiden smiled, keeping her lips tightly closed.

"What's your name?" River asked, feeling that such details were important before she removed any more of her clothing.

"Elise." The handmaiden smiled once more, revealing perhaps the most crooked set of teeth River had seen. "And stop your fretting. I've seen plenty of nakedness before. You're no different."

"I'm not fretting." River did her best to return the smile but came up blank. "I just prefer to do some things myself."

"Perhaps you'd be more comfortable dressing behind the screen then?" Elise led her to a corner of the room.

"Thank you." River found her smile and stepped behind an ornate timber screen to see a chair and a rack with a white dress hanging from it.

Her wedding dress. The first dress she'd wear as a woman instead of a Guardian.

She reached out to touch it, gasping at the fineness of the fabric. It was so... feminine. This was another word she knew existed but had never applied to herself. Guardians weren't feminine. They were tough. But why couldn't tough be feminine? Perhaps that would be something she could do as Queen one day. Teach the kingdom what it was like to be a real woman. Strong and fearsome. Certainly, if she had a daughter one day, that would be the first thing she taught her.

She stripped off the rest of her clothes and laid them on the chair, pausing to touch the coarse fabric. Would she ever wear these clothes again?

"Hurry now," Elise called over the screen. "You'll need some help with those clasps on the back of your dress."

River slipped the dress over her head and stepped out, turning her back to Elise so she could do it up.

"Oh dear," said Elise. "You are... rather a lot bigger than I realized. I've never dressed a Guardian before. I don't think we're going to be able to do much about this gap at the back. There's no way I can do up these clasps."

River felt a flush race to her cheeks. Was she really so big? She was the smallest in her family. Smaller than a lot of the Guardians. But still bigger than an ordinary human, towering over Elise. Would that be a problem for Prince Tate? Did he like his women petite? Because if that was the case, he'd be nothing but disappointed in her.

Elise tapped her foot on the floor and let out a satisfied huff.

"Actually, we can do this," she said, shuffling about on a bureau. "I have a ribbon I can thread around the clasps to hold them together. Nobody will notice."

With the cool draft tickling River's spine, she thought there was a good chance everyone would notice. Her only concern was just who *everyone* was. It wouldn't be anyone she knew. She'd been told to come here alone, much to the disappointment of her mother, who'd said she'd always wanted to see her daughter get married.

But then her father had reminded her of what an honor it was for their daughter to be marrying a Prince and that had put an end to her complaints. There could be no greater duty to their kingdom.

River straightened her spine and lifted her chin as Elise got to work behind her, pulling and stretching and threading until she was puffing and grunting with the strain.

"I think that's just going to have to do it," said Elise, stepping back. "Now, quickly, sit down for a moment while I sort out that horse's mane hanging from your head."

River sat down and closed her eyes as Elise pulled her fingers through her braid, in her best attempt to turn her into a princess.

She caught sight of herself in the mirror in front of her and watched her eyes go wide. River the Guardian had already gone.

"Who are you?" she asked herself, wondering what kind of woman would emerge in her place.

"I told you, I'm Elise."

"I'm River," she said. "I'm very pleased to meet you."

Elise nodded at her, too busy to realize that again, River had been talking to herself.

Today she was going to marry the Prince. Today was the first day of her new life that would be built on honor instead of strength. She could do this. And she was going to prove to everyone—including herself— that she was going to do it well.

TATE

THE NOW

*T*ate entered the throne room in a rush. If he hadn't been so used to racing through the cornfields in the morning, he'd probably be out of breath. He was running late after taking Pip her breakfast and hoped his bride wouldn't hold that against him.

But he quickly worked out that she was even later than him. Or perhaps she'd decided not to turn up at all? Unlikely, given how loyally the Guardians had served them in the past.

"Father." He dipped his head in a bow.

"Nice of you to show up," the King said, tapping his fork on the arm of his enormous throne, impatience burning in the blue of his eyes.

"Where is she?" A glimmer of hope ignited in Tate's chest that the nuptials had been called off. Although, he doubted it. His father had been adamant when they'd spoken earlier in the day that this wedding was going ahead.

"She's readying herself." His father stabbed his fork into his bowl of cauliflower, picking up a floret and shoveling it into his mouth. "Women like to look good on their wedding day. Your mother took days to get ready for our nuptials."

"What's she like?" Tate asked.

"Don't fret." His father rolled his royal eyes, chewing his cauliflower with an open mouth. "I chose you a pretty one. I don't want ugly grandchildren."

"But what's she like?" Tate asked again.

"I just told you she was pretty." His father frowned like there was something wrong with him.

Tate ignored the look and tried once more. "No, I mean, what's she like, apart from her looks? What's she like as a person?"

His father waved his fork in the air. "What does that matter? I swear, sometimes I wonder where you came from."

Tate winced. Would anything he'd do in life be enough for this man? Probably not. Maybe if he was able to produce him the grand-child he wanted, then he'd leave him alone, feeling secure in the knowledge the kingdom's future was safe. That was the one thing he could do to make this man happy. Perhaps that's why he'd agreed to it. But really, it didn't matter if he agreed. He was marrying a Guardian today, whether he wanted to or not.

"So, is this it?" Tate glanced around the throne room. This defi-nitely wasn't how he'd pictured his wedding day. His mother had told him stories when he was a boy of how when he found the woman he loved, the whole kingdom would come out to celebrate. Although, he supposed he was far from finding the woman he loved. All he'd found was a woman his father had described as pretty.

"What more do you want?" His father set down his bowl and picked up a large wedge of cheese, not bothering with a fork this time. "Weddings take preparation and I'm keen to get moving. I'm not getting any younger. Nor are you."

"I'm eighteen, Father."

"Yes and getting older by the minute. We'll parade you through the streets with your bride once it's done, if you like."

He didn't like. "Small and quiet is fine, Father. Perfect, in fact."

"The opposite of your wife." His father sniggered, tearing off a large chunk of cheese with his teeth and chewing it briefly, before spitting it out on the floor.

Tate looked at the macerated morsel and blanched.

"Tasted like piss," his father said, as if that made his actions more civilized.

Before Tate could reply, the heavy oak door swung open. He stopped himself from turning, not wanting to see the face of his wife just yet. He needed another moment to compose himself. Would his wife really be large and loud?

If only Pip were here to distract him. She'd no doubt whisper something ridiculous in his ear and he'd have to stifle a giggle.

"Your Highness," came a voice, far softer than the one he'd imagined a Guardian to possess. Was it possible his wife was small and quiet, after all?

He turned to see a woman standing in the doorway, curtseying. A woman. Not a Guardian, as he'd expected. A servant? No, she was wearing a wedding dress. This had to be his bride.

He glanced at his father to see what had gone wrong, only to find him nodding at the woman and gesturing for her to come in.

The woman straightened her back and stepped closer giving Tate the opportunity to study her. He decided she was indeed a Guardian. She was tall, even if not as tall as some he'd seen, and her arms, although slender, were lined with muscle. Her blonde hair had been brushed from the braid that Guardian women wore and fanned out in such a way as to create a softness around her features. His father hadn't lied. She was indeed pretty.

Remembering himself, Tate dropped to a polite bow and held out his hand to his bride, surprised to find he was shaking. To think that he'd barely blinked when a farmer had threatened him in the cornfield earlier in the morning and now here he was scared of a...woman.

She slipped her hand into his and he realized he'd forgotten to ask his father for her name.

"My name's River," she said, seeming to read his mind.

"And I'm Tate," he replied, surprised at her confidence.

"I know that," she said, seeming to suppress a smile.

"I do hope she's to your satisfaction," interrupted his father.

"She's lovely," said Tate, wanting to be polite, despite his brain crying out that there was nothing to his satisfaction about this moment. It was nothing personal against this woman...River. She seemed pleasant enough. It was just that he didn't love her. It wasn't possible to love someone you'd only just met. He should be marrying someone he loved. His mother had been very clear about that.

Tate stood tall and wondered if he had the better of River in terms of height. It was hard to tell. She was perhaps taller than him by a margin. Certainly, she was stronger. But was she faster? Was she smarter? Was she kinder of heart? He'd find all this out and more in the fullness of time.

"It's a pleasure to meet you." Tate squeezed River's hand gently.

She nodded and offered him a smile. "It's my honor to serve the kingdom as your wife."

Tate swallowed, wondering how much truth there was behind these words. Did she feel honored? Was she as pleased as her smile was leading him to believe? It was true the Guardians lived to serve their King, but none of them had ever been expected to marry a Prince before. They married each other, which was another thing they'd seemed quite happy with.

He pulled back his shoulders and puffed out his chest, wondering how he stacked up in River's eyes. She must surely have grown up expecting to marry a man who had muscles upon his muscles. Was he a disappointment to her with his lean frame and dark hair?

"Shall we get on with it?" his father asked. "I'll starve to death by the time this is finished."

Tate seriously doubted that, but led River a few paces forward, so they were standing side-by-side in front of the throne.

A Guardian rushed to the King's side and unrolled a scroll, holding it so the King could read the words that would tie Tate to this woman's side for the rest of his life.

"Citizens of The Bay of Laurel," the King began. "Well, there are a couple of citizens here at least... Citizens of The Bay of Laurel, we are gathered here…" The King rolled his eyes. "Blah, blah, blah… we don't need to read all this surely?"

Tate's eyes widened. Were nuptials official if they weren't read properly? Well, if the King said they were, then he supposed it didn't make a lot of difference.

"Tate, do you take this woman to be your wife?" His father waved away the Guardian and abandoned any pretense that these nuptials should follow protocol.

"I do." Tate was unsure if he should look at River or his father as he said this, opting to look at his shoes.

"And, River, do you take this man to be your husband?" his father asked.

"I do," said River, looking directly at Tate, making him feel guilty for not having done the same.

"Then so be it!" The King stood. "You're married. Now, off you go. Get to know each other and make me a grandchild. I have other business to attend to."

"Thank you, Your Highness," said River.

"I said, be off with you. Go and do what married people do." He waved his hand, a little too close to River's face and she blinked in response.

A Guardian burst into the room, holding a large tray laden with roast meat and a pile of potatoes so high Tate was surprised they hadn't spilled to the floor. It seemed Guardians had good balance as well as strength. There may not be a wedding feast planned as a part of these nuptials, however that wasn't stopping his father from celebrating alone.

"Come on," said Tate, placing a hand on the small of River's back.

Noticing he was touching bare skin, he withdrew his hand like she was made from fire. River's dress wasn't done up properly at the back, instead tied by a snaking line of silk ribbon, a strip of flesh visible from beneath her hair to her waist. Clearly, this dress had been made for a more petite bride.

He looked away from her back, not wanting to admit how hypnotizing this bare skin was. How was it that a hint of skin could be far more alluring than an expanse of it?

He took her hand and threaded his fingers through hers, realizing she was trembling ever so slightly. It seemed she wasn't as confident as he'd thought.

"Don't worry, I'm not going to hurt you." As soon as he said the words, he knew they were foolish. She was a trained soldier. She could hurt him if she wanted to, not the other way around.

"I know you won't hurt me." She blinked trusting blue eyes back at him.

The King may be desperate for a grandchild, but he couldn't have everything go his way. Sometimes people just had to wait. Tate was going to marry this woman with his heart before he ever laid a hand on her. Although, the way his heart was beating now, that may be a whole lot sooner than he'd originally thought.

ARIEL

THE NOW

*A*riel tied her dark hair under a scarf and leaned over the large cooking pot as she drew in the aroma. The spiciness of the turmeric mingled with the bite of the ginger, balanced out by the garlic Edison had dug from the fields earlier that morning.

The thought of her son, made her step back from the pot and sigh. What was she to do with him? She'd had such high hopes she'd be able to raise him to be better than the person she feared he was born to become. But with each day that passed, he was dashing her hopes more and more.

She got feelings like that about people. She could look at someone and immediately know if their heart was kind or cruel, or how far along the scale it sat.

This wasn't always a good thing. With Edison, she'd known the moment she laid eyes on him that his heart was black. Well, perhaps not black, but it was certainly a darker shade of gray than she'd like for someone so important.

She'd tried her hardest over the years to let in the light, but it was more difficult than she'd thought it would be. Especially as she was raising him on her own. Would having a father have made a difference? She guessed she'd never know. Time could be regretted, but it could never be turned back.

"Mother."

She jumped at the sound of her son's voice. He had a habit of interrupting her when she was thinking of him. Or was that just because she thought of him so often?

"Edison, good timing." She wiped her hands on her work dress. "Would you mind helping me move this pot from the flame?"

"Not sure why you bother. Your tonics aren't working. You're losing your touch." Despite his words, he lifted the pot from the flame and set it down to cool.

This was what she meant about his heart being gray. He could do something nice while saying something cruel at the same time.

"It has nothing to do with my touch," she reminded him. "These recipes are the result of generations of hard work and experimentation."

"Is this the new tonic?" He peered into the pot and waved the rising steam toward his nose.

"I've made some adjustments," she said. "I'm hopeful this will put a stop to the... problems we've been having."

"Problems?" He screwed up his nose. "I think it's a little more serious than that."

"Well, one day they'll be your problems, so I suggest you start helping a little more, rather than criticizing all the time."

When she got too old to make her tonics, Edison would take over, a thought that made her want to invent a tonic for her to live forever.

"Yeah, about that." Edison pulled out a chair from the table.

"What about that?" She took a seat of her own and waited to hear the words she was certain he was about to speak.

"I don't want to be the herbalist." He said the words like they meant nothing to him. "It's not the life for me."

"Edison." She drew in a breath and tried to slow the beating of her heart. Even though she'd been expecting this, it was still a shock to hear him say it at last. "Our family's been making tonics for generations, handing down the recipes and building the strongest army any kingdom has ever seen. It's our duty. Our future. There's no choice in that."

"It doesn't feel like my future." Edison folded his arms, his sandy blond hair falling across his face. "And what's the point of making tonics that are killing the Guardians, rather than making them stronger?"

"Edison! How dare you." His words had hit her like a slap. Making tonics was her life's work. Was he saying this was a wasted life?

"Face it, Mother. The reason the Guardians are strong is because they lift weights. The tonics you're making are doing them more harm than good."

She shook her head, unable to believe what she was hearing. She'd known Edison didn't share her passion for the tonics, but never did she think he was so against them.

"It's true, Mother," he continued. "You're old and have been smelling too many herbs to notice. I'm not spending my life doing a made-up job."

If Edison refused to carry on her work, who could possibly take over? Was the magic of the tonics in the recipe or was it in the fingertips of the person who made it? Edison had grown up in her kitchen. Would it be possible to teach anyone else how to do her work?

"This is *not* a made-up job," she protested. "Our work has helped build the strongest army any kingdom has ever seen. How do you explain the size and courage of the Guardians if not for the tonics?"

"They're dying, Mother. Three Guardians have died since the last full moon."

She didn't need him to remind her of that. This was something she was acutely aware of and had been working day and night to try to fix. *If* this did have anything to do with her tonics, then she had to find the answer.

"They're human," she said, fighting dark spots that were clouding her vision. "Of course they die. We die too. There's no proof it's the tonics."

He smirked at her in the same way he used to do as a child. "Are you as foolish as those useless cups I pour out for you each day?"

"Edison, that's enough!" She stood up and shouldered him out of the way of her pot so she could stir the steaming liquid. Dipping in a spoon, she sampled the tonic, wincing as the bitterness hit the back of her tongue, then smiling at its perfection.

Liquid gold. That's how she thought of it. It wasn't useless or foolish. Nor was she. There was only one person that label applied to right now.

"I'm going to the Bay to get you some more kelp," said Edison, once again confusing her with his kind actions contradicting his words. He knew she hated going to the Bay, so regularly made the trip for her. "But when I return, we need to talk about approaching the King to find a replacement. Someone else to help you with this nonsense."

"Edison, please." The last thing she wanted was for the King to turn his attention to her right now. Not before she fixed whatever it was that was broken and the Guardians were in perfect health once more.

"Enjoy your visit from Prince Tate." He smiled at her in such a way that if she didn't know him, she'd think he was being sweet. "I know he visits you while I'm gone. He's a bit young for you, don't you think?"

"How dare you!" Heat flooded Ariel's cheeks. It was true that Tate visited on occasion when Edison left the palace, but not for what Edison was insinuating. That poor boy had grown up without a mother. Being there for him when he wanted to talk was the least she could do.

She watched Edison turn his back and walk out of her kitchen.

Leaving the pot, she returned to the table and buried her face in her hands.

Edison was wrong about more than just her relationship with Tate. The tonics were just as powerful as ever. What was happening had nothing to do with that. The Guardians wouldn't be the fearsome army they were without her work. Their kingdom would be invaded and they'd all be thrown out of their homes.

The other kingdoms were already banding together and increasing their strength, which meant they were at more risk now than ever before. Forte Cadence, Wintergreen and more recently The Sands of Naar had called some kind of truce. These were very strange times they lived in.

She wished their King were the sort to consider joining the alliance instead of fighting against it. But that would never happen. One day when Tate was in power, things would be different. He was both brave and kind. He'd make an excellent King. But that would be years away. So, in the meantime, her job was to ensure their army was strong. How would they defend themselves if three kingdoms were to attack at once?

The tonics were helping, not hindering. How else could they work for so many years, then all of a sudden start to do the opposite?

She believed this with all her heart. She had to. For if she didn't, then her entire life and all the difficult decisions she'd made, had been a total waste.

RIVER

THE NOW

*R*iver allowed Prince Tate to lead her back to his bedchamber, her footsteps moving forward but her heart dragging her back.

She was loyal to the Prince. She wanted to serve him and be a good wife. But did she love him? No, she did not.

As she walked, she listed the things she knew about her husband.

He was tall for an ordinary human, albeit slightly shorter than her.

He was a Prince and would one day be King.

He had a sister that nobody had seen for many years, except when she sat at her window, which was practically always.

He had a handsomeness that wasn't present in his father, although it was possible that buried underneath all those rolls of royal flesh there was a handsome King.

And so far, he'd been kind to her.

It was doubtful he'd had any more say about this marriage than she'd had. He hadn't even been in the selection process. Did that make it better or worse? Would she like to have been selected by him?

She wasn't sure. Maybe he wouldn't have chosen her if he'd been there. Was that a good thing or bad?

She shook her head, trying to release these confusing thoughts. But still, they plagued her.

Prince Tate hadn't seemed too disappointed in the King's choice. She'd noticed the straightening of his spine when he'd discovered the way her dress was being held together and wasn't sure how that made her feel. Princes didn't look at Guardians that way. If she'd been wearing her tunic, she was certain he wouldn't have looked at her with that flash of longing in his dark eyes. At least he hadn't leered at her like Edison or made her feel foolish like Heath. He'd averted his gaze and done his best to reassure her that he'd never hurt her.

She was a woman now, not a Guardian. She needed to remember that. And men liked to look at women.

Prince Tate opened the door and stepped aside for her to enter his bedchamber.

Her stomach pulled together as if it had ribbons of its own holding it in place. No man had ever made her feel this nervous before. Was it because he was a Prince? Or was it because he was her husband? More likely, it was due to the King's instruction for them to make a baby. And despite how little she knew about being a woman, this was something her mother had made sure she knew about.

His bedchamber was large. The entire hut that her family of four lived in would fit inside, with room to spare. Light flooded in from a window, sending dappled patterns onto the large bed. She averted her eyes from the plush red quilt, not ready to imagine herself sleeping beside the Prince just yet.

Resisting the urge to slide into the nearest seat to ease her aching feet that'd been squeezed into shoes far too small for her, she went to the window and looked out. The view from here even more breathtaking than the one she'd had from the room Elise had dressed her in.

"We're a lucky kingdom," said the Prince, noticing her gaze across the fields.

"We are." River wondered if she was supposed to wait for him to make the first move or if she was supposed to remove her dress herself. Neither option sounded appealing at this point. But as she was determined to be a dutiful wife, she undid the braided silk belt that was tied around her waist, realizing she was going to need to ask him to help her undo the ribbon threaded through the clasps down her back.

"May I speak with you?" asked the Prince, not seeming to be able to look directly at her.

"Yes, Your Highness. Of course." She forced a smile to her lips.

"Please, call me Tate. I'm your husband now."

"Sorry. Yes... Tate." She had to force out this word. Would it ever sound natural to call the Prince by his first name, whether he was her husband or not? But he'd asked her to, so she had to try.

"This marriage was my father's idea," he said, confirming her suspicions. "I had no choice in this. Do you understand?"

She nodded, not certain she understood anything in this strange, new world.

"You're very lovely, so I don't want you to be offended by this. But... would it be all right if we..." He ran his hands through his hair and the tie that held it in a knot at the base of his neck slipped free.

She watched him with interest as he re-tied his hair, which she decided was a shame. She quite liked how he'd looked with it flowing free. Like he was a real human and not a neat and tidy Prince.

"Would it be all right if we waited a while to become man and wife in the way my father has instructed?" He spat out these words as if trying to get them over with. "I'd like to get to know you first."

She let out a deep breath and felt all her nerves flow free of her body, along with the expelled air. It seemed the Prince was a little unsure of himself, which was as surprising as it was endearing.

"I can wait." She did her best to look disappointed.

"There'll need to be a baby at some point," he continued. "But I see no rush. We're both young and healthy. Father need not know why it doesn't happen immediately. That occurs sometimes, I believe."

River nodded. "It does. It took my parents five years to conceive me."

"Five years!" His mouth fell open, although it shouldn't have. This length of time wasn't unusual for a Guardian.

"Our muscle mass reduces our fertility." She shrugged, not really understanding what muscles had to do with conceiving babies.

"Yet my father chose me a Guardian for a wife." His brows pulled together as he thought about this. "Curious."

"I'm not a Guardian anymore." River swallowed, wondering if she said this aloud enough times one day it would feel like the truth. "Perhaps he believes my fertility will increase in time."

"Or perhaps it's more important for him to have a few strong heirs, than a tribe of weaklings." Tate's shoulders slumped and River thought she could guess where his uncertainty about himself came from.

"Is that what your father thinks you are?" she asked. "A weakling?"

He blinked at her, not seeming to want to answer and she remembered she'd wondered the same thing about him before they'd met.

"I think it takes great strength to do what you did today," she said. "You married me when it wasn't your choice and you did it while treating me with dignity and kindness. To me, that's what a real man is. Your father should be very proud of you."

Tate's shoulders pulled back and a small smile spread across his strong features, lighting the darkness in his eyes. An unfamiliar flutter sparked in River's core as she looked at him, like some kind of flame had been ignited.

"Are your parents proud of you?" he asked. "How did they feel about this union?"

She took a step back and leaned against the windowsill, the aching in her feet matching the aching in her heart. She hadn't expected him to ask her about the family she'd been asked to leave behind.

"They were honored I was chosen," she said, swallowing hard. "As am I."

"I'd like to meet them." He stepped toward her and placed his hand gently on her shoulders. "River, when I told you after our wedding that I'd never hurt you, I meant that I'd never hurt you here."

He placed the palm of his hand over her heart, just inches from her breast and she felt as if the silk belt was still tied around her waist, constricting her.

"I'll never hurt you," he said. "This is my promise to you. I may not be able to be the husband to you that my father has ordered me to be. Not right now, anyway. But if it's all right with you, I'd like to be your friend."

River smiled. She'd never had a friend who wasn't a Guardian before.

"I'd like that," she said.

"Good."

She watched as he went to his bed and flopped onto his back, letting out a sigh.

"May I sit down, my Prince? I mean, Tate. I'm sorry, you did tell me to call you Tate." The soles of her feet were on fire now, like she was standing on a bed of nails.

"Of course." He hauled himself up so he was propped on his elbows. "You don't need to ask me if you can sit down. This is your home now, too."

"I'm sorry." She slid onto the chair and pulled off her shoes, sighing at the sweet relief of being able to wriggle her toes.

"Okay, this isn't going to work." He shook his head, his lips pressing firmly together. "We need a few rules."

Her head sprang up and she forced herself to hold his gaze. Had she been too quick to judge this man as kind? Was he offended by her feet? She should have remembered her manners and put up with the pain a little longer.

"First rule, you already know. You're to call me Tate."

She nodded. That, she could try to get used to.

"Second rule, you don't need my permission to sit or lie down or stand on your head. Understood?"

She nodded again, hiding a smile at the thought of standing on her head.

"Third rule. Please stop apologizing to me over trivial things."

She bit down on her bottom lip, wondering how many times she'd apologized. It couldn't be more than once.

"Fourth rule." He dropped the volume of his voice to a soothing tone. "I want you to trust me. Can you do that?"

"I can try," she said, not wanting to lie to him. Trust took time to build. And he scared her like no other man had before.

"Can I make a confession?" He got up from the bed and took the seat next to her.

"Yes." She smoothed down the fabric of her dress as she wondered what he could possibly confess to her.

"I'm a little scared of you," he said.

She couldn't stop the laugh that escaped her lips, instead, trying to catch it with her hand.

"Why would you be scared of me?" she asked. "You're the Prince! Your father is the King."

"True," he said. "But I'm still a man. Does that make sense?"

It made so much more sense than she knew how to explain. Perhaps a Prince and a Guardian weren't so different after all. They'd both worn titles all their lives that identified who they were in such an all-consuming way that it was hard to make sense of who they were as an individual.

"I think we're going to be very good friends," she said.

Tate smiled at her and in the warmth of the dark pools of his eyes, she knew she had nothing to fear.

It didn't matter if Tate had chosen her or not. They were in this together.

The tie slipped from Tate's hair once more and as it fell around his face, she drew in a sharp breath that fanned the spark in her core.

He reached for the tie, but this time she spoke up.

"Leave it, Tate," she said, with no hint of apology in her voice. Rules were rules.

EDISON

THE NOW

*E*dison flicked the reins, urging his mules to go faster. He was keen to get to the Bay and collect the kelp his mother required for her useless tonics. That should keep her quiet for a while. Then he'd be free to do what he was really going there for.

He knew his mother appreciated the help he gave her, just as he knew she didn't appreciate the sharpness of his tongue. But someone had to speak the truth! How else would she know what was going on around her? He was sick of holding back his words and had decided when he'd turned eighteen only recently that he'd speak his mind now that he was a man. He was tired of people treating him like a child.

Prince Tate had turned eighteen recently, too. The exact same day as Edison. And he was being treated so much like a man that the King had chosen him a bride. Where was Edison's bride? He wouldn't mind being betrothed to a Guardian. Especially one as appealing as River. Or even better, her sister, who'd have no choice but to be nice to him if it was the King's order. Not that she was able to be nice to anyone at the moment, lying in her bed.

He sniggered at the thought. Served her right.

Tate was in for quite a shock with his bride. The way she'd spoken back to Edison in the tavern was a disgrace. How dare she say he wasn't a real man! He'd only been speaking the truth when he'd said she wasn't a real woman. Guardians had stopped being real women many generations ago. They were mutants now, one glance could tell you that. It wasn't normal for anyone to grow so tall and strong. She was the freak, not him.

He flicked the reins again and as his mules finally got the message and increased their pace, he wondered what Tate was doing now. Humping his new bride, perhaps? If he was smart, he'd gag her while he was doing it. That guy had all the luck. He always had.

When they'd been young, they'd grown up like brothers, roaming the palace grounds together, with Pip trailing behind, begging them to include her in their games.

Back then, Edison had done anything he could to shake her loose, but Tate had always made excuses for her. He still did. She was as pathetic now as she was back then, looking out her window like she thought the world would come to her, even if she refused to go to it.

If only he'd been smart enough back then to realize the benefit in letting Pip tag long. Maybe then she wouldn't have shut him out. Maybe Tate wouldn't have either.

Both Tate and Pip had denied it, but he knew the truth of their feelings toward him. They'd pushed him away when their mother died, taking comfort in the company of each other, making it clear he was an outsider. Their grief bound them in a way that excluded him and he'd hated it. He still did. It'd been over a decade and he still hadn't found his way back in.

But he was going to change all of that. Because he had a plan. A plan that had nothing to do with becoming the herbalist and every-thing to do with the palace. It was about time he stopped living in the shadows while Tate got all the glory. They were two boys, born on the same day, but to two very different sets of parents. One set of parents meant Tate got to be King and the other meant Edison got to make tonics for the rest of his life, like he was some kind of servant. And he'd had enough. He was meant to be in the palace, he could feel it in his bones and taste it on his lips. He'd make a far better King than Tate would and if his birthright hadn't laid that path out before him, then it was time he paved it himself. There was more than one way to become King.

All he needed was some time alone with Pip. And finally, he thought he knew how to make that happen. He had the perfect excuse to be allowed into her bedchamber. And if he could get access to her room, then it shouldn't be too hard to gain access to her heart.

She clearly thought she was worthless. Why else would she lock herself in her room like that, allowing her health to deteriorate more and more each time the sun set and rose? He'd seen her at her window recently and her size was a real concern now. He could convince her that she was worthwhile, make her feel wanted. And then... well then, her health could deteriorate as much as she liked.

Once he had what he wanted, she could curl up and die just like her pathetic mother, he didn't mind. Or she could just stay in her room. It was the same difference really. She was practically a ghost haunting the palace right now anyway.

He saw a glimmer of blue ocean on the horizon and smiled. The Bay. The city this kingdom had been named after, before the King's great grandfather several times removed had built a new castle inland and brought his vision of the Guardians to life, fearful of another attack by Feldspar whose last attempted invasion had very nearly succeeded. Edison would get the kelp, find himself a willing whore, pick up the other supplies he needed and be back with plenty of time to put his plans into place.

Let his mother stew her pathetic herbs all she liked. He was stewing something far greater than her tiny brain could ever imagine.

PIP

THE NOW

*P*ip watched Tate creep out into the cornfield, surprised he hadn't waited longer before sneaking away from his new wife. Perhaps she should have realized he'd be keen to escape the palace and the Guardian who now slept beside him. It must be a strange feeling for him to share his bed with someone.

She glanced across at her own bed. Empty and cold, apart from her dolls staring back at her. There were no midnight conversations or the desperate pressing together of flesh happening under those covers. It was just Pip. All day. All night. Nobody to love her and nobody for her to love in return. Somehow, it felt worse now knowing that Tate had somebody, even though she was no more alone now than she'd always been.

It wasn't like Tate had even wanted to get married. That had been obvious. But she understood why he'd gone through with it. Their father was very difficult to say no to.

She both looked forward to and dreaded meeting his wife. The curious side of her wanted to see what she was like, but this would also involve his wife seeing what Pip was like. And she hated that. Nobody saw her these days. Except Tate, who brought her meals to her. And her father, who liked to stop by every now and then to tell her how disappointed he was with her. And her handmaiden, Elise, who cleaned up after her, but she hardly counted. Maybe she could ask Elise what Tate's bride was like? She'd said she helped her dress for her nuptials, but hadn't said much else. She needed to press her for more details. That would be better than having to go through the trauma of meeting somebody new.

Because if nobody new saw her, then nobody could judge her.

A gentle tap sounded at her door and she spun around. It was too early for her father or Elise. And she'd just seen Tate walk out into the cornfields. It couldn't be his wife, could it? Surely Tate would bring her to meet her himself.

"Who is it?" she called, only to hear another gentle knock in response.

"I said, who is it?" she shouted louder this time, going to the door.

But before she could get her eye to the spy hole, she heard a voice. "It's me."

Her heart skipped a beat and she stumbled back from the door at the sound of the voice of a boy she was once desperate to be her friend. Well, if she was honest, he was a boy she'd been desperate to be a lot more than just her friend. She'd had quite the infatuation with Edison when she was younger, with his fair hair, piercing blue eyes and a quick wit. A boy who'd made it abundantly clear that he didn't want her, almost as much as she wanted him. To this day, he remained the only boy she'd ever loved.

But what was he doing here now at her door? She knew he'd seen her looking from her window, but coming face to face with him was quite different.

She smoothed down her hair, wishing she'd had more warning. She may not love Edison anymore, but she still cared about his opinion of her. She didn't want him seeing how much she'd let herself go.

Sitting down on her bed, she folded her hands in her lap and concentrated on her breathing. She didn't have to let him in just because he knocked.

"Pip!" he called through the door. "I know you're in there. Let me in. I just want to talk to you."

She remained perfectly still, wondering how long she'd need to wait for him to go away. She'd promised Tate she'd never talk to him again. She couldn't break that promise when Tate had been so good to her.

"I have something for you." His voice was pleading now. "To help you. Please, let me in."

For someone who'd waited a decade to speak to her, he was certainly being very persistent all of a sudden.

"Leave it outside my door," she said, quite liking to be the one to be resisting his cries for attention for a change. He hadn't seemed to care one bit when she'd followed him around the garden as a girl, desperate to be included in the games he'd played with Tate.

Until he'd finally turned his eyes to her and things had gone so horribly wrong. Her life had never been the same after that. He'd said he wasn't to blame, but she blamed him nonetheless. When she wasn't busy blaming herself.

"Pip! Please."

She went to the door and fumbled with the cover on the spy hole. Lifting it, she peered through. And there he was, with only a piece of timber between them. She'd dreamed of this moment, never believing it would actually happen. If only she could see him a little more clearly. But for that she'd need a far bigger spy hole and for him to take a step to his left. Or she'd need to open the door.

Would Tate know if she let him in? He had secrets from her, after all. He'd never told her where he went in the mornings. No, she couldn't betray her brother like that.

"It won't take long. Please, Pip. I'd like to give this to you myself."

He held up his hand and she squinted but couldn't see what it was he wanted to show her.

"What is it?" She silently cursed her curiosity for getting the better of her. Some sister she was.

"I made you a tonic," he said.

"What for?" Her head sprang up. "I don't need one. And I don't trust your tonics."

"Let me in and we can talk about it. You do need this. I'm worried about you. I've seen you in your window. You don't look healthy."

She kneaded her hands, sorely tempted to let him in. Edison was worried about her? It seemed so unlikely. But with her mother dead and Tate newly married, who else was left to worry about her? She hated to admit it, but she liked the feeling of Edison being concerned about her.

She opened the door, just a tiny amount, enough for her to see Edison's face, clearly this time.

But where there stood a man with the bristles of a beard sprouting from his face, Pip saw the boy of her youth. Her heart lurched and she swallowed, glancing to the floor, wishing he wasn't seeing her like this. Time hadn't been as kind to her as it'd been to him.

She closed the door a little more, reducing the size of the crack.

"Come on, Pip." He tried to pry open the door, but she held it firmly. "Don't be like this. Not with me. We used to be so close."

"We weren't close," she whispered. "I wanted to be your friend, but you always ran away from me."

"I was just a kid! Boys always ignore the girls they like. Hasn't anyone ever told you that?" He pushed on the door again.

"You... liked me?" She could scarcely believe her ears.

"Of course I liked you," said Edison. "I still do. You were lots of fun. Whenever I ran away, I always hoped you'd chase me."

She opened the door, fully this time, and locked eyes with the boy who was now a man.

"That's better." His voice was soft, like a gentle promise. "Look at you. You're all grown up. A real lady now. A beautiful princess."

Pip stepped away from the door, unsure what to do with such a compliment, even if it was far from true.

"You can come in." She walked back into the room, thrilling at her rebelliousness, and waited for him to follow. It did sound like he had something important to tell her. Besides, he'd already seen her now and maybe what he had to say would give her something else to think about, instead of wondering when Tate would next grace her with his presence. She was no longer a little girl. It was time for her to decide for herself who she did and didn't allow into her life.

Edison slipped through the door and closed it behind him. Now that she could see him fully, she felt even more ashamed of her appearance. He was handsome. Extraordinarily handsome. That pull she'd felt toward him still existed, only now that they were grown, it was a different kind of force. One that made her stomach twist and her breath catch in her throat.

He put a small green bottle on her table and took a seat.

"I made you this tonic," he said.

"I don't want it." She perched on her windowsill, not wanting to get too close to him. "The last thing I need is to grow taller or broader."

"But surely you'd like to be stronger? Have more energy and think with a clear mind?" He pushed the bottle toward her. "This isn't the same tonic the Guardians drink."

"Is it the one you made for—"

"No!" he cut her off. "I've told you before it wasn't my tonic that did that. I made this one just for you. A brand new secret recipe."

"For me?" Her hands fluttered to her throat. He'd spent time creating something just for her? She was glad she'd let him in now. It would've been rude not to.

"I've told you, Pip. My tonics have never hurt anybody. Only helped them. I'd never hurt you."

She nodded, still not sure if she believed him.

"I've seen you in your window." He smiled at her and she noticed how blue his eyes were and how white his teeth. Perhaps he took a tonic to enhance his looks. "I want you to have the strength to leave your room. To be the girl you used to be."

Blood rushed to her cheeks. It'd been years since she'd felt so self-conscious that it manifested in the color of her face. Her hands fluttered to her cheeks, as she desperately hoped he hadn't noticed.

"What did you put in it?" She stepped closer to the table and took hold of the bottle, lifting it to her nose to smell. It had a strange nutty fragrance. She was certain she could detect chamomile in there, too.

"It wouldn't be a secret recipe if I told you that." He smiled at her and she dared to catch his gaze and hold it for a moment or two. "Drink it up."

She held it to her lips and wondered if it would kill her. Did she care? Was she even really living now?

"I don't really want to be stronger." She put the bottle back on the table.

"Come on, Pip. If you get a little stronger, you'll be able to leave your room. There's so much fun we can have together out there, just like when we were young."

"I'm happy here." She pushed the bottle back toward him. "I don't want to leave my room."

"But I want you to."

He reached for her hand and her knees went weak. His hand was so large and strong, making her own hand feel tiny encased inside his warm grasp.

His fingers rubbed her palm and she sat down before her legs gave way, but still, she clung to his hand. She wasn't ready to break the kind of contact she'd been craving all her life. Not yet. Maybe not ever.

"I've missed you, Pip," he said. "Thanks for agreeing to talk to me."

"You're welcome." She winced as her voice came out in a squeak. She was making a mess of this. Edison had grown up with the Guardians. She must look pathetic to him. He'd never visit her again if she behaved like this.

"You still have the dolls," he said, tipping his head toward her bed.

Yet more blood raced back to her cheeks and not because she was ashamed about her dolls. It was the thought of Edison seeing her bed. The place where she'd dreamed of him and thought about him and missed him with a deep ache in her bones. Seeing him look at her bed felt intimate, even though there was nothing intimate about it at all.

Still holding her hand, he leaned forward, sending her insides into meltdown. "Please trust me, Pip. I'd never hurt you. I made you this tonic to help you. I want to be your friend again. More, if you'll let me. I thought you wanted that, too. But if you don't..."

"But I do." She reached for the bottle with her free hand, lifted it to her lips and tipped it back. It was sweeter than she'd expected, a bit like Edison himself. Licking her lips, she wondered if she was hoping the tonic would really make her strong. Right now she didn't mind what it did to her as long as drinking it meant Edison would visit her again.

"I'll bring you another tonic tomorrow," he said, pushing back his chair and breaking contact between them.

"Yes, please." She clasped her hands together in her lap, trying to hold onto the feeling for a little longer.

"Thank you for trusting me," he said. "I know it wasn't easy for you."

"What will the tonic do to me?" she asked, desperate to prolong the visit.

"It'll make you strong and wash away your fears. We'll have you out of this room and running through the garden in no time."

She winced, not liking the sound of that at all. She didn't want to leave her room and run through the garden with Edison. She wanted him to stay right where he was in the safety of her room.

"Edison." She passed him back the empty bottle, a jolt passing through her gut as their fingers brushed. "I know I don't... look how I used to. You don't have to call me beautiful. I know what I am."

"Pip." He slipped the bottle into his pocket and placed a hand on her forearm. "You are beautiful. Now, let's work on getting you strong enough that you can show the world some of that beauty again."

"Thank you," she said, putting her hand over his. There could be no harm in letting him believe she wanted to leave her room, just as long as he didn't stop visiting her. She wasn't sure she could wait another decade before seeing him again.

"See you tomorrow?" he asked.

She smiled as she nodded. "I'll open the door a little more quickly next time."

He laughed. "See, beautiful and funny, too."

She watched him leave, then shifted to sit in the chair he'd vacated, looking at her bedchamber as if through his eyes.

Was she really beautiful? Tate said so. And now Edison. But her mirror didn't, not that she'd looked in it for years, having covered it over with a blanket. She didn't need to look in it to know she was as fat as she was useless.

But one thing she couldn't doubt was that since drinking the tonic, she certainly did feel strong and calm. Was that the tonic Edison had given her, or had that been the effect of Edison himself? A man who her brother had banned her from seeing when she was a girl. But now that she was a woman, her promise didn't seem so important to keep. It was broken now anyway. And as she knew better than anyone, once something was broken it was almost impossible to put back.

TATE

THE NOW

*T*ate hating handing out bad news. Especially when the bad news was worse than bad and he had to deliver it to a wife he barely knew.

"What's wrong?" River asked, the moment he walked into his bedchamber. *Their* bedchamber now.

Pip had often told him he wore his mood on his face, but he hadn't believed her until now. He tried to rearrange his facial expression into a more neutral one.

"Sit down." He patted the back of a chair and nodded at River.

"Tell me what's happened." Her feet remained planted on the floor.

"Please sit down," he tried again. This wasn't news to give someone while they were standing up.

She reluctantly lowered herself into a chair and blinked at him with the pale blue of her eyes as she waited for him to speak.

He pulled up a chair close beside her and drew in a deep breath, wondering how to phrase what he had to say, and deciding it'd be best to just spit it out.

"Your sister passed away overnight."

River's hand flew to her mouth as she let out a noise that reminded him of a rabbit caught in a trap. She knew what was happening and desperately didn't want it to be true.

"I'm so sorry." The words choked in the back of his throat with their uselessness.

She shook her head, still not seeming to be able to find any words of her own.

"The herbalist's working hard to find out what the problem is." This would be of little comfort but he wasn't sure what else to say. "We're going to get to the bottom of this."

"It's too late for Daphne."

He nodded, unable to deny the truth of this. He knew better than anybody how impossible it was to bring someone back once they were gone. Pushing thoughts of his mother aside, he focused on his wife, patting her awkwardly on the hand.

"I should've been there with her." Streaks of tears were flowing down River's face now. It was the first time he'd seen a Guardian cry. He didn't even know they could.

"It's my fault you weren't there." The heavy ache he'd felt in his chest when he'd first heard this news increased in weight, like a stone against his ribs. "I'm so sorry. Please, go to her now. Your family needs you."

"But you're my family now." She blinked, wiping away her tears and pulling back her shoulders. There was the Guardian courage he was familiar with.

"Oh, River," he said. "Of course I'm your family. But that doesn't mean you have to say goodbye to the family who raised you."

"That's... that's not what your father told me when he selected me. He was very clear that I was expected to leave them behind."

Tate shook his head, realizing the disappointment his father had for him ran both ways. How could anybody try to cut someone off from their family like that?

"Go and visit them." He kept his voice gentle, in the same way he spoke to the injured rabbits.

"My duty is to you now." She bit down on her lip and looked at him, each blink of her eyes breaking his heart just that little bit more.

"Then I request that you accompany me, while I visit your family to pay my respects."

River's forehead wrinkled and she tilted her head, more than aware he was saying this for her benefit.

"Please," he said, standing and reaching out his hand. "This way you can tell my father that you were following my orders."

River didn't need to be asked twice. She got to her feet and took Tate's hand, her eyes brimming with tears. "Thank you."

He sighed, wishing she wouldn't be so polite. He was never going to get to know her if she kept up those walls. He wanted to see the true River. The one who'd shocked him by boldly requesting he let his hair fall free. Perhaps the problem was that she didn't seem to know herself. The woman she was now that she was no longer a Guardian. She had as much to learn about herself as he did about her.

"Come here," he said, pulling her close to his chest and wrapping his arms around her.

She returned the embrace with stiff formality at first, then melted into him, sliding her hands around his waist and resting her face on his shoulder as a quiet sob shook her body.

"I'm so sorry," he said again.

"No apologies." She lifted her head from his shoulder to look at him. "If a rule is good for me, then it's good for you, too."

"That sounds fair."

He took her by the hand and led her from the palace and out to the garden. He was glad to have been able to offer her some kind of small comfort, even though he suspected nothing he did would be able to take away the pain of her losing her sister. If anything happened to Pip, he'd be devastated.

But he knew Guardians were tough. Brave. They faced their troubles with stony faces and heads held high. Seeing tears fall from River's eyes had been huge. Was it because she was no longer drinking her tonics in the morning? It'd only been a couple of days since the wedding. Surely, they weren't so powerful that they had such an immediate effect when she'd stopped taking them.

More likely it was just the gravity of the news itself.

They followed a path to a tall hedge, behind which was the Guardians' village. Tate used to come here often as a boy, searching for Edison to come out to play or to talk to Ariel about her magic potions, as he'd liked to call them.

But he'd come here far less regularly since his mother died, avoiding Edison rather than seeking him out. He visited Ariel only when he knew Edison wasn't around, feeling uncomfortable every time he stepped through the hedge. Not because he wasn't made to feel welcome, but for the opposite reason. The Guardians treated him like he was some kind of supreme being, bowing to him and stopping their conversations mid-sentence when they noticed him. Had they done that when he was a child? Perhaps they had, but he hadn't noticed it. Or perhaps children didn't garner as much respect as when they were grown.

He tightened his grip on River's hand, aware that now he was seeking comfort from her as well as handing it out.

They went through the opening in the hedge and past the tavern where the Guardians took their meals and tonics. Behind the tavern was the kitchen and the small home the herbalist shared with Edison. He was probably back there somewhere. But Tate didn't want to think about him right now. His focus was on River.

The Guardians' small huts were dotted around the landscape. The way their thatched roofs clung to the mud-brick walls reminded Tate of the hats he sometimes saw the farmers wearing.

Everywhere he looked, there were Guardians training. Running, jumping, lifting, climbing; their hard muscles glistening in the sun, male and female alike. He glanced at River and tried to imagine her in her Guardians' tunic, putting herself through these grueling exercises. Did she miss it? Would her hard muscles turn to soft flesh now that she was no longer using them?

As they passed, groups of Guardians would stop what they were doing and bow their heads to show their respect. If they were curious about River in her new royal clothing on the arm of a Prince, they didn't show it. She was a Princess now and it was their job to serve her. They treated her as they did any other royal.

River bowed her own head, holding back her tears. She didn't seem to want the attention of these people she'd grown up beside. All she wanted was her family. All she wanted was to grieve.

"Over here." River tugged on his hand, taking him to one of the huts on the outskirts of the village.

Before they reached the door, it flew open and a female Guardian stood before them with her arms outstretched, as if she'd somehow known her daughter had come home.

River ran into her mother's arms and they held each other in silence, tears unnecessary to convey the sadness they felt. Tate pushed down a pang of longing for the comfort of his own mother's arms. This wasn't about him.

"Come in." River's mother let go of her daughter and stepped aside.

"I'll wait out here," said Tate, not wanting to intrude on such a personal moment.

"No, you won't," her mother said, with nothing but love in her eyes. "You're my son now. You'll join us inside."

Tate felt a pain stab him in the chest and for a moment he thought he might weep the tears that River had been holding back. He realized for the first time that he didn't just miss his mother. He missed *having* a mother.

He stepped into the small hut and into his new bride's life.

RIVER

THE NOW

*R*iver knew it was her job as a Guardian to stay strong. But how was that possible when every cell of her body felt like it was tearing apart.

Daphne was dead. Her sister who'd been younger than her, stronger than her, taller than her and undoubtedly an all-round better person than her. If Daphne died, then what hope did anybody else have, least of all River.

She watched her brave mother usher Tate into the small home she'd grown up in. There were no rooms in this hut. Everything they needed was all in this one open space. But her family hadn't needed a large home. All they'd needed was love, something that seemed to be distinctly lacking in River's new home in the palace. Although, there was no denying a bond was developing with Tate. It wasn't love though. Not yet. But the spark had certainly grown into a small flame.

As her eyes adjusted to the dim light, she saw her father sitting beside Daphne's bed. His head was in his hands and she wondered if he knew she was there. Daphne was still on the bed, and River averted her gaze, not ready to see her sister's cold face just yet. She'd never seen a dead person up close before and wished the first time wasn't someone she cared about so much.

"Father," she said, placing a hand on his back.

He jolted and looked up at her, his face stony, his eyes empty pools. Never before had she seen him like this.

"River? I barely recognize you." He stared at her, having never seen her like this either.

She wore her hair down around her shoulders now and the palace seamstress had made her several dresses that fit without ribbons struggling to pull them together at her back.

"It's me," she said, holding out her arms as her father stood, anticipating his warm embrace. The hug from Tate had given her some comfort, but it was her father's arms she craved right now.

But instead, he dropped to a bow. "It's nice to see you, Your Highness."

River's stomach fell. She didn't want him calling her that. Nor did she want him bowing to her. He was the man who gave her life. Her mother hadn't treated her like that just now. This was ridiculous! She knew Guardian blood ran strong and loyalty and service to the royal family were paramount, but this was taking things too far.

So, she stepped closer to him and wrapped her arms around his waist, forcing him upright, his hands hanging limply by his side. She continued to hug him, waiting for him to return the affection, but he held still.

"Please, father," she said. "I need to know you love me. I'm still your daughter."

With these words, his arms engulfed her as he pulled her close, his giant Guardian body dwarfing her.

She relaxed into his familiar warmth, realizing how much she'd missed him.

Then, letting go of her with almost as much urgency as he'd taken hold, he went to the door and left the hut.

"I don't understand." River shifted her eyes from the door to her mother as she slowly shook her head.

Her mother forced a smile that said she didn't want to explain, so River tried again. "Does he blame me for Daphne's death? That I wasn't here to look out for her?"

"Oh, no. Of course not." Her mother rushed to her side.

"Then what is it?"

Her mother sighed, taking the seat her husband had only just vacated and looked from Daphne and back to River, her eyes filling with tears that would never fall. "He feels like he's lost both his daughters."

"But that's not true." Tate stepped forward to join River at her side.

She'd almost forgotten he was there, he'd been so quiet until now. Did he feel uncomfortable intruding on what was an excruciatingly personal moment? Perhaps now he had some understanding of how she felt in the palace.

"Just because River's now my wife, doesn't mean she's no longer your daughter," said Tate.

His words flew straight from his lips to River's heart. She may not have married the sort of man she expected to, but there was no doubt she'd married one who was kind. And what more important quality could there be in life than kindness?

"Thank you." Her mother smiled up at Tate, her thoughts no doubt mirroring River's own. "Please excuse my husband leaving just now. We're trained to bury our emotions no matter how intense they are. It makes us stronger as warriors."

Tate nodded. "People kill for hate. They kill for love. Emotion is what drives us to be better people and it's what causes us to be worse. There's nothing wrong with letting our feelings show."

River hesitated, not sure how to feel about this. Tate was questioning everything she'd been raised to be.

"Please forgive me." Tate's eyes fell on Daphne's lifeless body. "Perhaps I should wait outside for you. You need some time here."

"Thank you." She didn't want to agree, but he was right. She needed to talk to her mother. And she needed to say goodbye to Daphne. Tate may be her husband, but he hadn't known Daphne.

"I'll be right outside if you need me." He stepped outside and closed the door behind him.

"He's a good man," her mother said, reaching for her hand. "I'm relieved for you."

"Were you worried?" Her mother hadn't shown this concern when she'd learned the King had selected her. The only sign had been with the words her father had refused to say.

"A Guardian never worries," her mother said.

"What do you think of what Tate just said about emotions?" she asked, not sure she'd have an opportunity to speak to her about this later. "Is it right for us to keep pushing them down until they burst out in a flood?"

"I'm not sure. I'd need to think on that. All I know is that your husband may be just what this kingdom needs. And with you beside him, The Bay of Laurel will be stronger than ever before."

There was a pride in her mother's face. No matter what reservations she may have had about River's marriage, there was a part of her that was undoubtedly as honored as she'd claimed to be.

"I feel our kingdom is getting weaker lately, not stronger." River looked at her sister's wasted body, not yet able to drag her eyes to her face.

"I don't mean strength of muscle, River. I mean strength of heart."

River squeezed her mother's hand back. There were so many more layers to this woman who raised her than she'd realized. Why was it that she was only discovering it now that they no longer lived under the same roof? Sometimes distance sharpened perspective, rather than blurred it.

"Do you mind if I sit with her for a bit?" she asked, motioning to the chair.

"Of course." Her mother stood. "I know you loved her, too. I'm going to wait outside with your Prince."

River sat beside Daphne and waited until they were alone. She lifted her sister's hand from the bed. It was cold and heavy.

Slowly, she shifted her eyes from Daphne's hand, to her chest, to her neck, to her face.

"Oh, Daphne!" She let out a gasp and pushed back her tears in the way she'd been taught to as a child, but it was no use. They spilled out anyway, just like they had when Tate had first delivered the news. "Oh, Daphne."

Her beautiful sister no longer looked like her sister. Her face was so relaxed without her smile to hold it in place that she looked like a different person. If it weren't for the familiar slope of her nose, or the tilt of her eyes, or curve of her chin, River might be convinced it was someone else who lay in this bed. But it was Daphne. There was no doubt about it. This was her sister.

"Thank you for being my sister," she said. "Not that you had a choice in that."

She paused, as if expecting Daphne to open her eyes and reply.

"I'm going to find out what happened to you," she vowed. "I promise you that. And I'm going to flatten whoever's responsible."

Then lifting her sister's hand to her lips, she kissed her fingertips. "Love you, Daph."

Before she could let her emotions take hold too fiercely, she stood and joined her mother and Tate outside the hut.

Tate's face lit up to see her, not with joy, but with something else she couldn't quite put her finger on. Was it respect? Admiration? Having spent her life suppressing how she felt, it was going to take some time to unravel the knot of feelings inside her.

This man had come into her life and changed it in so many ways. And in time, she may have the power to change many more lives.

Tate reached out and placed a hand on her back in such a way that it made her feel like not only did she marry Prince Tate... she felt like he married her.

PIP

THE NOW

*P*ip set down her favorite doll on her bed and stroked its
faded dress, spreading it out like a fan.

Ariel, the herbalist, had knitted her a set of woolen dolls as a gift
when she was born. It seemed her talents stretched beyond the
kitchen, as the dolls were exquisite. There was a King and Queen doll,
a Prince and a Princess, and a male and female Guardian.

Pip's favorite, of course, was the Princess doll, who she'd somewhat unoriginally named Prin. The doll had long, blonde hair, just like
her and two bright blue crosses carefully stitched on for eyes. Her
pretty dress was pink, not the sort you could remove, but knitted in as
part of the design. What Pip especially liked, was that Prin was beautiful. What a shame, she hadn't grown up to match that part of her
Princess doll.

"It's time for your sleep now, Prin," she said, using the same tone
her mother had used when she'd been a young girl.

Prin looked back with her sewn on eyes, unblinking.

Then, hearing a noise in the passageway, Pip leaped off the bed and ran to the door to look through her spy hole. But seeing it was only a maid passing by, she quickly returned to the bed, to check on Prin.

"You're still awake!" She put her hands on her hips and tutted. "All right then, I'll tell you a story. That should help you sleep."

Pip drew up a chair next to the bed and imagined she was her mother telling her younger self a story. She knew it was childish to play such games at the age of sixteen, but with little else to do in her bedchamber, this was something she was reluctant to let go of. It reminded her of happier days. And it wasn't like she had anything else to do, except stare out her window or watch people through her spy hole.

"Once upon a time, there was a beautiful Queen who was married to a handsome King. They had a daughter they loved very much. They named her Snow, for she had the fairest skin and blondest hair that anybody had ever seen."

Pip's hands fluttered to her own hair that her mother had once combed into soft waves and she wondered if her mother had changed this part of the story to match her own appearance. Or perhaps she'd made up the entire story.

"But sadly, the Queen died when Snow was still a young child…"

A familiar lurch gripped Pip's stomach. This was another part of the story that matched Pip's own life. But thankfully the next part was different, so she pressed on.

"The King remarried soon after and his new wife became step-mother to Snow. But she was a wicked stepmother who was jealous of Snow's beauty. She'd look into a magic mirror every day and ask who the most beautiful woman in the kingdom was, happy to hear it was her. But when Snow grew from a girl into a woman, the mirror changed its answer and the evil Queen flew into a terrible rage to hear the mirror speak Snow's name."

Prin looked up at Pip, not seeming to be growing any sleepier, so Pip lifted the corner of her blanket from her bed and tucked her in a little more. When her mother had told her this story, she'd never gotten sleepy either.

"The Queen had a huntsman take Snow into the forest to be killed, but she begged for her life and the huntsman let her run away, as long as she promised never to return to the palace. Now, this plan might have worked if not for the magic mirror that continued to insist Snow was still the most beautiful woman in the kingdom."

Pip hesitated, remembering how her mother had told her many times that she was the most beautiful girl in The Bay of Laurel. Back then, she'd smiled at her mother and believed her. Why then, had she had such trouble believing Edison when these same words had come from his mouth? Was the difference in the person who spoke them, or the ears that heard them? But there was no time for such wonderings now. Prin was waiting for the rest of her story.

"And the mirror was correct, as Snow was indeed still alive, having wandered deep into the forest where she found an abandoned cottage. She swept it out and made it her home where she lived happily until one day an old woman knocked on her door to give her a shiny red apple. Not realizing the old woman was the Queen in disguise, Snow took the apple and bit down into it. Of course, the apple had been poisoned and Snow fell immediately to the ground."

Pip cleared her throat, aware of the raspy tone to her voice, perhaps because she hadn't used so many words at once for a long time.

"Now, this might sound like a terrible way to end a story, but it isn't. For, you see, Snow was only asleep, not dead. And soon after, a Prince from a faraway kingdom happened upon her cottage when he was riding through the forest. Falling in love with her at first sight, he bent to the ground and scooped her into his arms, placing a gentle kiss upon her lips. Snow opened her eyes and the Prince took her to his kingdom so they could live happily ever after."

Pip smiled, wondering what it would feel like to have Edison press his lips to hers, then realized she'd forgotten to tell Prin the ending to the story.

"So, the next time the Queen talked to her mirror, she was pleased to hear that at last, she was the most beautiful woman in the kingdom. The mirror wasn't lying, of course. It was only telling the Queen half the truth and Snow was able to live the rest of her life with her loving Prince by her side, free from the wicked Queen."

She pulled the blanket up so it covered Prin's face. "Good girl, you're asleep now."

She knew she hadn't told the story properly and decided to ask Tate about it later. Had their mother told him the same story when he was young? Or being a boy, had she told him stories of dragons and soldiers instead of princesses and queens? It was getting harder and harder to remember all the details. She was certain she'd accidentally changed it over the years. She had a faint memory that in the version her mother had told her, there'd been a group of strange little men in the cottage when Snow had arrived, but perhaps she'd just imagined that. Her mother had a book with the story of Snow written down in it, but that had disappeared not long after she'd died. Or had it been before? If only Pip had looked after it! How could she have been so careless to have lost it? She should have taken it from her mother's room and kept it safe always. Then she wouldn't have to try to remember all the details of the story. She spent so much time alone, thinking, that sometimes it became difficult to tell the difference between what she remembered and what she imagined.

Maybe Edison's tonic would change all of that. He'd said it would make her strong and wash away her fears. But what was she scared of exactly? Nothing really, which of course meant she was scared of everything.

She went to her bureau and combed her hair, noticing it was thinner than it used to be. Just another thing that made her feel ugly.

But Edison didn't seem to think so. He'd come to her bedchamber every morning for six days straight now, armed with his tonic and his compliments. And he was right, she was feeling stronger. But she still wasn't certain if it was the tonic, or his words? Maybe it was both.

It felt good to have forgiven Edison. If indeed there was anything to forgive. He insisted he'd done nothing wrong and despite her memory screaming at her that this wasn't true, she knew she couldn't trust her memories. The story of Princess Snow was proof of that. Tate had been over-reacting when he'd told her to stay away from Edison after their mother's death. This was yet another thing she needed to talk to him about. If only he weren't so preoccupied lately with his wife. He didn't have nearly as much time for her since he'd gotten married. Some days he'd practically thrown her breakfast at her and run away.

Edison didn't do that, though. He lingered in a way that made her feel like he never wanted to leave. And she didn't want him to, either. It was far more interesting talking to him than it was to Prin, mainly because he talked back. And unlike Tate, when Edison talked to her, he had excitement in his eyes instead of sadness.

She was certain she could trust him. He wouldn't be spending so much time with her if his feelings weren't genuine.

Whatever the case, for the first time in such a long time, Pip felt like she had a future, instead of only having had a past. And that felt so good.

EDISON

THE NOW

"*His* is Majesty will see you now."

The Guardian stood back and held the door for Edison, who marched through as if it were his own father he was here to see.

He bowed in front of the King's throne, knowing he must wait to be addressed before rising to his full height.

"Edison, my boy." The King put down the bowl of string beans he was eating and smiled, a green strand hanging between his front teeth. "How are you? It's been a long time since you came to see me."

Edison let out a slow breath as he stood, having been unsure as to what kind of reception he'd get. But whatever grudge Tate seemed to be holding against him, thankfully it didn't seem to be shared by his father.

The King stuck a finger in his mouth and fished out the vegetable matter from between his teeth, flicking it and watching it fly across the room with a satisfied smile.

Edison cleared his throat. "I was giving you time to grieve the loss of your Queen." He hoped this sounded reasonable. How could he tell the King the reason he hadn't been seen around the palace was because the Prince had shut him out? If the King wasn't aware of this, then it was best to keep it that way.

"She's been gone for many years now, Edison." The King seemed almost confused. Perhaps his feelings for the Queen hadn't run particularly deep. His own memory of the Queen was that she was pretty enough, but not especially interesting. Whatever the case, her husband certainly didn't seem to be mourning her loss too greatly.

"The years have passed quickly, Your Majesty," said Edison.

"Indeed they have." The King smiled at him, although it did little to set Edison at ease in his presence. If he were to become King one day, would people treat him with the same level of fear? He hoped so.

"Y-yes." Edison scolded himself for losing his voice. He had to get to the point, but timing was everything. He didn't feel quite ready yet.

"I always did like you, you know," said the King.

Edison couldn't have stopped the grin that spread across his face, even if he'd wanted to. A compliment like this from the highest ruler in the land was rare. He hadn't come here to receive such praise, but was certainly happy to accept it.

"Thank you, Your Majesty. And I've always had great respect for you." He bowed his head to show his sincerity.

"And what brings you to see me today?" The King reached over for another bean and poked it into his mouth, chewing loudly.

Edison averted his eyes, disgust burning the back of his throat. The King had doubled in size since Edison was a boy. He wasn't sure what he'd been eating, but it had to be a lot more than bowls of beans. Perhaps eating vegetables made him feel like he was being healthy.

"I'm here to speak to you about a delicate matter, I'm afraid." Edison steeled himself to deliver the speech he'd been practicing all night. "But one I fear I cannot hold from you for a moment longer."

"Speak freely, my boy." The King reached for his cup of wine to wash down his beans.

Edison swallowed, then as he lifted his head, he brought forward the life-changing words. "I'm afraid I don't wish to take over as the herbalist from my mother when the time comes. I feel there are better ways I can serve the kingdom."

Almost choking on his wine, the smile fell from the King's face and he set down his cup. He wasn't taking this news as well as Edison had hoped.

"And what better ways might these be?" asked the King.

"It's the Guardians," said Edison. "There's growing unrest amongst them."

"I've heard a few have perished recently. But wouldn't you be best placed to aid them by following your path as our future herbalist? A few adjustments to the tonics should set them right." He raised his eyebrows and waited.

"I'd like to suggest a different approach," said Edison. "I fear the tonics need more than just a few adjustments. The way they are right now, they're doing more harm than good."

The King's eyes opened wide and he sat forward. "That's quite a statement. Do you realize how many palace resources have gone into those tonics over the years? Are you telling me that's been a waste?"

"I'm aware, Your Majesty. Which is why I'm bringing this to your attention. The tonics were an important key in developing the Guardians' strength in previous generations, but the problem is that it's started to give them too much courage."

"But courage in a soldier is a good thing, is it not?" The King reached for the last few beans, looking at his empty bowl like it'd offended him.

"It is," said Edison. "Usually."

"Go on," the King urged, biting into the beans as they slid between his teeth.

Edison may not have the King on his side just yet, but he certainly had him interested, which was a good starting point.

"The Guardians are becoming unruly," said Edison. "I live beside them, so trust me that I know. Just the other day a female Guardian ruthlessly insulted me for no reason whatsoever when I handed her a tonic." He decided to omit that it was the King's new daughter-by-law he was talking about, not feeling this would aid his case. If the King were to verify the story with River, he may receive an exaggerated and inaccurate version of events that didn't paint him well.

"They're growing far too confident," Edison continued. "I believe the tonics are to blame. The courage it gives them is being misused. I understand why you chose to marry one to your son, however, the message this has sent to the Guardians is that they're now equal to us. Equal even to you. Putting that together with the recent unfortunate deaths, we now have rumors of a rebellion on our hands."

"A rebellion against me?" The King's face went just as pale as Edison had hoped it would.

"I'm afraid so, Your Highness. You know just how strong the Guardians are. If they were to turn against us, I'm afraid there's nothing that could be done to stop them. How would we defend ourselves against an army so strong? You only have to look at what happened in Forte Cadence not all that long ago. Their King had no chance when his army turned."

Now the King's face went from white to green and Edison was concerned he hadn't seen the last of those beans. Had he really never thought about this possibility before? Was he so certain of his army's loyalty that he'd never considered what might happen if they rebelled? Of course, there had been no such talk of any rebellion in The Bay of Laurel, but Edison could see it in the Guardians' eyes. And if they were thinking it, then surely it wasn't so different to them saying it. He wasn't lying to the King, merely keeping him one step ahead.

"What do you suggest we do?" asked the King.

His use of the word *we* warmed Edison from the inside.

"It's time to show the Guardians some discipline. Put them back in their place. They're servants and soldiers, not equals. If you don't act quickly, I'm afraid the rebellion may become more than just talk. It will become a serious and imminent threat."

The King shook his head, clearly shaken. "And you have a plan?"

"I practically grew up inside the walls of this palace, despite living amongst the Guardians. I understand how this kingdom works—not as well as you do, of course..." He hesitated, hoping his words hadn't tripped him up, but when the King didn't seem perturbed, he continued. "If you make me Master of the Guardians, I'll oversee the tonics to ensure they're corrected to maintain the Guardians' strength but reduce their confidence to make them more submissive. And I'll ensure we have no further premature deaths. That's something I believe I can fix immediately. I'll also overhaul the Guardians' living conditions. No more residing in family groups, we'll divide the village into two. One half for the males and the other for the females. I'll personally select who breeds with who. No more marriages, no more relationships, no more alliances. It's time to treat them as the army your ancestors dreamed they'd be. One that's not just strong and courageous, but loyal and compliant."

The King glanced at his empty bowl and nodded slowly. "Interesting. And you believe these changes will be enough to stamp out any signs of a rebellion?"

"I do." Edison nodded, keeping his expression suitably grave. "Their loyalty to you will be restored and they'll be ready to protect you against any threat of invasion in the coming years. As you're aware, our enemies are getting stronger. They've aligned in a way that's most dangerous to our kingdom."

"This is true. It's been of growing concern to me, but my advisors have been unable to provide me with as much reassurance in all our meetings as you've been able to in just this short conversation. Your approach may be just the solution I've been searching for."

"Yes, Your Majesty." Edison straightened his back and tipped up his chin. This was going even better than he'd imagined. "It's time to get tough."

"And who would you be overseeing to make the new tonics?" asked the King. "Your mother?"

"She's still useful, Your Majesty. She may have lost her touch, but nobody knows their way around the kitchen like she does. Under my guidance, I feel that things can be improved."

The King looked at Edison and nodded slowly. "Yes, she's been loyal and discrete over the years. She saved my son's life when he was an infant, did you know that?"

"That was a long time ago." Edison hadn't come here for the King to be reminded of how well his mother had served the kingdom. This was supposed to be about his future, not hers.

"What you propose is indeed of interest," the King said.

Edison's chest deflated as he anticipated the 'however' that was certainly to come next.

"However... I need to know that I can trust you. I can't possibly make such drastic changes to the kingdom without being absolutely certain I can believe what you have to say." He scratched his chin as he thought. "I think I'll send you on a quest."

"Yes, Your Majesty." Edison ignored the fluttering in his stomach. Surely, he'd be able to pass whatever quest the King had in mind. "I'll do anything to prove my loyalty to you."

"I want you to go to Wintergreen." The King sat up in his throne, his eyes shining. "Take as many Guardians with you as you feel you need. They have an apothecary where an Alchemist produces elixirs of oils that bring about miracles."

Edison wondered what miracle the King was after and waited for him to explain. Procuring some oils shouldn't be too difficult a task, especially with several Guardians in tow.

"I want you to seize one of their elixirs for me." The King thumped his fist on the arm of his throne. "Every bottle of it they have."

"Seize?" That sounded a little more forceful than necessary, but Edison was undeterred.

"Yes, seize. I don't want you to give them one pebble in exchange. You're to take the oils by force. Just like the Guardians, it's time our enemies know who's in control here. We don't ask for anything. We take it. Do you understand?"

Edison nodded, pleased the quest didn't sound overly difficult. "I'll seize the oils, Your Highness. May I ask which oil it is that you require?"

"It's a delicate matter, I'm afraid." The King lowered his voice, despite there being nobody else present. "Nobody else knows, so if word gets out, I'll know the source. Do you understand?"

"Yes, Your Majesty. I won't say a word to anybody." Edison bowed to show his sincerity.

"I'd like a supply of fertility oils, as a wedding gift to my new daughter. I'm keen for her to hurry up and provide me with an heir. As you're no doubt aware, Guardians aren't known to produce more than two or three children per female. We need to enhance the Princess's fertility so she can deliver me at least a dozen strong heirs."

"Forgive me, Your Highness, but I'd be more than happy to make the new Princess a tonic to enhance her fertility."

"I'm curious about these miracle oils." The King waved his hand as if Edison were no more than an annoying fly. "And you said yourself that our tonics are doing more harm than good. Fetch me the elixir I desire and let Wintergreen know who's in charge here. If you succeed, I'll consider your request."

Edison caught his smile before it reached his lips, not wanting the King to see how excited he was by this prospect. Just as the King had been unable to imagine his army turning against him, he was similarly blind to the idea of Edison's loyalty wavering. Because if Edison was made the Master of the Guardians that meant the world's strongest army would be under his control. He'd be able to overthrow the King with ease, leaving him as the greatest ruler the land had ever seen. He may not have royal blood, but he'd make a far better King than Tate, who was as weak as he was stupid.

Edison bit his tongue to stop himself from asking the King what would happen if he failed in his quest, and the taste of iron flooded his mouth. Failure wasn't an option. He didn't need to ask about the consequences to know they wouldn't be good. Death was a common reward for failure in this kingdom.

At least he was wise enough to have a backup plan. And Pip was doing so well at helping him with that.

"I'll make the preparations," said Edison. "Thank you, Your Highness."

He pulled back his shoulders and strode from the room. Things hadn't gone quite as well as they could have. He'd have preferred to be handed his new title without having to earn it. Or at least been given a promise of it upon his success. But things could certainly have been worse.

His hand went to his throat, searching for the hemp cord he'd worn since he'd been a boy, before remembering he no longer wore it. So, he ran his fingers through his hair instead.

All he had to do was acquire an elixir using whatever force he felt was necessary. He could do that. And when he did, he was going to be able to do so much more. So very, very much more.

TATE

THE NOW

ate was back in the cornfield, running between rabbit traps, his eyes darting around for any sign of a farmer.

It felt good to be out here, even if the good he was doing was only small, it made a big difference to the energy in his soul.

It was a stressful time watching River grieve for her sister. The pain her emotions were triggering in Tate's own heart was a little confusing. Because it told him in the short time that he'd known River, he'd already grown to care about her. He wondered if it was because she was his wife, or if it was because of who she was as a person? Perhaps it was a little of both.

A trap in the distance stole his attention and he dashed toward it, his eyes fixed on the dark shape thrashing about inside the metal jaws. Please, let him not be too late to help this poor creature.

He skidded to his knees and felt his hair slip from the tie that'd been holding it. He brushed it out of his eyes as he bent to the rabbit, relieved to see the trap had caught it by its tail. This was rare, but fortunate. A rabbit could survive without this ball of fluff on its rear.

"Hey, little friend," he said, taking hold of the rabbit's torso and wincing as it bit him.

He adjusted his hold, away from the rabbit's mouth and got to work on the trap, easing it open until the rabbit came free. Taking some balm from his pocket, he wiped it across the rabbit's severed tail and let go.

The rabbit raced away, gone in seconds.

"No problem! Happy to help!" Tate laughed as he got to work on resetting the trap and disabling the spring mechanism.

Hearing a movement behind him, he spun around. A farmer was bound to catch him one day. He'd been certain he'd been alone.

But it wasn't a farmer.

"River." His eyes scanned his wife's pretty blue dress. "You startled me."

"I followed you." She folded her arms and tilted her head as he got back to work on his trap.

"I figured out that much already," he said. It was a little surprising she'd succeeded in following him like that, although she was trained for battle, he reminded himself. Just because she no longer dressed like a Guardian didn't mean she was no longer as skilled as one. "But why?"

"I wanted to know where you went each morning." She tilted her head as she watched him work.

"You could've just asked." He finished with the trap and stood, wiping his hands on his already filthy trousers.

"Would you have told me?" she asked, holding his gaze.

"No."

She smiled. "Then you know why I followed you."

"Where did you think I was going?" He motioned with his head for her to follow him. It was time to get back to the palace anyway. Pip would be waiting for her breakfast.

"To meet a lover," she said, plainly.

"Well, perhaps I was." He smiled at her, liking that she cared enough about this as a possibility to find out. "I do love rabbits."

"I can see that. But, why Tate? Why do you do it?" She looped her hand in the crook of his arm and his heart skipped a beat.

"I can't lie in my bed knowing there are creatures out there suffering. Well, ones that I can help, anyway." This was the simple truth of it. He didn't know if she'd understand, but she was his wife. He needed to learn how to trust her.

"But Tate, there are rabbits all over the kingdom. There are hundreds of farms with many thousands of rabbits caught in traps right now. Why would you bother to save just that one you let go? What difference did it make?"

"Well, it made a difference to that one, didn't it?" He winked at her to show he knew how crazy it sounded.

She sighed. "Oh, Tate. How can I argue with that?"

"Who says you have to argue? You know, I've never told anybody about what I do out here."

"Not even Pip?" she asked, looking up at Pip's window in the palace.

"I told her once, but she didn't believe me. Does that count?" He followed River's gaze to Pip's window, frowning when he thought he saw an unfamiliar shadow in the window.

"Did you see that?" he asked. "Is there someone in there with her?"

"I don't think so." River squinted, trying to get a better look.

"The light plays tricks sometimes," he said, trying to convince himself just as much as River. He'd ask Pip about it later when he took up her breakfast.

"I'd like to meet Pip," said River. "Will you take me to her?"

"She's not great with meeting people." He pulled his eyes from the palace and back to the path ahead.

"Are you worried about what she'll think of me?" River let her hand fall from Tate's arm and kicked at the ground as she walked.

"No! Of course not." He wondered what he was worried about and realized it was the opposite of what River had suggested. "I'm... I'm a little worried about what you'll think of her."

"You're embarrassed of her? Tate, what's wrong with her? Why doesn't she leave her bedchamber?"

He stopped walking and reached for River's arm, pulling her to a stop. A conversation like this needed his full attention. He'd trusted River with his secret about the rabbits—not that he'd really been given a choice in that—but could he trust her enough to let her into Pip's life?

"I'm not embarrassed of her," he said, wanting to be clear. "I love Pip. It's just that she's not well. You'll notice that the moment you meet her, but it's not her physical appearance that makes her unwell, it's her mind. She has a problem with food. It started when our mother died and I have no idea how to fix her."

"Is that why you save the rabbits?" River's eyes filled with what could only be described as love.

"I don't understand," he said.

"You save the rabbits because you can't save Pip. It makes you feel like you're doing something."

He took a step back like he'd been punched, the shock of her words completely throwing him for the simple reason that she was right. He'd been blind to what had been so obvious to her.

"I'm sorry," she said, misunderstanding his reaction.

"No, River. You're right. You're completely right. And I think you should meet Pip. Today. Right now. Come with me while I take up her breakfast." It didn't matter if Pip was apprehensive about meeting River. She'd be good for her. Perhaps she'd be able to fix her in the way Tate hadn't been able. And if there was one thing he'd learned about River already, it was that she wouldn't judge Pip. For the state of her body, or the state of her mind.

For all his father's faults as a man and as a King, Tate thought that maybe for once he'd done something right. He'd chosen Tate the best wife he could ever have dreamed of.

PIP

THE NOW

*P*ip pressed her eye against her spy hole as she waited for Tate. Her stomach growled to remind her that he was late. At least she'd had time for her body to absorb Edison's tonic without interference.

She smiled at the love Edison had been showing her, going to all that trouble to make her a special tonic, then bringing it to her to make her brave and strong. The days were passing so much faster now that she had his visit to look forward to. He really did seem to care about her. She wished she'd never doubted him. To think she'd spent all these years blaming him for something he clearly had nothing to do with. Coincidences happened sometimes. But if he was innocent, did that also put her in the clear? She wasn't sure she was ready to absolve herself just yet.

She sighed and stood back from the door. Why was it so much easier to forgive someone else than it was to forgive yourself?

Going to her bed, she picked up Prin, cradling her as she thought about her mother's death. The details were getting hazy now, in the same way the story of Princess Snow and the poison apple was starting to fade. Only this was worse, as she didn't often give herself permission to think about it to remind herself of exactly how it'd happened. But now that she'd been having her daily tonics, perhaps it was safe to think about it with a clearer head.

Her mother had been beautiful and kind. But she'd also been sad for no reason anybody could explain. She'd slept a lot, more than any normal person, having had the herbalist make up a tonic of skullcap to assist her. Sometimes she'd sleep for what seemed like days on end and Pip would sit on the end of her bed waiting for her to open her eyes and play with her.

She remembered the day Edison had approached her in the garden. She'd been only six years old at the time but even then, she'd felt aware of Edison's presence in a way that didn't seem normal. He'd always had that effect on her. Like they were connected in some strange way. She still couldn't explain it. That feeling remained with her today.

Edison, who was only eight years old himself at the time, had slipped a small jar of tonic into her hand and told her if she switched it over with her mother's regular tonic she'd wake up and be healed.

Delighted with this prospect, Pip had thanked Edison and crept into her mother's darkened room ever so quietly and swapped her afternoon tonic with Edison's preparation.

And he'd been right. Her mother had consumed the tonic and been more alive than Pip remembered ever seeing her.

The following days were the happiest of Pip's life. She'd meet Edison every morning in the garden for the special tonic, go to her mother's room and make the swap, then spend the afternoon with her while Tate and Edison ran through the garden pretending they were Guardians in battle.

But then just as quickly as her mother's health had returned, it vanished. She began sleeping even more than before, her skin turned a strange yellow color, and a fever broke out that refused to go away.

So Pip stopped giving her Edison's tonic, just in case that was the problem. And then… well, then she died.

And Pip blamed Edison, despite him insisting that without his tonic she'd have died far earlier and Pip should be thanking him for giving her a chance to spend some quality time with her before she died.

Not knowing what to believe at the time, Pip had confessed to Tate and he said even though Edison probably had nothing to do with it, they could never be sure. He made her promise never to speak to him again.

But now she'd broken her promise and let Edison back into her life. She knew it was wrong, but had to admit that was part of the reason it felt so good. She was doing something dangerous and the excitement of that burned in her core.

A tap at her door made her jump. Tate was here, almost as if he'd heard her thinking about him. She shouldn't have been surprised, given she was expecting him.

But when the door opened, she was most definitely surprised to see he wasn't alone. There was a tall, blonde woman standing beside him. His mysterious wife, who she still wasn't sure she was ready to meet.

"Pip, this is River," said Tate, not waiting to be invited in before heading for her table to place down her breakfast tray.

River curtsied and Pip tried to push down the blush she felt creep into her cheeks. It'd been a long time since anyone had curtsied to her. Even Elise didn't bother anymore when she came to tend to her room.

"Hello, River," she said, glad she'd fixed her appearance as much as possible when she'd woken, even if that had been for Edison's benefit, not River's. "Nice to meet you. Please, come in."

River went and stood beside Tate, and Pip was surprised to see an ease between them, almost like they'd known each other for years. It unsettled her. She was used to being the most important person in Tate's life. She'd never thought for a moment when he got married that she'd be displaced, especially given their father had been the one to choose his bride. Even more reason that she need not tell Tate everything that was going on in her life. Edison never made her feel like she was second best. Well, not anymore he didn't.

"I like your doll," said River.

Pip's flush deepened to realize she was still clutching Prin in her hand. She threw her onto the bed as if she weren't her most prized possession and crossed her arms, wondering what River thought about her so far. If she was shocked or disgusted by her, she was doing a good job of hiding it so far.

"You must be hungry," said River, trying another topic to break the silence. She was persistent, Pip would give her that. Not surprising for a Guardian. "Don't mind us. Please, eat."

"She never eats in front of anyone," said Tate. "No matter how often I ask her to."

"*She* is right here," said Pip, trying not to pout. "And *she* will eat later, thank you."

"Don't be like that," said Tate, putting his hand on River's back, despite his words finally being directed at her. "What's up with you lately?"

"What do you mean?" She blinked at him, certain she hadn't been behaving any differently, even though her whole life had changed the moment she'd allowed Edison to step through her door.

"You're different somehow." He left his wife's side to go to her, and suddenly the attention she'd craved from him didn't seem like such a good thing after all. "You look different. Your hair is…clean. You're wearing new clothes."

She stepped back, both pleased that he'd noticed and annoyed. If he found out Edison had been visiting her, she was in big trouble. Who knew what her father would do to her. Or Edison!

"Was there someone in your room this morning?" he asked.

She blanched as her heart threatened to explode. "No!"

"I thought I saw a shadow through your window," he said. "Are you telling me the truth?"

"You caught me out! It was one of my many lovers who visit me every day." Hopefully, a half-truth would be more believable than a blatant lie.

"It's your attitude, too." Tate bit down on the inside of his lip as his head tilted. "You're not behaving like yourself."

"Leave her, Tate," said River, putting her hand on his arm. "She told you it was nobody. I was with you and I didn't see the shadow."

"You were with him?" Anger bubbled in Pip's empty stomach. All these years she'd been asking where he was going in the morning, and now he'd not only told River, but he'd taken her with him!

River nodded. "I followed him. He wouldn't tell me where he goes, either."

"And where does he go?" Perhaps this was her opportunity to find out at long last.

"I've told you before," Tate said. "I set the rabbits free in the cornfield."

She huffed. It seemed she was going to have to wait a little longer for him to tell her the truth. Perhaps she'd be able to get it out of River a little more easily one day.

"Pip, I don't mean to give you a hard time," said Tate. "It's just that I'm worried about you."

She felt her resentment for her brother melt away as she looked into the depths of his dark eyes. That was two handsome men who were worried about her now.

"Sit down and let me fix your hair." She reached for the strands of hair that had flown free of the tie Tate normally wore.

"River likes it like this," he said, glancing at his wife, whose cheeks turned a dark shade of pink. Just how far had things progressed between these two?

"But father doesn't like it," she said. "He'd shave you bald before you could say roast potatoes with dripping."

Tate sighed and sat down, allowing her to pull his hair into a knot, handing her a tie from his pocket. He must go through hundreds of these each year. His hair was almost as restless as he was. She liked fixing his hair, finding it a way to express affection for her brother without looking him in the face. She didn't deserve his love.

No, that wasn't right. Perhaps she did. Edison said it wasn't her fault her mother died. She'd helped her live her last days to their fullest. She was dying anyway. Some people were just born weak. Edison said she had to rise above that. She had to be stronger than her mother had been. He was helping her.

"Don't worry about me," she said to Tate, stepping back, satisfied his hair was princely once more. "I'm fine. I've never been more fine, in fact."

"We'll let you eat, then." Tate stood and gave her a kiss on the cheek.

"Do you mind if I visit you sometimes?" asked River. "It can get lonely here in the palace."

Pip found herself smiling. "That would be lovely. We can be sisters."

River moaned in a strange way and Tate rushed to her, putting a protective arm around her. Pip remembered too late that Tate had mentioned that River's sister had died recently. The last thing she'd want right now was a new sister.

"I'm sorry," said Pip. "I didn't mean…"

"It's okay." River's eyes filled with moisture. "Having a sister would be nice. I do miss my sister. She was my best friend."

"Off you go," said Pip, not sure what to do with a Guardian's tears. "Go and make me an aunt."

"Not you, too." Tate rolled his eyes.

As they left, Pip thought that being an aunt would be nice. She could play with the child in the gardens and be the kind of friend she'd always wished she'd had as a child. If it were a girl, she might even give her niece her set of dolls. It was about time she stopped playing with them. They'd have such fun together. It would be just like she was a girl again herself.

But she'd have to leave her bedchamber to do that. Could she do that? Maybe. But then again, maybe not. Perhaps just thinking about it was the first important step.

ARIEL

THE NOW

"Where are you going?"

Ariel watched as her son prepared a sack of various essentials.

"I told you. A King's quest." He smirked and she saw his father's face embedded in his features. She was thankful he didn't look more like him.

Ariel sighed, hoping this quest was an invention of her son's mind. What possible mission could the King send her son on? His job was to work by her side, not gallivant around the kingdom pretending he was a Guardian, like he'd done with Tate as a child.

"And who will help me while you're gone?" she asked.

"You have plenty of supplies. I've made sure of that. You'll have to serve your tonics in the tavern yourself. Just don't kill anyone while I'm gone."

Edison chuckled and Ariel went to her kitchen, needing a rest from her son's presence before she decided to kill him.

She didn't trust him. She never had, really. But now it was different. Now that he was grown, he wielded far more power than he had when he was a child.

She knew he'd been sneaking out somewhere in the mornings and had followed him as far as the palace itself and seen him slip inside one of the doors used by the servants. But what was he doing in there? And did it have anything to do with the tonics she'd discovered him creating in her kitchen when he'd thought she'd been asleep? The two had to be linked.

But what exactly was he up to?

Perhaps Edison going away on his mysterious King's quest was a good thing. It would give her time to think without the distraction of him being there.

If only she could gather the courage to speak to the King herself. Although, his soul was almost as gray as her son's, so she didn't expect that would do her much good anyway.

"Things are going to be different when I return," said Edison, following her into the kitchen. It seemed there was no getting away from him right now. Not until he'd said what he was so eager to tell her.

"How so?" She was unable to inject the pretense of energy into her voice. Being his mother had been so much more tiresome than she'd anticipated.

"If I succeed in the King's mission, you'll be answering to me from now on." He puffed out his chest, pushing his blond hair back from his forehead. She knew it was wrong, but in that moment, she couldn't help but think how the ugliness of his soul had seeped into his face, much like it had with the King over the years.

"You said you didn't want to be the herbalist." She sat down and waited for him to finish saying whatever it was he'd followed her in here to say.

"I don't," he said. "You can keep that job. But at least I'll be able to instruct you on how to do it properly."

It was at that moment that Ariel had her first black thought all of her own, causing her to wonder if her own soul was gray, or full of light as she'd previously believed? She could end Edison's life with ease any time she liked and he'd never see what got him. She could make it look like pneumonia or heart failure or that he'd slipped away in his sleep. She knew all the recipes. They were written down in a special book she kept in a metal chest buried in the parsley patch, safe from her son's hands, after she'd found him studying it as a boy.

But could she kill this son she'd raised? A son who once she'd loved? She didn't think so, which was what made her think that her soul was indeed more light than gray.

"Good luck on your quest," she said, with no further words for him. There was nothing she could say that would turn him around. She knew this as she'd spent the last eighteen years doing everything she could. But now she gave up. He was a lost cause. She'd be better off spending her energy coming up with ways to outsmart him than seeking ways to try to let the light into his soul.

"Is that all you have to say?" His frown was one of disgust.

"It is." She buried her face in her hands and waited for him to leave.

"No wonder you're killing everyone with your tonics," he muttered, leaving her in peace at last. "You're pathetic."

Was she really killing everyone? That sweet Guardian girl, Daphne, had been the latest casualty. Was that really her fault? She still found it so hard to believe. Edison had to have something to do with this. There was no other logical explanation. Did that make her a bad mother to be convinced of such a thing?

With Edison gone on his quest, it would give her a chance to find out for sure. If the Guardians returned to health, she'd know he'd been interfering. And if they didn't. Well, then she was the worst kind of mother there was.

EDISON

THE NOW

*E*dison rode ahead of the two carts of Guardians being hauled by the kingdom's strongest mules. It was frustrating having to slow the pace of his horse to allow them to keep up, but it was necessary. Besides, they needed to get used to following him. Because when he returned, victorious from the King's quest, he was going to be their master. Life was going to change in more ways than their small brains could ever imagine.

He sniggered at the thought they were helping him succeed. They may be brave and they may be strong, but they were also ridiculously stupid. Yet another reason why they needed to be pulled into line. The Guardians were given far too much freedom.

His plan was to head to the river that formed the border with Wintergreen, tie up the mules at the base of the mountain and make the remainder of the journey on foot. The Guardians would never get their carts across the water, but the walk would do them good to maintain their fitness. Not that the apothecary was too far from the border. Perhaps a day's journey at most. But thankfully there was no need for Edison to have to take a single step, given that his horse could swim.

The sooner he was back at the palace, the better. He couldn't wait to get started with his new life. It was so close now, he could taste it. He may not have been born a Prince, like Tate, but he was going to be so much more powerful, proving that brains were more important than birthright.

He followed the road over a crest and a giant rocky mountain range came into view. They were nearly there. He'd never seen this mountain range before, but knew it was the dividing point between four of the world's five kingdoms. Much bloodshed had taken place here in generations gone by as the kingdoms tousled for power and borders were established.

And if he could see the mountains, the river wasn't far. It'd be nice to dismount and stretch his legs. They'd spend the night here and attempt the river crossing at first light. The sun was already getting low in the sky and crossing at night would be far too dangerous, even with a dozen Guardians in tow.

As the mountain loomed closer, Edison reduced his pace to shorten the distance between himself and the Guardians. Their risk of an ambush was greater the closer they got to the shadows. Although, if the stories were to be believed, the three other kingdoms that bordered the mountains were united in peace now. What a ridiculous concept. Kingdoms were meant to invade, not align. It was just lucky The Bay of Laurel's King hadn't been stupid enough to enter into any such agreement. He didn't need to with his strong army. And that was what Edison was here to prove. The Bay of Laurel called the shots.

The mules pulling the two carts of Guardians were tiring and their pace slowing. Frustrated at how close they'd come and how long it was taking, Edison decided to believe the rumors of peace and ignore the threat of an ambush. He took off ahead, his horse just as desperate as he was to reach the water.

He rode to the base of the mountain and dismounted at the river's edge near an impressive waterfall. His eyes scanned the water from where it crashed into the river right up to the summit of the rocky mountain, marveling at the height it had to fall. He'd never seen anything like it.

While his horse drank, he removed his shoes and rolled up the legs of his trousers so he could cool his feet and wash his face. There'd be no swimming at this time of night when the temperature was about to plummet. He'd never get dry again before morning.

The Guardians had forced their mules into a gallop now, the panicked expressions on their faces making it clear they were unimpressed by Edison leaving them behind. The King had been very clear they were to protect him at all costs.

The thundering of the mules' hooves shook the ground and the leaves of the trees that clung to the side of the mountain quivered in response.

As the Guardians got closer, the thundering grew in strength and Edison emerged from the shallows of the river to watch, frowning at the intensity of the noise, audible even over the crashing of the waterfall. Something wasn't right. The rumbling was too loud and growing louder still. Two carts of mules could never make this kind of racket. Was there an echo?

He looked up the mountain, gasping to see a wall of boulders hurtling down, gravity pulling them faster and faster as they bounced and rumbled their way to the ground below.

"Watch out!" His voice was swallowed by the mountain as pain gripped him around his thumping chest.

The mules reared up and tried to turn around, restricted by the heavy carts attached to them. They panicked and turned anyway, uprighting the carts and spilling out the roaring Guardians, who hit the ground and scrambled in an attempt to get to Edison to keep him safe.

But they needn't have bothered. Edison was a safe distance away. It was the Guardians themselves who were in danger, with the boulders heading straight for them. Their desperation to get to Edison only slowed them down, tangling them in the chaos, their feet unable to find purchase on the rumbling earth.

As stones and boulders smashed onto the dirt, the Guardians with their carts and mules were sent flying and a cloud of dust erupted, masking the carnage from Edison's barely-blinking eyes. This didn't seem possible. Of all the times for these stones that'd sat on that mountain since the beginning of time to decide to fall, it had to be now. Why, now? Not when Edison had come so far. Returning to the palace a failure wasn't an option.

Edison stepped backward into the water, distancing himself further from danger as he waited for the last boulder to fall and the cloud to clear. His horse had already started its swim across the expanse, desperate to get away. Edison followed, splashing and kicking and propelling himself to safety.

He threw himself on the bank of the other side of the river, catching the reins of his horse just in time before it ran off into the dusk.

"Easy now," he said, unsure if his horse could hear him. "Easy, boy."

The pain in his chest was subsiding now, replaced by the screaming of his lungs for air, as the realization of how close he'd come to death hit him.

He pulled himself to his feet and peered across the river. The rumbling ceased and the waterfall soon became the only noise to be heard above the horrible panting Edison was aware was escaping from between his clattering teeth.

Had anyone survived?

As the dust was slowly taken by the gentle breeze, he saw a large pile of rocks where once there'd stood man and beast. Surely nobody could survive being crushed and buried under that. It was impossible.

With a sense of great dread, he had to accept that his Guardians were gone. There was no point in going back to look for survivors. It was a shame, but he reminded himself that it was better than if a group of real humans had been killed.

Somehow, Edison had escaped. If he hadn't ridden ahead of the Guardians, he too would be dead right now. He'd made the right decision. This whole trip would've been a waste of time if he hadn't survived.

Or was it still a waste? Surely, he couldn't go on to the apothecary alone? He was wet, cold and shaking. Not in any kind of fit state for such a journey.

And how would he demand the Alchemist hand over the elixir the King desired without the Guardians standing behind him? He didn't pose nearly a great enough threat on his own.

But the King was adamant he needed the fertility elixir to provide him with a hoard of babies he'd call his grandchildren. But they were babies Edison would call freaks. Because their mother would be a Guardian. They'd be abominations that needed to know their place. Crossbreeding them with pure blood humans was wrong on every level. Just another reason why Tate couldn't possibly become the King, because that would make his firstborn child heir to the throne and what kind of kingdom would The Bay of Laurel become with a freak seated upon the throne? He'd rather die than see that happen.

This was why he must continue on and complete his quest

A movement on the other side of the river caught his eye. A mule had somehow survived the rockfall and was trying to get to its feet, having pushed its way out from under the rubble. But its reins were pinned under a boulder and it was unable to stand.

Edison looked back to the water, contemplating for the briefest moment if he should cross the river again and cut the mule free. It seemed a waste of energy to save a beast with a brain even smaller than the men it'd transported here.

No, he couldn't put himself at risk for a mere animal. That would be even more foolish than risking himself for a Guardian.

He had a quest to complete for the King and nothing was going to get in his way.

He squeezed some water from his shirt and climbed back onto his tired horse. He had to press on. His destiny depended on it.

RIVER

THE NOW

*R*iver knocked on Pip's door and waited. The breakfast tray was heavy, even for her strong hands. There was so much food on there, all for one person. But it wasn't her place to comment on that. Tate had asked her to see if she could get Pip to open up to her. He thought Pip needed a friend. And she owed Tate that much at least. He'd already done so much for her, treating her with such gentle respect.

"It's River," she called out when there was no answer. "I have your breakfast."

"Where's Tate?" Pip opened the door a crack and her eyes narrowed.

"He asked me to bring this to you today."

"Why?" She opened the door wide now and River saw a very different Princess to the one she'd met only days earlier. Her locks of blonde hair were a mess and she had dark circles under her eyes.

"He had other business to attend to and didn't want you to go hungry." This wasn't strictly a lie, albeit not entirely true. "May I come in, please?"

Pip stepped aside to let her pass.

She placed down the tray and stood, wringing her hands, waiting for Pip to invite her to take a seat. Surely, she didn't expect her to leave straight away?

"Are you feeling well?" asked River, despite Pip's disheveled appearance indicating that she wasn't at all well.

"Not especially." Pip sat on her bed, picked up her doll, then set it back down again as if remembering herself.

"May I sit down?" River put her hand on the back of a chair.

Pip pursed her lips together, then nodded slowly, while River did her best to reserve her judgment of this girl her husband adored.

"What's it like?" asked Pip.

"I'm not sure what you mean." River sat down and smoothed out the fabric of her skirt, still unable to get used to the softness compared to her Guardians' tunic.

"What's it like being married to my brother?" asked Pip. "Being... I don't know... being a real person. You know, instead of one of those freaks."

Pip crossed her arms and waited for River's response, unaware of how offensive she'd just been.

"Guardians are real people." River tried to keep the venom out of her voice, doubting she'd succeeded. "Who told you otherwise?"

Pip bit down on her bottom lip. "Nobody."

Who had this girl been talking to? Someone must've put these ideas in her head. River knew Tate didn't think like this and he was the only friend Pip had. Unless it was the King himself? But that didn't make sense either. Nobody would choose a *freak* to marry their son and provide them with an heir.

"Guardians are very much real people, Pip." River sat forward in her chair. "Perhaps you'd let me introduce you to my family one day? You'd like them and I'm sure they'd like you."

River bit down on her own lip now, conscious of her lie. Her parents wouldn't like Pip one little bit if she spoke like that. But maybe they could help convince her that they were ordinary people with the same hopes and dreams as anybody else. Although, there was something about the way Pip spoke that make River feel like she was testing out these ideas rather than believing them herself.

"I can't meet them." Pip crossed her arms. "You know I don't leave my bedchamber."

River drew in a breath, reminding herself that she hadn't come here for a fight. She'd come here for the exact opposite reason. Tate had wanted them to be friends, although that was seeming less and less likely the more words that came out of Pip's mouth.

"I meant that perhaps I could bring my family here one day to meet you," she explained, speaking more slowly than usual to reinforce her point.

Pip shook her head. "I don't see visitors."

"You saw me."

"I don't get a choice in that. Not at the moment anyway."

She was talking in riddles now.

"At the moment?" asked River, hoping she might start making more sense.

"One day things will be different. Ed—" Pip stopped talking as if she'd suddenly become mute.

"Ed?" River prompted, hoping the rest of that word didn't result in the name of a man she'd come to despise.

"I didn't say Ed." Pip cast down her eyes, clearly hiding something.

River pulled her lips into a smile, deciding to bide her time before she pressed her on this. "I'd like to be your friend, Pip. Your sister, too, if you'd let me. I want you to know you can trust me."

"Do you love Tate?" asked Pip.

Now it was River's turn to dodge a question. How could she explain her feelings to Pip when she didn't even understand them herself?

"Tate is the kindest man I've ever met," she said.

"Everybody knows that." Pip waved her hands in front of her as if to shoo away River's words, a gesture River had seen the King use. "But do you love him?"

"Yes." River was unsure if this was true, but aware it was the answer Pip was seeking. Could love bloom so quickly? She admired Tate and couldn't help but notice how handsome he was, especially when his hair slipped free and fell around his face. But was that love? It was the beginnings of it, certainly.

"He loves you," said Pip. "I can tell by the way he looks at you."

"Would you like to get married one day?" asked River, trying to steer the conversation in a safer direction. Tate wasn't here to speak for himself and it seemed unfair to talk about him like this.

Pip nodded and a huge smile spread across her face. "Definitely."

River sat forward, hoping Edison didn't have anything to do with the certainty of Pip's answer. "Do you have anyone in mind?"

"No," said Pip, a little too quickly.

"Are you sure about that?" River laughed in a failed attempt to keep the conversation lighthearted.

"I'm hungry now," said Pip. "Would you mind?"

"Oh." River stood, realizing she was being asked to leave. "Of course."

As Pip hauled herself off the bed, the top button from her dress fell open revealing something around her neck. River tried to shift her eyes away but couldn't.

Pip was wearing Edison's distinctive hemp cord. It had to be his. Nobody else had one like that with three different strands of colored hemp woven together.

River pulled back her shoulders and reminded herself that she was a Guardian. Handling a difficult conversation was nothing compared to what she'd been trained to do.

"Pip, when you said Ed earlier you were about to say Edison, weren't you?" She looked Pip directly in the eye, daring her to lie.

Pip cowered, like the *real* person she was and shook her head.

"He was the shadow Tate insists he saw in here," said River. "Why else would you be wearing his necklace?"

Pip's hands flew to her throat and she pulled her dress together to cover the cord.

"He's the man you hope to marry, isn't he?" pressed River. "And I'm going to bet he's the one planting awful ideas inside your head. Ideas that sound very much like things Edison would say."

"Please don't tell Tate!" Pip fell to the floor and clutched at River's dress. "Please! He might tell Father, who'll make me marry a Guardian like you. And I won't. I just won't!"

"Why? Because you don't love a Guardian? Or because we're freaks?"

"I'm sorry, River! I am! I don't think you're a freak. The truth is, I don't know what to think anymore. All I know is that I love Edison. I know he doesn't always say the right thing, but he means well. He's a good man and he's been helping me get better."

"I'm not going to say anything." River knew she wouldn't be able to keep this promise. She wanted to win Pip over, but her loyalty was to her husband. He needed to know the truth so he could protect his sister.

Because River wasn't sure exactly what Edison was up to, but she knew one thing for sure. And that was that he was up to no good.

EDISON

THE NOW

*E*dison tied up his horse at the drinking trough and ran his fingers through his damp hair.

He'd traveled through the night, the journey to the apothecary taking far longer than it was supposed to. He had no idea where he was going in the dark and was freezing cold in his wet clothes. He'd clung to his horse, shivering, as he led it in circles, desperately trying to draw some warmth from the animal's back.

If those stupid Guardians hadn't raced so fast toward the mountain, it wouldn't have rained those rocks down on them and left him alone and stranded. He'd be waking up on the other side of the river after a good night's rest.

When the sun had come out at long last, he'd climbed off his horse and tilted his face to the sky, willing the rays to dry his clothes and warm his bones. But all it'd done was turn his clothes from wet to dank and his bones from freezing to just plain cold.

Eventually, he'd had to ask a passerby for directions to the apothecary, just about weeping for joy when he'd finally arrived.

The apothecary was a large building with a smaller store tacked onto the end. The building wasn't anything special, but he had to admit the garden around it was something else. Edison hadn't realized gardens like this existed. Paths were lined with lavender and rosemary, leading through manicured gardens of roses, and there was a gazebo in the distance with trails of jasmine crawling all over it like a flowering spider's web.

In The Bay of Laurel, plants were grown in rows to optimize their food production, not to enhance their beauty. He'd never really thought about a garden being beautiful before, but there was no denying that's what this was. His mother would love it. Pip probably would, too, if she could transport herself from her bed to the gazebo. Women liked pretty things like flowers, even if they were almost as useless as the women themselves.

He took a step toward the apothecary, his nose wrinkling at the overpowering strength of the fragrances pouring out. He could smell peppermint and cinnamon and possibly lemon. It wasn't all that different to his mother's kitchen, although these foods were being prepared to be consumed with the nose instead of the mouth

Foolish, really. What use could sniffing an oil do? It needed to be taken into the body directly for the goodness to be properly drawn from it. This kingdom should come to The Bay of Laurel to steal their tonics, not the other way around. The King was a fool to have sent him on this quest.

But fool or not, the King was the one in power and if Edison wished to take his place, he had to play his game.

He pushed open the door to the apothecary, still unsure exactly what his plan was. Would the King even know how he acquired the oils? Just as long as he got them, that was all that mattered. But the coins he'd brought with him had been buried underneath a mountain of rock along with the Guardians. Apart from the clothes on his back, all he had to offer was a tired horse and he needed that to get back home.

A wave of aromas assaulted his nostrils as he stepped inside. It would be enough to send him turning around and walking away, if it weren't for the warmth of the room. He saw walls and shelves lined with tiny bottles of oils, but his eyes skipped straight past these to a fire burning in a hearth at the opposite end of the room. He went immediately to it and rubbed his hands together, not caring what smells he had to put up with, just as long as he got to feel the heat of the fire.

A woman who was busy restocking the shelves, halted the tune she was humming and looked up at him and smiled.

"Hello," she said.

Edison found himself smiling back, then reminding himself he was here to stamp his authority, he switched to a frown.

"You look a little cold," the woman said. "Would you like a hot cup of tea?"

"Bring me your Alchemist," he said, puffing out his chest, while he continued to warm his hands. "And a cup of tea."

The woman went to a counter, poured some steaming liquid into a mug and handed it to him.

He gulped it down, only stopping to wonder what was in it after he'd drained the last drop. Surely it hadn't been poisoned? She didn't know that he was her enemy yet.

"I'm afraid our Alchemist is very busy," said the woman, continuing to smile at him despite his hostility.

"And I'm afraid I don't care." Edison thrust out the empty mug and increased the intensity of his stare.

"Let me see what I can do." She took the mug and scuttled through a back door, shaking her head as she went.

Edison forced himself away from the fire and paced the shelves, wishing the bottles were labeled so he could take what he needed and leave. Perhaps he should do just that? Pick up any old thing. How would the King possibly know the difference? He stuffed a few bottles in his pocket just in case.

The back door opened again and a young man came through, frowning at him. His features were even fairer than Edison's or any of the Guardians. His hair was practically white, his skin translucent, and his eyes more like the sky than the depths of the sea. He looked only perhaps sixteen years at best. Certainly no older than Pip.

"I'm the Alchemist," the man said. "You asked to see me?"

"Is this a joke?" asked Edison. "You're little more than a boy."

"I'm as old as I need to be." The Alchemist raised his eyebrows, not seeming to feel the need to defend himself.

"I've been sent by the King," said Edison, pulling back his shoulders. This Alchemist was younger than him, which meant there was no way he could be wiser. Edison could outsmart him.

"King Ari sent you?" asked the Alchemist.

"No. The real King." He rolled his eyes. "The King of The Bay of Laurel. I've traveled far to see you."

"The real King, hey?" The Alchemist laughed to himself in a way that was most unsettling. "My sister will find that amusing when she next comes to visit."

"Your sister?" asked Edison, wondering what a stupid girl could have to do with this.

"She's married to King Ari," the Alchemist said. "They've reached out to your *real* King on several occasions, but he's clearly a busy man."

The Alchemist's sister was the Queen of Wintergreen? Why hadn't the King mentioned this to him? Surely this detail was important.

Edison scratched his head as he tried to figure out if this was a good or bad development. The Alchemist was more powerful than he'd anticipated, which meant he could either crush him harder or help him fly higher.

"You've come here alone?" the Alchemist asked, leaning to look out the window.

"I have an army of guards following behind me," said Edison, moving to block the Alchemist's view of the window "They should be arriving any moment now. The strongest army the world has ever seen and they're under my command."

"They won't come too close to us here." The Alchemist didn't seem to be the slightest bit intimidated.

"How can you be so certain?" Edison returned to the fire to feel some warmth on his back.

"Our friend and neighbor, Forte Cadence, has whispered for our protection," said the Alchemist. "Any army who tries to get close will fail. They'd protect you too if you joined the alliance."

"What does *whispered for* mean?" Edison wondered if what the Alchemist had just said could possibly be true. Had the Guardians been stopped by a crumbling mountain, or were there greater forces at work here? Surely it was just a coincidence. Nobody could whisper for a mountain to fall.

"You ask a lot of questions," said the Alchemist. "But you're not giving me many answers."

"I need your fertility elixir." Edison stepped forward and sneered. "Every bottle of it that you have. Quickly now."

The Alchemist threw back his head and laughed. "Is everyone in your kingdom like you?"

"What? Dangerous?" Edison gripped the Alchemist by the front of his shirt.

"No." The Alchemist turned a purple shade, but didn't drop his calm exterior. "Rude."

Edison tightened his grip on the young man. He could kill him if he wanted to. But would that satisfy the King? Probably not. Best to frighten him without taking his life.

"I can't get the elixir for you... if you don't let go of me," puffed the Alchemist.

"That's better." Edison let go, pleased to have some compliance at last.

The Alchemist brushed himself down and turned to a shelf to pick up a bottle, unscrewing the lid and spilling the contents over his counter.

"Oops!" he said. "Sorry, I'm a bit shaken."

An aroma filled the air, swirling in the room. Edison breathed in the floral scent. It figured that a fertility elixir would be made from flowers. Delicate and pathetic like the women who needed to use them. As he breathed it in again, he felt his pulse rate lower and an unexpected wave of calm washed over him.

The Alchemist turned and took a dozen more bottles from the shelf, placing them in a small hessian bag. Then he retrieved a dozen more and tied up the bag with a piece of string, watching Edison carefully as he slid them over to him.

"Thank you," said Edison, then remembering himself, he added a sneer.

"Happy to help." An amused expression returned to the Alchemist's smug face. "Whatever the *real* King needs, don't hesitate to ask."

"Tha—" Edison caught himself in time and breathed in a sigh of floral relief. "Good. He will call on you again and we expect you to comply."

"Oh, and in case you wondered, they're for indigestion," said the Alchemist.

"What are?" Edison took a step to the door, not liking the unfamiliar feeling taking hold of him in here.

"The bottles in your pocket." said the Alchemist. "A perfect choice for a kingdom that powers itself on food."

Edison felt a flush rise to his cheeks. How had this man known about that? He'd put the bottles in his pocket well before he'd come into the room.

"This won't be the last time I see you," said Edison. "Work on your attitude for next time."

"Oh, I'm certain this will be the very last time we meet," the Alchemist replied. "Safe travels now."

Edison opened his mouth to reply but this only served to provide him with another large dose of elixir. He'd be the most fertile man in the land by the time he returned.

He sniggered at the thought of Pip providing him with a litter of royal babies. She was already wearing his necklace, given to her as a sign of his affection. She knew it was his most prized possession, having been given to him by his father. It was the only piece of his father he had. Women were suckers for gestures like that and Pip was no different. She was probably crying her eyes out for him right now.

He left the apothecary and its annoyingly smug Alchemist and returned to his horse, who'd moved from the trough to feed on a clump of daisies.

It was good to be back out in the fresh air. The more he breathed, the more that strange feeling of calm left him. His clothes had dried out nicely, he had warm tea in his belly and a bag full of elixirs for the King.

He may have lost his army of Guardians, but he'd succeeded in the King's quest. And he'd done it all alone. That was even better. The King would be sure to be impressed.

He hoped.

Because if he wasn't, then Edison was a dead man.

TATE

THE NOW

*T*ate pushed open the door to the Guardian's tavern and glanced around. He knew Edison wasn't here, but even when he was away, his presence seemed to lurk in the shadows.

There were a few Guardians milling around. Each of them stopped and bowed when they saw him.

"Please, no need for that." Tate held up his hand. "I'm just passing through."

He went to the back of the tavern and through to the kitchen, finding Ariel bent over a pot, sampling her latest tonic. Tate sniffed the air, certain he could detect grape juice.

"Tate!" Ariel straightened, set down her spoon and went to him, taking hold of each of his hands and holding them gently. "You're here."

Ariel always made time for him, but never stopped to bow at him and he was glad for it. She'd turned out to be an unlikely friend to him over the years, almost like a mother-figure, in some ways. It'd been a while since he'd seen her, so had been glad to learn that Edison was away. Nobody seemed to know where he'd gone, or at least been willing to tell him. River said she'd heard he was on a quest for the King, but Tate's father had denied that. But he'd said it in a way that made Tate certain he was lying. How was he supposed to rule the kingdom one day when his father never told him what was going on?

"Have you been well, Ariel?" He let go of her hands to peer into the pot. Yes, definitely grape juice. There was no mistaking it.

"I'm very well, thank you." Ariel smiled at him, and he detected a sadness in her eyes, making him wonder if he should press her on this. But this wasn't unusual for Ariel. There always seemed to be secrets hidden behind her eyes, like she wanted to tell him something, but couldn't.

"Is this a new recipe?" he asked.

She nodded. "Just experimenting with a liver tonic."

"What's in it? I can smell grapes?" She liked it when he talked about her tonics. If she wanted to talk to him about anything else, it would come out in time.

"Yes, grapes, blueberries, beetroot, and some coffee beans. It tastes quite astringent. Try some."

She handed Tate a spoon and he dipped it in, then sipped on the dark liquid. Ariel was right. It was acidic. But in a surprisingly pleasing way.

"You think the Guardians' livers are failing them?" He attempted to dip his spoon back in, only to have Ariel slap away his hand. She was very strict about not putting a spoon from your mouth into a communal pot. He liked that she applied the same rules to him as anyone else, as one of the rare people who treated him like a person instead of a prince.

"It seems so." She sighed deeply. "Yellow skin, nausea, fever, weight loss. It all points to the liver. But I don't understand. It can't be their tonics. They've been drinking them for generations. Why would it suddenly be poisoning them now?"

"It won't be your tonics." Tate's shoulders sank to see the beginnings of tears in Ariel's eyes. She took her work so seriously. It was her life. He hated to think of a time when Edison would take over from her. Because likely by then it would be when Tate was King, which would mean he'd no longer be able to avoid his former friend.

"Do you know where Edison is?" asked Ariel, taking a basket of spinach from a high shelf and sorting through it, removing any leaves that had wilted.

Tate shook his head. "It seems to be a mystery. Is he giving you trouble?"

"He always gives me trouble." Any pretense of a smile fell from her face. "You know that."

"But worse than normal?"

She looked into his eyes, then seeming to decide to trust him, she nodded. "He says when he returns that he'll be running my kitchen. I'm to take his orders."

Tate considered this. A mother's instinct was rarely wrong. Particularly a mother who was as astute as Ariel. And what she said made some kind of sense. If Edison was on a secret quest for the King, it was very possible if he succeeded that he could be put in charge of the kitchen as his reward.

"I didn't think Edison was all that keen to take over as herbalist," said Tate. "He always said as a boy that he had other ideas for his future."

Ariel nodded. "That's right. Which is why I'm certain he's up to something."

"I'll talk to my father." Tate set down the spoon he was still holding. "See if I can get him to tell me anything. I've heard a rumor Edison's on a quest for him, but my father denied it."

"He's been sneaking out every morning." Ariel pushed her dark hair out of her eyes. "Going into the palace, not long after you go for your morning walk."

"Oh." A sick feeling gripped Tate around the middle. Was Edison the shadow he'd seen lurking in Pip's room? He cursed himself for doubting what he'd seen with his own eyes.

"You suspect what he's up to?" Ariel's eyebrows darted up as she placed a hand on Tate's arm.

"Pip's been acting very strangely lately. You know how much she doted on Edison as a child."

"Oh." It was Ariel's turn to be surprised now. "Tate, do you think…"

"I don't know." It was true. He didn't know what to think. Or more to the point what to say. He was going to need some time to think this through before he spoke to anyone about this. Including Ariel. If Edison was wooing his sister, it spelled nothing but trouble. Maybe River had found out something when she'd taken Pip her breakfast this morning. He'd talk to her about it later.

"Do you think he has plans to marry Pip?" asked Ariel. "To become a Prince rather than the herbalist."

"I hope not." Tate swallowed hard, but the sick feeling in his stomach remained.

"Tate, listen to me." Ariel lowered her voice. "I want you to be very careful. My son… he's dangerous. And ambitious. You know that. Having his sights set on Pip won't be enough. He won't be happy to be the husband to a Princess. But the husband to the Queen… well."

Tate took a step back as he tried to absorb what she was saying. The only way Pip could ever be Queen was if he died before he produced an heir. He knew Edison was dangerous, that wasn't news, but was he *that* dangerous?

He should never have pushed Edison so far away when they'd been children. Because sometimes your enemies could do you far more harm when they were far away than when they were within arm's reach.

"I have to go." He stooped to kiss Ariel quickly on her cheek. He needed to talk to his father. And he needed to do it now.

"I mean it, Tate," she called after him. "Be careful!"

Tate jogged back to the palace, hoping to catch his father before he retired from the throne room to his bedchamber. This couldn't wait until morning. If Edison really had been visiting Pip then both their lives may be in danger.

"Father!" He approached the throne just as the King stood up, a pile of crumbs scattering to the floor around his feet.

"I'm tired, Tate. I've been dealing with the problems of the people since sun-up. You'll understand just how draining this is one day. Can it wait until morning? I'd like to retire to my bedchamber now and eat my dessert."

Tate shook his head. "I need to talk to you now."

The King sat down again heavily and sighed. "What is it?"

"It's Pip." Tate slowed his breathing, trying to choose his words carefully.

"Phillipa?" A look of alarm crossed the King's face. He may ridicule his daughter, but deep down somewhere in his heart, he loved her. Perhaps he loved who she once was. Or was it who he still hoped one day she'd be?

"She's okay," Tate added. "For now. It's just that... I've been told someone has been visiting her in her bedchamber. Every day, for a while now."

"Who?" the King sat forward, strumming the arm of his throne.

"Edison." Tate swallowed as he waited for his father's reaction.

His father stopped his strumming and gripped the timber arm of the throne so tightly his knuckles turned white. A contrast to the purple flush staining his face.

"You must tell me where he is," said Tate. "For Pip's sake, as well as your own."

"I sent him on a quest," he said, almost as if he'd never denied this. "With a small army of Guardians for protection."

"What kind of quest?" Edison wasn't strong and he wasn't clever. What quest could he possibly complete for the King?

"I needed him to fetch me something." His father waved his hand, as he did when he didn't wish to elaborate.

"What was it?" asked Tate, not deterred by a waving hand.

"They traveled by carts pulled by two of our strongest mules," he continued, without answering Tate's question. "One of the mules returned to the palace this morning, having chewed through its reins. It was quite badly injured, I believe."

"What do you think happened?" Tate decided to check on the mule later to see if there was anything he could do for it.

"I think Edison failed. That's what I think happened. And his failure cost me some of my best Guardians. You know how many generations it's taken to breed them so strong. They're not toys that can be dispensed of. They're a crucial part of the safety of our kingdom. A failure like Edison isn't worthy of my daughter. We must put a stop to whatever's happening between them immediately. That's if he's still alive."

The doors to the throne room burst open, and right on cue, Edison came stumbling in, followed by two Guardians.

"Edison?" Tate could barely recognize him. Normally so well-groomed, Edison was covered in mud and looked pale and exhausted.

Edison limped toward them and collapsed to his knees beside Tate, keeping his attention firmly on the King. The Guardians stood by, keeping a close eye on him, ready to jump in if required.

"Forgive me, my Lord." Edison blinked up at the throne. "The quest didn't go as planned, but I've succeeded. You'll be pleased with me."

"Pleased?" the King bellowed. "I'm not pleased! You failed me. Where are my Guardians?"

"They're... well... I'm afraid there was a terrible accident. They were crushed by falling rocks. It was—"

"Silence!" boomed the King.

Edison hung his head and stilled his words.

"Were there any survivors, apart from the mule that returned this morning?" asked Tate, hoping at least some of the Guardians had made it. River was going to be devastated by this, just as she was starting to accept what had happened to her sister.

"No," said Edison. "Only one mule that I set free when it became trapped."

"I saw the reins myself." The King narrowed his eyes. "They'd been chewed through, not cut with a blade. Are you telling me you bit them with your own teeth?"

"N-n-no! Of course not," said Edison. "The mule chewed through as I was trying to reach it. I dragged away some boulders so it could get out."

The King shook his head, not seeming to believe this any more than Tate did.

"And the Guardians?" asked Tate. "Did you drag away boulders so they could escape?"

"They were too...heavy." Edison's eyes darted around the room. "No ordinary man can shift a boulder. I'd need a Guardian for that."

"But you just said you moved some boulders away from the mule." Tate crossed his arms and sighed. This man was so foolish, he hadn't even taken the time to think up a story that made sense.

"They were smaller boulders." Edison's voice dropped to a whisper, as he realized he was tangling himself in his lies.

"I've heard enough!" The King stood from his throne and reached for his sword, knocking a bowl off his table and scattering breadsticks across the room. "You were responsible for those Guardians and I'll crush you, just like you crushed them!"

The Guardians stepped forward and took Edison by each arm, holding him captive at the King's mercy, although Tate seriously doubted his father was fit enough to successfully swing a sword.

There was a gasp behind them and he turned to see River at the door, her mouth agape to see the King standing over Edison, cowering on the floor with his hands over his head.

Just as Tate was about to motion at River to leave, she turned and ran. He'd need to find her later. He couldn't go after her now. There was too much at stake.

"Did I frighten your wife?" the King asked, turning his attention to Tate.

"She's fine," said Tate, hoping this was the case. "She's a Guardian. She's seen worse than this before."

"And have you?" asked his father. "You've been protected all your life. One day you'll be King and you'll need to be stronger than this. Look at you, shaking like a little girl."

"I'm not shaking." Tate looked at his hands to see they were indeed trembling.

Edison had been like a brother to him growing up. He may not trust him now, but he didn't wish death upon him. Ariel would be devastated. She may not trust her son either, but still, he was her child.

"What would you do with this failure before us?" his father asked, his attention still firmly planted on him.

"I'd put him on trial," said Tate, wondering how this had become more about him than it had Edison.

"Yes!" Edison struggled against the Guardians, his face lit with hope. "A trial! I can explain everything."

"He's had his trial," said the King. "The injured mule was his trial. This man has failed me. And failure's not an option. Not now and not ever."

The King stepped down from his platform and stood beside Tate, holding out his sword.

"Show me what kind of King you'll be, my son. I want to see for myself. Deal with this failure and deal with him now."

As Tate held out his hand to take the sword, every cell in his body wanted to push it away. Killing Edison would solve so many problems. He couldn't possibly marry Pip and murder his way to the throne if he were dead.

But... this wasn't how he dealt with things. Violence wasn't the answer. It was never the answer. Proving he could kill a man wouldn't make him a better King. It would make him a far worse King. Because it would make him like his father. A man who Tate had reluctantly come to accept was perhaps the worst kind of King of all.

"Do it," his father said.

"Forgive me," Tate muttered, as he swung the sword over his head.

PIP

THE NOW

*P*ip stood with her eye pressed up against the spy hole in her door, watching people in the palace come and go. Servants, cooks, and Guardians walked up and down the passageway with such purpose, all just as busy as Pip was bored. It was getting late in the evening and there wasn't much to see from her window in the fading light.

She'd seen River walk past a few moments ago. She was the only one who didn't walk with purpose. She walked as if she was in a magical land, taking in her surroundings. She'd soon get used to the palace. It was early days.

Pip blinked to see River coming back down the hallway, only this time she was in a hurry and she had her hand cupping her mouth as if something dreadful had just happened. Was Tate okay? Whatever River had just witnessed, it couldn't have been good.

"River!" Pip opened her door and called out to River, who was quickly disappearing down the passageway.

"River!" she called again, feeling sweat break out on her forehead. It'd been a long time since she'd poked her head out of her doorway like this.

River slowed, stopped, then turned around, as if she'd have preferred to ignore Pip's calls.

"Come here. Please?" Pip couldn't go to River, but she had to know what happened. It would be impossible to wait until Tate came in the morning to find out. That was assuming he was all right to be able to tell her.

River dropped her hand from her mouth and came to Pip, standing at her doorway, not seeming to want to come in this time.

"What happened?" asked Pip. "Is Tate okay?"

River looked confused, then nodded her head. "Tate's okay."

"Then who is it?" Pip let out a long breath. "Someone must be hurt. Is it another one of your Guardians?"

"It's… never mind." River shook her head and looked to the floor, her feet shuffling as if they wanted to run away. "It's nothing."

"River! Tell me what's happened." Pip reached for River, but she backed away, out of her grasp. "I may not be able to leave my room, but I'm no fool. Something happened just now. What's going on?"

"It's…"

"It's who? It's what?" A pain shot through Pip's jaw. "Talk to me, River!"

"It's Edison." River spat out the words, like she'd just swallowed poison.

"What about Edison?" Pip realized too late that she'd stepped out of her bedchamber and was now standing in the passageway for the first time in a shameful number of years. "What's happened to him? Is he back?"

River nodded. "He's back. And your father's about to have his head."

Pip heard a cry escape her lips almost as if her soul had flown out of her body and taken on a life of its own. This couldn't be happening. Not Edison! She'd only just found him again. She couldn't bear to lose him. Her father may as well take her head if he were to take Edison's.

"You have to stop this." This time she took hold of River, grasping her by her arms. "Please, you have to go back and stop it."

"I can't stop this," said River. "I have no power to stop such a thing."

Pip yelped. "I love him, River! Please, help me. Please. You know what it's like to lose someone you love."

These words hit River hard, their impact visible in the way she flinched.

"I might not have the power," said River, her voice softening at last. "But you do. You're the princess. Your father won't listen to me, but he might listen to his own daughter. Go to him. Now! It's your only chance."

That wasn't possible and River knew it. She couldn't walk down that passageway and not just because she was wearing a nightgown.

"I can't do it." She let go of River's arms to clutch at her hands. "I can't."

"You can." River wriggled out of her grasp and turned Pip to face the direction of the throne room.

Pip scanned the hallway. It was longer than she remembered. Although the ceiling felt lower and the walls closer in. She sucked in another breath, fighting to get the air into her lungs. Then, gripping onto Edison's necklace with her free hand, she clutched it, reminding herself why this was important. He'd let her wear this as a promise that he'd always love her. But now his safety depended on her. He'd come to her room to save her life, but now it was her turn to save him. She couldn't let him down.

"Will you help me?" she asked River. "I can't do this alone."

River looked to the ceiling, let out a long sigh, then held out her hand. "Hold my hand and put one foot in front of the other. I've got you."

Pip did as she was told. Then she stopped, unable to pull enough air into her lungs to continue, the oxygen being used to keep her heart racing and her fingers tingling.

"Close your eyes," said River. "Keep hold of my hand."

Doing as she was told, Pip took another step.

"Imagine you're walking around your bedchamber," said River. "I'll lead you. But Pip, we need to keep moving forward. And you need to hurry."

River pulled at Pip's hand, and she followed with her eyes kept firmly closed. She told herself that this was her bedchamber. Right now, they were walking toward the window. They turned a corner and she imagined they were walking to her private washroom. Another corner and they were heading toward the bed. She could do this. She really could. Just one foot in front of the other. One hand in River's and the other on Edison's necklace.

She heard a door open and recognized the smell of her father's throne room immediately. It didn't matter how long it'd been since she'd smelled it, she'd know that combination of leather, wood, blood, and power anywhere.

"Pip!"

Her eyes sprang open at the sound of Edison's voice and she ran forward, not caring where she was or who would try to stop her.

Edison was kneeling in front of her father's throne, a Guardian standing on either side of him, one holding each arm. Her father sat in his throne and Tate was standing over Edison with his sword held over his head, ready to end the life of the man Pip loved.

"No!" she screamed, throwing herself at Edison, and clinging to his chest. But with his arms firmly pinned, he was unable to embrace her in return.

She saw her father shake his head as he waved at the guards to let go of Edison. His arms wrapped immediately around her and he pulled her close. She was the one who'd brought him safety, yet somehow, he was the one making her feel safe.

"It's okay, my darling," he whispered in her ear.

"How could you?" she hissed at Tate.

"I didn't, actually," said Tate, lowering his sword.

"Children." The King strummed his fingertips on the arms of his throne. "This is just like the old days. Although, I must say I'm surprised to see you here, Philippa. It's a miracle you remembered your way through the palace to find your way. You had a guide, though, I see."

Pip loosened her hold on Edison to see River shrink a few steps away.

"You can't kill him," Pip said to her father. "Please, Father. If you decide he must die, then please kill me, too. I'll throw myself from my window if you don't."

"Pip!" Tate shook his head, disappointment brimming in his traitorous eyes. She'd never forgive him for this. To think if she hadn't called out after River, he'd have killed the only man she'd ever loved.

"I mean it." Pip shifted her gaze back to her father. "Edison's everything I live for. We're going to be married. I love him, Father. Please, don't kill him. Whatever he's done, it has to be a mistake."

"It *is* a mistake." Edison pulled himself into a stand and reached out a hand to help Pip up. "I've been trying to tell you, Your Majesty, that I succeeded in your quest. Not only that, but I succeeded alone. I did the job of ten men all by myself. This should be rewarded, not punished."

"So, now you tell me how to do my job, do you?" The King shook his head.

Pip didn't like the tone he was using. Nothing good ever came from that tone.

"The Guardians were killed by a rockslide," said Edison. "I cannot be blamed for that."

A gasp sounded from behind Pip, and River came forward once more to stand beside Tate.

"Who died?" asked River. "Which Guardians were sent?"

Edison shook his head. "They were nameless Guardians. Nobody of note."

A look of pure hatred spread across River's face as she shared a brief glance with the two Guardians who'd stepped aside. These were their people Edison spoke of. But it wasn't his fault. He just saw the world differently. What was the shame in that?

"No Guardian is nameless,' said River.

"Having been miraculously spared by the rockslide, I pressed on ahead," said Edison, ignoring River's protest. "It was at great personal risk to my own safety, and I faced the Alchemist to deliver your message. Fearful for his life and sensing my authority, he handed over these elixirs, with the promise to supply you with anything else you require in future."

Pip watched as Edison untied a hessian sack from his belt and handed it to her father. What kind of oils could her father have possibly wanted so badly that he'd risked Edison's life to get them?

"You took your time to tell me this." The King accepted the sack and opened it to extract a small bottle. Removing the lid, he tipped some oil into his hands and sniffed at the floral fragrance quickly filling the air.

"Interesting," he said. "But a bit too womanly for me. It's a perfume more suited for a female."

He held the bottle out in River's direction.

"For my new daughter," said the King. "Put some on immediately. It will please me."

Pip huffed at her father's words. His new daughter? He already had a daughter! He didn't need a new one. Edison had gone to the trouble of retrieving these oils surely they should be for the King's daughter by blood.

River accepted the bottle, not seeming grateful at all.

"Go on. Put some on," said the King, in such a way it was a command rather than a question, smiling as River complied.

The power of the fragrance strengthened and Pip crossed her arms, wishing for a bottle of her own. She wanted to smell like flowers, too.

"There's plenty more, my love," said Edison, sensing her disappointment as he put a protective arm around her shoulders.

Pip smiled as a wave of floral calm washed over her. Everything was going to be okay.

"She's not your love," sneered Tate. "Get your hands off my sister."

"I quite enjoy putting my hands on your sister." Edison stepped toward Tate, clearly feeling braver than he had when Pip had first burst into the room. Although, now that the urgency of the situation had calmed down, she realized her fear had been irrational. Tate would never have taken Edison's head. He didn't have it in him, no matter how much he might like the idea of it. Her brother was a gentle soul.

"You've put your hands on my daughter, have you?" said the King, drawing the attention back to Edison.

Pip felt herself flush. "Not in that way, Father. Edison is a man of honor."

Tate laughed at these words. "Never will you find a man with less honor than the one before you, my sister."

"That's not true!" cried Pip as Edison removed his arm from her shoulders to bow before his King.

"I would like to ask for your permission to marry your daughter," he said.

Pip's legs went weak, in much the same way they had when River had led her from her bedchamber. Edison really did want to marry her! She couldn't decide if it felt like she'd woken from a long dream or if she'd just slipped into one.

As a child, her mother had talked about the Evernow. A time when you were happy to live your life right now in the moment, not wishing for the past or yearning for your future. Never before had Pip experienced such a feeling. But she finally knew what her mother had meant. She'd never been happier than she was right now. Edison loved her. And more than anything, she loved him.

"I need some time to think on this," said the King.

"But Father!" Pip protested.

"Enough, Philippa. I was tired and hungry before this nonsense began. Now I'm starving and exhausted. Leave me now. All of you. And return at sun-up for my decision. I cannot think with you here. It's been a long and arduous day. Edison, I'm afraid you're going to need to spend a night under guard."

"No!" Pip cried out. "This is entirely unnecessary."

"It's just for one night," her father said, waving for the Guardians to take him away. "We can't have your love running away now, can we?"

The Guardians seized Edison in a way that seemed a little more forceful than necessary.

"Edison would never run away and leave me," begged Pip. "Let me stay with him instead."

Her father didn't seem to feel it necessary to answer this latest plea.

"It's okay, Pip," said Edison, his bravery making her love him even more. "I'll see you tomorrow, my darling."

"She's not your darling," roared Tate in a voice Pip didn't recall having ever heard before.

"That's what you think." She walked from the room, unable to bear being witness to Edison being dragged away by those monsters. She didn't need River's help to find her way back to her bedchamber. If Edison could be so brave, then so could she. He loved her. For real. He hadn't just said it to her in the privacy of her bedchamber, he'd said it to her family.

She turned the corner that would lead her to her room, feeling more like she was floating than putting one step in front of the other, in the way she'd arrived here.

There was no way her father would take Edison's life now. She'd saved him in just the same way he'd saved her.

River may have been the one to lure her out of her bedchamber, but it was Edison who'd truly set her free.

RIVER

THE NOW

"We need to talk," said River, slipping her hand into Tate's as they walked from the throne room.

She noticed he didn't squeeze her hand back like he normally did. Was he upset with her for fetching Pip? An act that'd ultimately prevented him from killing Edison. She'd thought he'd be glad. But after hearing Edison speak about the Guardians as if they were livestock, she wasn't so sure she was glad. Were some people better off without air to fill their lungs?

"Perhaps we should speak outside." Tate changed direction and led her out a side door.

River was learning her way around this labyrinthine palace now and knew they'd step out into the strawberry patch. She liked it out there, with the innocent red berries all lined up in neat rows. Surely nobody could get upset while standing in a strawberry patch?

"I need to talk to Pip," said Tate.

"She's not ready to hear you yet," said River. Sometimes it wasn't so much what you said to someone, it was when you said it. And Pip's ears were going to be closed to Tate for some time now. He needed to catch her at the right moment if he wanted her to listen.

They walked down one of the rows of strawberries, both seeming to be waiting for the other to break the silence. The fading light was casting long shadows in front of them, but neither of them were concerned by the approaching dark.

"Why did you go and get her?" he asked. "I was shocked to see you both there."

"I didn't get her. She saw me walk past her door and called out to me. I didn't want to tell her what was happening. I promise I didn't, but she got it out of me. I felt so sorry for her. She was so distressed at the thought of losing Edison."

"You knew she loved him?" He stopped walking to turn to face her in the falling darkness.

"I've only known since this morning. When I took Pip her break-fast, she was wearing that braided cord Edison normally wears around his neck." Her fingers fluttered to her own neck. "You must know it. It's very distinctive. I'd recognize it anywhere. So I asked her about it and she confessed everything to me, begging me not to tell you."

"Why didn't you tell me?"

"I didn't have time!" She turned to him to make sure he believed her. "I wanted to, but you were nowhere to be found. I'm sorry, Tate. I really am very sorry."

He nodded, seeming to be happy to take her at her word. Then, wrapping his arm around her, they walked on.

"I'm sorry," said River, prepared to accept her portion of the blame for what had been an all-round disastrous day.

"I'm the one who's sorry," he said, letting go of her hand to wrap an arm around her shoulders.

They reached the end of the strawberry patch and headed into the citrus orchard behind it. The temperature of the air cooled under the leafy canopy, but the warmth of Tate's body kept River feeling snug.

"What happened?" asked River. "I couldn't believe my eyes when I saw you holding the sword above Edison's head."

"I couldn't believe it either. You know that's not me." He paused briefly to look at her.

"Of course I know that. That's why I was so surprised."

"I went to my father to talk to him about Edison before he arrived." Tate walked them further into the orchard, keeping his voice low. "Father said Edison had gone on some kind of quest, but one of the mules had returned to the palace severely injured."

"Was he concerned?" asked River, snuggling in closer.

"No, he was furious! Those mules were carting the Guardians that Edison took with him. And if the mule broke free, he knew something had gone terribly wrong. Edison was the one in charge and he may not value the lives of the Guardians, but my father certainly does. I've never seen him so angry."

River nodded, pleased to hear this. She couldn't bear to learn that the King shared Edison's hateful opinion of her people.

"Then Edison walked in," said Tate. "He told all sorts of lies and Father decided to take his head."

"So, how did you end up with the sword?" This was the question she'd been wanting to ask this whole time. She needed to know what kind of man she'd married. Was he the sort who saved rabbits from the cornfields or one who took a man's head in the palace? Or was it possible to be both? Were people black and white, or did everyone have shades of gray?

"My father handed me his sword." Tate kicked at a stone on the ground. "He insisted if I'm to be King one day, I needed to prove myself and take my first life."

"He was testing you." River shook her head. From what she knew of her husband so far, there was no way he'd be able to kill a human. Especially one he'd grown up with like a brother, no matter how insipid he'd become.

"And then you appeared," he said. "I hated you seeing me like that. I wasn't sure what to think when you left."

"I'm so sorry, Tate. I had no idea what was going on when I walked in."

"Please stop apologizing. Maybe it was for the best. You got Pip to leave her room. Nobody's been able to do that for so many years now. You've given me hope for her future. Now, we just need to make sure that future is free of Edison."

"You had your chance to be free of him," she said. "But your heart is far too kind to take that option. I don't believe you would have done it, even if you hadn't been interrupted."

"Probably not." Tate screwed up his face and let go of her to kick at another stone. "But maybe it would be better if I had. He said such awful things about the Guardians. Am I terrible to think that we'd all be better off if Edison had lost his head?"

"Only if I'm terrible, too." River's shoulders sagged. "I thought the same thing. Perhaps we're a perfect match, after all."

"River." Tate turned to her and lifted his hand to her face, rubbing his thumb across her cheek. "The more I get to know you, the more I think you are my perfect match."

River's stomach pulled into a knot and in the fading light, she focused on the spark in Tate's eyes and held onto it.

"We're perfectly terrible," she murmured, hoping this would be the moment Tate would lean into her and press his lips against hers. She'd found herself yearning for this moment more and more with each day that passed. He was her husband in name, but lately it felt like he was becoming her husband in her heart as well.

His eyes were drawn to her mouth and she waited. Given they were such a similar height, there was no need for him to even dip his head. All he needed to do was step forward.

But he remained frozen to the spot, seeming unable to do with his lips what his eyes desired.

But she was a Guardian, strong and brave. She could do this. She knew he wanted it.

She reached her own hand to Tate's face, feeling the roughness of his stubble underneath her fingertips. He wasn't neat and tidy, like a

Prince should be, but she liked the manliness of the shadow of his beard and his untamed mane of dark hair.

They leaned in at the same time, their lips finding each other's as darkness settled on the kingdom and light filled their souls.

The kiss was gentle for only a moment, before it became desperate and searching. They needed comfort, they needed release, but most of all, they needed love.

"You're the husband I dreamed of," breathed River as they reluctantly broke away. The palace had too many eyes to take things further out here.

"You're the wife I didn't know I wanted in my life." The white of Tate's teeth flashed in the moonlight, as he pressed his forehead against hers and smiled. "And now you're the wife I can't live without."

"We have to be up early," said River. "You need to sleep."

Tate nodded. "Then I think you should take me to bed."

She thought she saw him smile again and was glad he couldn't see the flush racing up her neck.

She'd been sleeping beside this man for many nights now and had felt nothing but safe. But now that things between them had shifted, this arrangement seemed filled with danger.

And she had to admit, she loved it.

EDISON

THE NOW

*E*dison struggled against the grip of the Guardians as they hauled him back into the throne room, certain they were using more force than necessary. He took note of their faces, despite the fact they all looked the same. They'd live to regret this. He still had plenty of that special tonic left. The one he liked to give to all the Guardians who disrespected him.

"Get your hands off me!" he cried, although his words seemed to have the opposite effect and they gripped him tighter.

How dare the King treat him like some kind of criminal! He should be thrown a street parade, not having his life threatened with a sword that looked a little too sharp for Edison's liking, even if Tate had been too gutless to use it.

He let his legs fall limp and the Guardians dragged him toward the King's throne like he weighed nothing at all. Picking up his feet, he scrambled his way forward. Now wasn't the time to look pathetic.

The King was already seated with a bowl of buttered carrots in his lap like he was here for the entertainment. He picked up a carrot and bit into it, letting the butter drizzle down his chin. Tate and his Guardian wife sat to one side of him and Pip on the other. Thankfully, they didn't seem to think now was a good time for a snack.

Edison locked eyes with Pip who looked like she was about to lurch herself out of her seat and run to Edison. She was his best hope out of this mess. If it weren't for her, he wouldn't be alive today. But then again, if it weren't for him, she'd still be in her room playing with the hideous dolls his mother had made her, so he guessed they were even.

"Stay where you are, Philippa," the King instructed.

"Do as your father says, my love." Edison made those eyes at her that she seemed to like so much. She was so easy to play. All women were. Although, River's sister had proven a little more difficult unfortunately, but she hadn't been a real woman anyway.

There was a floral scent in the air and Edison sniffed at it, his nose crinkling until he realized it was the fertility elixir he'd retrieved from the Alchemist. The King must be insisting that River wear it. He really was desperate for that half-caste grandchild. Just as well the elixir was almost definitely completely useless. That Alchemist didn't seem like he knew the first thing about anything. He wasn't even a man yet.

Although, if there was a chance the elixir worked, then he really should get Pip to breathe it in. The sooner she carried his child, the safer his position in the kingdom would be. He glanced again at the King's sword, a reminder that his current position was far from safe. It was more than possible he'd be put to death in a matter of moments.

He knelt in front of the King and bent his head, hoping to be granted a pardon for the sin he'd never committed. He'd succeeded at his quest! But he kept his mouth silent as he waited.

"Edison," said the King. "You've caused me a sleepless night."

Edison could guarantee it wasn't as sleepless as the one he'd just spent, locked inside a cell.

"I'm sorry, Your Majesty." He kept his head bowed, afraid if he spoke, he might undo any favorable decision the King may have arrived at overnight.

"As you're aware, you've angered me with—"

"Father!" Pip cried out, making Edison wince. Did she not know how to stay quiet? He tried not to lift his head to scowl at her.

"Philippa, my daughter. One more word from you and I'll have you removed. Do you understand?"

"Yes, Father," she whispered.

"Now, where was I?" Edison heard the King crunch down on another carrot. "Yes, you angered me, Edison. You left with a dozen of my most valued Guardians and all that returned, other than yourself, was one injured mule."

"I'm sorry, Your Majesty." Edison dared to look up at the King, not liking how this was sounding. Perhaps he needed Pip to interrupt, after all.

"But as you pointed out to me, you succeeded in the quest I asked you to complete." The King smiled. "This pleases me. You made an excellent point yesterday when you said that you managed to do the job of ten men alone. I fear I was too hasty in my judgment of you."

Edison let out the breath he'd been holding. This sounded more promising.

"Father!" cried Tate.

"I haven't finished!" The King held up his hand. "As the Princess pointed out to me, she's become quite… attached to you."

"I'm attached to her, too, Your Majesty." Edison looked across at Pip to see her cheeks flush. Putting his head back down, he waited.

"I wouldn't normally encourage such an attachment. You're not a…suitable choice… for the Princess. However, you did something that nobody else has been able to achieve for many years now."

Edison tried to swallow, but his mouth was dry.

"You got Philippa to leave her bedchamber," said the King. "Which means you've succeeded in pleasing me twice."

"Father, may I speak now?" asked Tate, leaning forward in his seat.

Edison suppressed his eyes from rolling. Just when he was getting somewhere. There was nothing Tate could say to improve his situation here.

"Go ahead." The King waved a carrot at the Prince.

"I agree that Edison's life should be spared," said Tate. "I don't believe his actions have been severe enough to warrant his death."

Edison smiled at Tate. Perhaps their childhood friendship meant something to the Prince after all. Or was he doing this for his sister? It was hard to tell.

"However, it'd be wrong to allow him to go back to his life as it was before," added Tate.

The smile fell from Edison's face as he steeled himself for Tate's next words.

"He must be sent far away," Tate sneered. "To another kingdom, if possible. You can't allow him to marry Pip!"

"I can't?" The King raised his eyebrows. "Yet another person telling me how to do my job."

Edison held his breath as he waited for the King to continue. The last thing he wanted was to be banished from the kingdom! Where would he go? Certainly not to Wintergreen with all those flowers everywhere, or that strange kingdom that whispered for rocks to fall on people's heads.

"You wanted me to prove to you how I would behave as King," said Tate, holding his father's gaze. "And that would be the decision I'd make."

"Edison will not return to his old life," said the King.

"Excellent." Tate smiled as he crossed his arms.

"But it won't be the life you suggest," said the King. "He'll remain in this kingdom."

"Father!" Tate stood up.

The King held up his hand for Tate to sit, but he remained with his feet planted on the ground.

"Edison has asked two things of me," said the King. "Firstly, to marry my daughter. And secondly, to lead our army of Guardians."

"No!" Now, River leaped from her seat to stand beside Tate. "Forgive me, Your Majesty, but that would be a very bad outcome for the

Guardians. You said yourself that Edison was responsible for the deaths of the dozen he took with him to Wintergreen."

Edison winced. Why did everyone have to keep mentioning that!

"River's right," said Tate, holding his wife's hand in a way that seemed far too intimate for two people married for convenience. "How can he be in charge of a whole army, when he failed so badly with only a dozen of them? They're already dying as it is. We can't afford for things to get worse."

Edison cursed under his breath, as he saw the first signs of his special tonic backfiring, when it'd done nothing but serve his purpose so far. Wiping out a few Guardians who deserved no better, and making his mother look incompetent had been easy. Overseeing them to a return to health would be even easier. All he'd need to do was dispose of the responsible tonic. But what if the special tonic was what prevented him from achieving an even greater plan? He'd never forgive himself. It would be like sacrificing a queen to take a pawn. Very poor play indeed.

"It's no wonder I've lost my appetite when I'm surrounded by such fools," said the King, throwing his bowl to the table with a clatter. "The reason I'm considering Edison's request is *because* the Guardians are dying. Things can't get much worse and he has some bold ideas that may be worth testing."

Edison let out a slow breath. Maybe the special tonics had been a genius move after all. A move that would allow him to take all his opponent's pieces in one swoop.

Now Pip rose to her feet. "If Edison succeeds and restores the Guardians to health, then I'd like you to grant him permission to marry me. Please, Father?"

"I'll commit to no such thing at this stage." The King shook his head slowly. "Enough decisions have been made for one day."

"So, what exactly are these bold ideas?" asked Tate, directing his question at Edison.

"I wish to take charge of the tonics by overseeing the herbalist to make some improvements." Edison tried to decide how many of his ideas he should reveal. Change was often better received when it was meted out, rather than given in one large dose.

"I heard about this," said Tate. "And it's ridiculous. How could you possibly claim to know more about the tonics than a woman who's been making them all her life?"

"How did you hear about it, Tate?" Edison raised his eyebrows in River's direction. "Did my mother tell you during one of your special visits?"

"Where I get my information is none of your business!" Tate scowled, which lit a spark of joy in Edison's belly.

"Enough squabbling!" The King rolled his eyes. "Edison believes his skills could be better used to build a stronger army."

"And what are these skills?" asked River. "He's only just become a man. And not much of one at that."

Edison waited for the King to silence her. What position did she hold to insult him? But to his annoyance, she was allowed to get away with her insolence.

"Answer my wife's question," said Tate. "What are your skills?"

"I have fresh ideas," said Edison, being as vague as he could manage. "New approaches."

The King cleared his throat. "Edison wishes to separate the Guardians into two camps."

Edison winced at the King's words, knowing they would cause the animosity he was trying to avoid. "He'll control their breeding and reformulate their tonics."

"Their *breeding?*" River stood, unable to disguise her disgust. "The Guardians are not livestock to be bred. We're humans, just like you. Humans who've dedicated our lives to serving our King. We do it because we have love in our hearts for our kingdom. Treating us like animals will only turn us from soldiers into slaves."

"You're no longer a Guardian," said the King. "This is none of your concern. Please take your seat and be silenced or I'll have you removed."

At last, the King had put the freak back in her place. It was just a shame it'd taken so long.

Edison watched River sink into her seat and shake her head, ignoring Tate's attempts to give her comfort. They were certainly a strange couple. It was just as well their relationship wouldn't survive long enough for them to bring their half-caste into the world. He knew just the tonic to make sure of it.

"Father," said Pip, stepping forward. "May I work with Edison? With the tonics, I mean. I'm curious to learn more about them. Otherwise, I'm afraid I'll lock myself in my room once more."

"I don't see why not." The King picked up his bowl, his appetite seeming to have returned. "Edison, do you have any objections to that?"

Only about a thousand of them. But none he could voice here. "No, Your Majesty."

"And what about Ariel?" asked Tate. "Where does this leave her?"

"She may continue to work in the kitchen," said Edison. "Under my watchful eye, of course. There's plenty of work to be done."

"She taught you everything you know," said Tate. "This isn't right."

"It's always unfortunate when the apprentice outgrows his master." Edison did his best to give Tate a reassuring smile.

And that's exactly what was happening here. Edison had outgrown not only his master, but the entire kingdom. It was time to shake things up. He'd spent his whole life learning from everyone else. It was time they learned a thing or two from him.

PIP

THE NOW

*P*ip pulled down her bonnet over her eyes so she could only see her slippered feet treading lightly on the path in front of her.

She'd thought she'd be okay to leave the palace but the reality of it was far more frightening. Perhaps she should've asked Tate to escort her, but that would be a bit hard considering she wasn't talking to him right now.

She could do this. She knew she could. If she just looked down at her feet and pretended she was in her bedchamber, then she'd be all right.

A sparrow darted across the path and she jumped back a step. That didn't happen in her bedchamber. She was going to have to get used to this, along with a thousand other things.

Slowing her breathing, she pulled her bonnet down once more, ignoring the sweat that'd broken out on her forehead. Maybe she should go back?

She turned around and took a step toward the palace, her racing heart slowing just at the thought of the safety of her bedchamber.

But then she thought of Edison and her steps stopped once more and she turned. It didn't matter how much this frightened her, she had to press on. The herbalist's kitchen wasn't far. She could do this. For Edison. He'd see how brave she was when she had to be.

Besides, she really did want to learn more about the tonics. One of them in particular. She'd been fascinated with them as a child, spending time with Ariel in her kitchen, watching her work her magic. But that was before her mother died. After that, everything had changed.

She took off toward the tavern, keeping her head down and her steps fast. The sooner she got there, the better she'd feel. It wasn't far. She used to walk this path all the time as a young girl. She could do it again.

Would Ariel recognize her? Probably not. She looked different now. Older. Taller. Bigger in every way possible.

Pip breathed a sigh to reach the tavern and she stepped inside, letting go of her bonnet to clutch at her chest. Having walls around her, made her feel instantly safer. Only a few more paces and she'd be at the kitchen.

She kept her head down, unaware if anybody was watching her from one of the tables. She wasn't here for them. She was here to see Ariel.

The familiar smell of the kitchen rushed up her nostrils, and she felt the years fall away and once again she was a small girl grinning at Ariel from her doorway.

"Pip!" cried Ariel, looking up from her chopping board. "I can't believe it."

It seemed Ariel had recognized her after all.

Unexpected tears filled Pip's eyes to see the woman who'd once been so kind to her. Then remembering what Edison had told her about his mother, she steeled herself against her. She wasn't here to rekindle a friendship. She was here to learn. Not that Edison seemed to think there was an awful lot his mother could teach her. But he'd said if she learned the basics from her, then he could teach her the refinements.

Ariel went to Pip and put a hand on each of her shoulders, seeming to want to hug her, but sensing that wasn't what Pip wanted.

"Oh, my poor girl," said Ariel. "What's happened to you?"

Pip's back stiffened at the bluntness of her words.

"This isn't healthy," Ariel said. "Look at you! What are they feeding you in that palace."

"You think I like looking like this?" Years of anger flared in Pip's chest. "I can't help it. No matter what I do, I'm still the fattest princess this kingdom has ever seen."

"Pip, you're not fat," said Ariel.

Pip looked to the floor, tired of everyone telling her this. She'd spent her whole life with people telling her she wasn't fat, but she knew exactly what she was.

"Pip, listen to me. You're not fat," Ariel said, again.

"Do you have a tonic to make me thin?" asked Pip, biting down on her tongue. She wasn't supposed to ask this so soon. Her real reason for wanting to be here was something she'd planned to keep to herself for a little while, and here she was blurting it out at the first moment.

"Come with me." Ariel led Pip from the kitchen through a small door at the rear. Pip had never been in here before, having always assumed it was a storeroom, when in fact it was the herbalist's house. Which made it Edison's house. She looked around with interest, imagining her beloved living inside this space.

It was a small home, jammed with a lifetime's worth of belongings, including Ariel's bed. There was another door off to the side where Edison must sleep, given she could only see one bed. A large mirror stood to one side and that's where Ariel took her now.

Pip turned her head not wanting to see herself, but Ariel positioned her in front of it and held her still.

"Tell me what you see," said Ariel.

Reluctantly, Pip shifted her gaze. In her own room, the blanket still hung over the mirror. It'd been years since she'd seen herself and she barely recognized the girl she saw before her now.

"What do you see?" asked Ariel, standing beside her.

"Me. And you." She attempted to smile at Ariel in the mirror, wondering why she was doing this to her. Perhaps Edison was right and his mother was losing her mind.

"And what do you look like?" asked Ariel. "Describe yourself."

"Fat," said Pip, the word that'd haunted her for so many years, spilling from her mouth automatically. "I'm fat."

"And do you think I'm fat?" asked Ariel.

"Of course not!" said Pip. Ariel had always been slender.

"Now look at yourself, comparing yourself to me, and again, tell me what you see."

Pip dragged her eyes back to herself, comparing the broadness of her shoulders with Ariel's, the width of her waist, the angles of her face.

And suddenly it felt like the blanket in her bedchamber had fallen away, not from her mirror, but from her eyes, and she was seeing herself properly for the first time.

She raised her arm and saw the protruding bones, turned sideways to see that her waist was little wider than her arm, and her cheeks were sunken and hollow. Ariel, who was so slender, was at least twice her size. Could it be true? Could she really be so thin, when she'd spent her life believing the opposite?

"Pip, you've never been fat. Not for a single day of your life," said Ariel. "Tate's said for years now how worried he is about your weight. He told me how thin you'd gotten, but I didn't realize how serious it was until just now when I saw you for myself."

Pip looked back at the mirror. Could it be a trick? Was she really thin, when she'd been convinced she was fat?

"Pip, how long has it been since you ate anything?" asked Ariel.

"I eat." This wasn't a lie. She ate everything Tate brought her, which was enough to feed three men.

"And then what do you do with it?" Ariel's eyes were dark and serious.

"Nothing," said Pip, averting her gaze.

"You bring it up again, don't you?" Ariel put a gentle hand on her back.

Pip stepped away from her, shocked at how Ariel could know such a thing.

"Have you been spying on me?" Was that how she'd recognized her so easily. "Has Elise been telling tales as she's emptied my chamber pot?"

"Oh, Pip. No, of course not. I can see it for myself. There's no way you could be eating and look like this. There's not an ounce of fat or muscle on your bones. You're starving yourself to death, my poor girl. And you've been doing it for years."

Ariel looked so upset that Pip's eyes were soon welling with tears of her own. She'd forgotten how a mother's love felt. And Ariel may not be her mother, but she was the next best thing to the mother she'd lost, despite the missing years between them.

"Why, Pip?" asked Ariel. "Why are you doing this to yourself?"

"I don't..." Pip paused, not sure how to explain something she didn't even understand herself. "I don't deserve to eat."

"Oh Pip," said Ariel, reaching for her and wrapping her arms around her. "Sweetheart. That's not true."

Pip hesitated, then accepted Ariel's love, catching sight of their embrace in the mirror and noticing how frail she looked beside this healthy woman.

"It's okay," said Ariel. "I'm going to help you. I'm glad you came to me. We're going to make you well again."

Tears spilled freely from Pip's eyes and she wondered why she hadn't come to Ariel sooner. She'd thought she hadn't been worthy of a mother. But maybe it was a mother who'd be the one to make her feel worthy once more.

"What's going on?"

Pip's head snapped up to see Edison standing in the doorway, his face contorting into a series of strange expressions as he tried to figure out what he was witnessing.

"Edison!" Pip let go of Ariel and rushed to his side to show him her loyalty.

"This was a terrible idea to have you here." He put out his hand to hold her at a distance. "Go back to the palace, Pip. I'll come and talk to you about this later. In the meantime, have a good think about what you're doing."

Pip hung her head once more and went to leave, but Ariel darted forward and took hold of her arm.

"She's staying here," said Ariel. "Look at her, Edison. She'll die if she goes on like this. She needs help."

"She's fine," he said.

"She's not fine!" Ariel held out her palms and shook her head. "How could you let this poor girl believe she's fat, when clearly she's starving to death?"

Edison bit down on his bottom lip. "How long do you think she has?"

This was when the room started to spin and Pip had to reach out to hold onto Ariel to stop herself from falling. Because yet another thing had just become perfectly clear. Edison wasn't asking how long she had because he didn't want her to die. It was more like he didn't want her to die *yet.*

TATE

THE NOW

*T*ate made his way through the cornfields. It was early and there was no need to run today. The sun had barely peeked up from behind the hills.

He yawned, thinking about River sound asleep in his bed. He'd had to be extra quiet to leave without her noticing. It wasn't that he didn't want her company today, more that he just wanted to be alone to sort out all the thoughts swirling in his mind.

River. Pip. Edison. Ariel. His father. There was just far too much going on right now. Everyone competing against each other instead of working toward common goals. This was no way to run a kingdom. The royal family were meant to be the leaders, but how could they lead when they all wanted to walk down different paths?

Tate wasn't sure how he was going to put a stop to Edison. All he knew was that he had to. He'd spent all of yesterday and most of the night talking through the possibilities with River. Well, to be fair they hadn't talked all night, but they had been awake. Part of the night had been dedicated to exploring each other, learning and bonding. He felt so close to her now. Far closer than he'd ever felt to another human, Pip included.

Pip had held herself at a distance ever since their mother died. She'd taken it so hard, blaming herself. That blame had no doubt led to her health problems. He was at a total loss to know what to do about that. His sister was disappearing in front of his eyes. It didn't matter how much food he brought her, she just got thinner.

He plucked a leaf from a corn stalk and shredded it in half. He'd let Pip down. He just didn't know what he could do that would save her. She was so vulnerable. It was no wonder Edison had been able to swoop in and influence her like that.

Putting Edison in charge of the Guardians was a disaster. Tate was shocked his father was even entertaining the idea. But short of murdering his father to take the crown, what could Tate do about it, except continue to voice his disgust?

Seeing a mass of brown fur in one of the traps, he went to the injured rabbit, crouching down and feeling the faintest sign of a heartbeat. There was no hope for this poor little one.

He opened the trap and lifted the rabbit to his chest. It didn't even move to register it was aware of the contact.

"Sorry, little guy." Tate squeezed the small furry body with one hand and felt the heartbeat ebb away with his other. At least this poor creature's last moments were one of human kindness.

He put the rabbit back in the trap and closed it. The farmer would be none the wiser and could still make rabbit stew for dinner tonight. But at least Tate had been able to put an end to the suffering. He really hated those traps.

Maybe River was right. What difference was he making out here? Was he doing this for the rabbits or was he actually doing it for himself? Did it make him feel like some kind of hero to rescue these defenseless creatures each morning? Or was he just rescuing them because he wasn't certain how to rescue his sister? He couldn't make things better for Pip, but he could make a difference for the rabbits. It all seemed so stupid now that he thought about it.

Deciding to abandon his traps for the morning, he turned back to the palace. If River was still asleep, maybe he could crawl back under the covers next to her and get some sleep.

As he got closer to the palace, a noise reached his ears. He stilled his footsteps and tilted his head as he listened. It was the sound of marching. Heavy boots stomping on the earth. Were they being invaded? Had Edison stirred up something in Wintergreen and now they were paying the price?

His steps quickly became a jog, then a run, as he ran toward the source of the noise. The Guardians' village. A strange place for Wintergreen to attack. In years gone by when battles had taken place, the palace was always the first target, which was exactly why it no longer greeted their enemies from its former vulnerable position in the Bay.

It wasn't until he got closer that he realized there were no shouts or cries to accompany the sound of battle. Just boots marching.

And one voice shouting.

Edison's.

Tate increased his pace, emerging through the gap in the hedged fence to the Guardians' village, then ground to a halt as he took in what was before him.

The village was a shambles. Belongings had been taken from the huts and piled up in broken pieces. Doors to what had once been proud homes swung open and a sense of profound sadness hung in the air.

Looking toward the training fields, he saw that Edison had separated the Guardians into two groups, with men in one and women in the other. They were lined up in neat rows with a large space running down the middle.

Tate ran to them, gutted to see the defeated look on the Guardians' faces. Eyes were red and cheeks were stained with muddy tears as they kept their eyes focused on the back of the person in front of them. One young female Guardian broke her gaze to look at Tate, pleading with her eyes for help. The Guardian next to her had a large purple bruise on her face. This was outrageous! What had Edison done to these people? He'd broken them!

An army may fight for you out of fear. But didn't Edison know that when they fought for you out of love and respect, their power would be far greater? It seemed Edison was even more foolish than Tate had believed.

He watched Edison now, pacing up and down the space between the Guardians, using a sword for a walking stick as he inspected his marching army.

"Faster!" he shouted at a male Guardian, tapping him roughly on the back of his legs with his sword.

The Guardian picked up his pace to fall in step with the others, keeping his eyes focused straight ahead.

Edison nodded his approval, before shifting his gaze to the females, using the tip of his sword to lift the tunic of a young Guardian, while he smirked, drunk on his power.

"What are you doing?" Tate called out. That Guardian could've been River not all that long ago. How dare he abuse his position like that.

The sound of the marching softened and slowed ever so slightly.

"Keep marching!" Edison commanded, his sneering face pointed at Tate.

"What do you think you're doing?" asked Tate.

"Training my army," said Edison, puffing out his chest.

"Training them for what?"

"We're going to invade Wintergreen," said Edison. "King's orders."

"You couldn't even keep a dozen of them alive on one simple quest," said Tate, shaking his head. How could his father have approved such a thing? "How can you possibly invade a kingdom?"

With these words, Edison stepped toward Tate with his sword held out in front of him.

Silence filled the fields. The marching had stopped and the Guardians turned to look at Edison. He may be their master, but they'd been bred for generations to protect the royal family. And that included Tate.

Edison put down his sword and took a step back from Tate.

"March!" he cried. "I didn't tell you to stop."

The Guardians resumed their march. Tate could command them to kill Edison right now, and they would. Put him out of his misery in the same way he'd shown the rabbit mercy, earlier that morning. But Edison wasn't a rabbit. He was a snake. And snakes needed to be outsmarted not crushed under a boot, in case their poison leached into the ground. He was determined to be a better leader than his father. One who ruled with compassion instead of fear.

"You're so weak," spat out Edison, glaring at Tate.

Perhaps it wouldn't be so terrible to crush just one snake. Especially if it was a snake determined to bite him. But then he reminded himself how devastated Ariel would be to lose her son. He couldn't kill him. He had to find a way to see if he could be redeemed first. If there was even an ounce of hope, then he had to explore that.

"Just so you know," said Edison. "If the roles were reversed, I'd have had them kill you right now, you spineless fool. And your freak of a wife."

The Guardians paused their march once more and looked at Tate for direction.

"Kill him," said Tate, the temptation too great and exploding in his chest like a bolt of lightning. Nobody threatened River like that. Especially not Edison.

The Guardians abandoned their lines to form a circle, with Edison and Tate in the middle. But it was Edison in their focus, their hatred for him just as great as Tate's own. The circle began to close and Tate was swallowed into the first row as the two Guardians closest to Edison wrestled his sword from his hands and took hold of his arms. A third Guardian placed his large hands around Edison's neck.

Edison thrashed and squirmed. "No!" he cried out. "I'm your master and I command you to take your hands off me."

The Guardians turned to face Tate, seeking his final approval for the slaughter of the man who'd appointed himself as their master.

"You are *not* our master," said the Guardian with his hands around Edison's neck, as he tightened his grip.

"No," Edison gurgled, his face quickly turning purple. "No!"

"*I* am your master," boomed a voice from the back of the crowd. "And take your hands off him."

Tate spun around, just as a path opened up between the Guardians to reveal the owner of the voice.

The Guardians let go of Edison immediately, letting him fall to the ground. They may have been acting on Tate's instructions, but there was only one person who overruled him.

The King.

Tate watched his father stride toward the center of the crowd to stand beside Edison, who was now struggling to his feet.

"What's going on here?" The King directed his question at Tate.

"Somebody had to stop him." Tate put his hands on his hips and glared at his father. "He's treating the Guardians like animals, not people."

"They're an army." Fire burned behind his father's eyes. "An army that I instructed to follow Edison's commands. You had no right to interfere."

"And you had no right to appoint him to such a role." The words flew from Tate's lips before he could stop them. The King may be his father, but he wasn't known for his mercy or his love for his children. "You must put a stop to him."

The King seemed to think about this for a moment.

"Tate, you are my son, but you have failed to act when your kingdom needed you. Edison may not be doing everything right, but at least he's trying. That shows strength and courage."

Edison stood tall now, smirking at Tate like he'd done as a child whenever he'd beaten him in a game. But this wasn't a game! The future of the kingdom was at stake.

"Father, you don't know the first thing about me." Tate stepped in front of Edison, hoping his father would look at him; not like he usually did, but properly, seeing the man he was instead of the man he wanted him to be. "Appoint me to the Guardians and I'll show you what a strong force they can be."

"What?" said his father, with a smile so bitter Tate could practically taste it. "You'll rescue them like you rescue your precious rabbits in the cornfields?"

Ice gripped Tate around the core. "You know?"

"Of course, I know. It's my job to know." The King's smile morphed into a sneer. "You accuse me of not knowing the first thing about you. Perhaps it's you who doesn't know me. You've done nothing but disappoint me your whole life."

"But... but... I don't..." Tate grimaced as the words refused to come out. His father must've had him followed. But when? And what else had he seen? What kind of a father spied on his own son?

"Rescuing rabbits in the cornfields?" Edison laughed, clutching at his sides as if it was the funniest thing he'd ever heard. "Oh, how very sweet, Prince Tate. Or should that be Princess Tate?"

"Take him away," the King commanded his Guardians. "To the dungeon.

At last, his father had seen sense. With Edison locked away, they might be able to set things right. But when two Guardians took hold of his own arms, he realized his father hadn't been talking about Edison.

He'd been talking about him.

RIVER

THE NOW

*R*iver pushed open the door to Pip's bedchamber, disappointed to find the room empty. She'd been hoping Tate was here. His side of the bed had been cold when she'd woken and she'd waited all morning for him to return from the cornfields, disappointed he hadn't asked her to go with him.

She'd thought after the closeness they'd shared over the last couple of days that things between them might be different. But it seemed it wasn't so. Not only did Tate not ask her to come with him, but he hadn't returned. River had eventually convinced herself that he'd taken Pip her breakfast and ended up staying to talk to her about Edison.

However, he wasn't here and nor was Pip for her to ask about his whereabouts. Maybe she'd gone to help Ariel, like she'd said she wanted to. It was strange to think of Pip leaving her room, but River was proud of her newfound courage. If only it hadn't been Edison who'd been her incentive.

River left Pip's room and headed out of the palace. She'd go to the tavern and see if Pip was there. Maybe she'd find Tate on the way.

As she took the path toward the Guardians' village, a sick feeling built in her stomach. Something wasn't right. As soon as she stepped through the hedge, her fears were confirmed. It wasn't the strewn belongings piled up outside the huts that gave it away, it was more the feeling hanging in the air. There was a quiet sadness hovering over the village like a dark cloud.

Rushing to her parents' hut she stepped inside, gasping to find four male Guardians seated around the table. The hut looked entirely different. Her mother's quilt was missing from her bed and the angel that Daphne had made from straw was missing from the shelf above her bed.

The men stood and bowed when they saw River.

"Where are my parents?" she asked.

The men looked to each other, clearly not wanting to answer.

"Are my parents all right?" Her heart rate picked up. What had Edison done to them?

"They're safe," one of the men said. "For now."

"Then what's happened here?" River's hand dragged through her hair as she tried to make sense of what her eyes were telling her.

"Edison," another of the men said. "Edison happened. The King has put him in charge of the Guardians. Says he's our master now."

"But what has he done to you?" she asked.

"Dragged us from our beds in the middle of the night and made us empty our huts," said the tallest of the men. "He's divided the village in two. Men to the south. Women and children to the north. He forbids contact between families. We're not allowed to see our wives or children."

River's heart lurched to see the beginnings of tears in his eyes. Guardians may have been bred to be brave, but they still had hearts. You can't tear a man from his home and family and expect him to be okay, no matter what tonics he's been fed.

"I'm going to fix this," said River. "I don't know how, but I'm going to put this right. I've been talking to my husband and we're going to figure this out."

"Oh," all four Guardians said at once, looking to the floor.

"What?" she asked. "You don't believe I can fix this?"

"No, it's not that," one of the men said. "It's just that... well, haven't you heard? About the Prince, I mean."

River took a step back, unsure what she was about to hear, but certain that she wasn't going to like it.

"Heard what?" she asked, when nobody seemed to want to explain further. "Please, speak freely. I may be dressed like a Princess, but I assure you that I'm still very much a Guardian. I'm one of you. You can talk to me."

"Your husband," a Guardian said. "He... well, he..."

"Please, spit it out," she said, too impatient to care for manners.

"There was an incident in the cornfields," the tall Guardian said, taking over once more. "Edison was making us march, for no reason other than to make us march. He was humiliating us, lifting up the tunics of the women and throwing out jibes at the men. Your husband heard the marching and came to stop Edison. But Edison only turned his anger on Prince Tate, taunting him and boasting of how he was going to invade Wintergreen."

"Is my husband alive?" she asked, needing to have her worst fears answered immediately.

"He is. But the King heard the altercation and had Prince Tate sent to the dungeon."

River pulled out a chair and sat down, her legs shaking so hard she thought she might collapse.

"The dungeon?" she asked, despite being certain she'd heard correctly. "The King sided with Edison over his own son?"

"I'm afraid so."

"This can't be happening." River buried her face in her hands, not wanting these men to see how deeply affected she was.

"Your husband's a good man," said the Guardian. "We always thought it, but after what he did today, now we know it. He's brave and selfless."

"He is." River swallowed back her grief. Surely the dungeon was only a temporary punishment to keep Tate out of the way. The King wouldn't lock him up forever. He was desperate for her to produce an heir, something that would be impossible with her husband in a dungeon.

"I'm sorry, Princess." The Guardians shuffled their feet, not seeming to know what to do with themselves.

"I need to find Princess Pip," she said, standing up and brushing down her dress.

Pip may be angry with Tate right now, but she loved him. He was her brother. She wouldn't want to see him locked in a dungeon. And if she'd been able to convince the King to spare Edison's life then surely, she could convince him to let Tate go free.

"The Princess is with the herbalist," said the Guardian.

"Thank you. And thank you for being so frank with me just now. I meant it when I said I was going to fix this. And I needed the truth for that."

She left the hut feeling like there was no place left in the world she could call home now. That's why she needed to find Tate. He was her home now.

EDISON

THE NOW

*E*dison laughed as he watched his Guardians run around the field. He wanted them to be fast as well as strong. Endurance was important in a battle.

"Faster," he hissed as one of the females ran past him, slower than even his own mother could run.

"Please, Master," she puffed, coming to a stop in front of him. "I can hear my baby calling for me. I must feed him for him to grow strong."

The Guardian pointed to the cluster of Guardian children beside the field, all freaks in the making. The older children were caring for the younger ones, something Edison thought was a genius idea. Why waste the skills of a fully grown Guardian, doing something that really wasn't all that difficult? Babies needed to be fed and changed and not much else. Feeding them from the breast made that a little more complex and was something he was going to need to give some consideration. Was it really necessary? Surely there was a tonic that could take care of that?

"Five more laps of the field and you may feed your child," he said, feeling rather generous this morning.

The ungrateful Guardian didn't seem all that pleased with his answer. She really didn't know how lucky she was. He could have had her killed for questioning his training routine. Or she could join Tate in the dungeon. After all, he seemed to be very keen on the Guardian women, so he'd quite like that.

The Guardian turned her back and continued her training and Edison shook his head once again at the slowness of her pace.

He didn't think it was possible to be any happier than he was right now. Although, he may need to reassess that when he became the King of The Bay of Laurel. His mother believed in the Evernow, saying she was perfectly happy to enjoy her life right now living in the moment, but he'd never heard a bigger load of rubbish. What a ridiculous concept! Why be content with what you had right now, if you knew it was possible to have more?

To *be* more.

Everything was falling into place so beautifully. He could almost taste his victory. He had the Guardians, he had Pip, and now he had Tate conveniently out of the way. He sniggered to think of the precious Prince locked away in a dungeon. Hopefully, the King would leave him there for a while so he could have a good long think about his place in life.

Edison should've been the King's son, not Tate. He would've made him proud. Anybody could see how embarrassed the King was of his children. So embarrassed that he'd had his son marry a freak of nature in an attempt to redeem himself with strong and worthy grandchildren. But there was going to be no need for that. Pip would produce the true heir. An heir who carried the strength of Edison's blood. And in the meantime, while the child grew, Edison would be able to lead this kingdom. He just had a few unpleasantries to get out of the way first.

A flash of color caught his eye over near the tavern as he saw Pip emerge. She was wearing a pink dress with a matching bonnet that she had pulled down over her eyes. After his mother's protests, he'd agreed to allow Pip to continue to learn in the kitchen. His mother had a point about Pip's health. She was even thinner now than she'd been when he'd first started visiting her. He needed his mother to build her up a bit if she was going to live long enough to marry him and bear his child. The tonics he'd been giving her had given her a good start, but he was far too busy right now to think about that. Masters needed to delegate.

He waved at Pip, but soon realized she was never going to see him.

"Guardian," he barked at the next soldier to run past. "Fetch me the Princess. Tell her I wish to speak with her."

The Guardian nodded twice and took off after Pip, leaving Edison smiling at how efficient it was to have an army of slaves.

He watched as the Guardian spoke with Pip, then held out his arm as she took hold of him and allowed him to lead her back to Edison. This wiped the smile from Edison's face.

"Get your hands off her," he said to the Guardian, who quickly removed his arm from Pip's hold.

Pip stopped where she was, a few feet away from Edison, her face pointed down underneath that stupid bonnet.

"Look at me," he said to her. Then turning his gaze to the Guardian. "And you, get back to your running."

Pip had tilted her head up just enough that he could see her peeking out at him from under her bonnet.

"What's wrong with you?" he asked, shaking his head. She was behaving like some kind of lunatic. He hoped his children wouldn't turn out like that. He'd need to make sure he kept them well away from her to stop her influencing them with her ridiculous behavior.

"I'm still adjusting to being outside." Pip dipped her gaze once more.

He noticed she was shaking. "You have a whole army here who'd lay down their lives to protect you. You have nothing to be afraid of."

"They didn't protect Tate." Her words were so quiet he'd had to strain his ears to hear them.

"Your brother told the Guardians to kill me!" He tried to suppress the rage building inside him, but it was impossible. "Are you not on my side? I thought you said you loved me."

"I do," she said, just a little too quickly. Had her feelings for him changed? Despite being fairly certain her feelings were going to be irrelevant for his plans, it'd be easier if she was on side for now.

"Pip, my love." He reached out and took her hands, disappointed to feel her squirm, rather than eagerly grasp him back. "Let me walk you safely back to your bedchamber."

"But don't you have work to do here?" she asked, giving his hands a pathetic squeeze.

"They can take a break."

He looked toward his running Guardians, waving his hands and shouting for them to finish. Several of the women ran toward their children like they were attached with an invisible cord.

"There," he said to Pip. "They run when I say run and they stop when I say stop."

He'd thought she might be more impressed than she seemed. Women were so difficult to please.

Looping her hand through the crook of his arm, they set off to the palace.

"Did you learn much today with my mother?" he asked.

"I did," she said, the eagerness he knew so well returning to her voice, as her expression filled with confidence. "She knows so much. She has a tonic for everything."

He sighed and stopped to look at Pip. "Pip, my darling. She doesn't know everything. You've seen the Guardians are dying. I told you that I just want you to learn the basics from her. I'll teach you what you need to know. Have you been drinking the tonics she's been giving you?"

"Yes. I do feel a little stronger."

"Excellent," he said. "Just don't overdo it. You don't want to get fat for real."

The stricken look on Pip's face was just what he'd hoped for. Far preferable to the confidence she'd displayed only moments ago.

Besides, he genuinely didn't want her to get fat. He liked how scrawny she was. It made her vulnerable, a quality which was the most attractive of any trait a woman could possess. If he'd wanted a woman who was big and strong, he could have married a Guardian. All he needed her to be was strong enough to bear him a child.

"My mother can be dangerous," he said. "Don't trust her. I'm the only one who truly loves you. Always remember that."

"Yes, Edison." She gave him a hollow smile.

Great. His mother may not have been poisoning the Guardians, but she was most definitely poisoning Pip. Only it wasn't with her tonics, it was by poisoning her mind.

"I don't want you to go back to the tavern," he said. "It was a bad idea. I want to teach you myself. That way we can spend more time together. I can bring your tonics to your room."

"But you're busy," she said.

"Not too busy for the woman I love." He smiled to cover his lie. Not only was he too busy, but there was no way that he loved his woman. He just couldn't see his way out of this. She was too important right now for him to risk their relationship. Whatever poison his mother had been feeding her mind with, he needed to find the antidote and win her back. It couldn't be that hard.

He paused to tilt her chin up toward him, stooping to place a gentle kiss on her lips. Only instead of it making her quiver in the way it usually did, it made the shaking in her hands increase.

"I have some wonderful news for you," he said. "I spoke to your father just now and he's granted me permission to marry you. And he's keen for it to happen as soon as possible."

"But... but he said he wanted you to prove yourself first." She reeled back from him and he had to squeeze her hands tighter to keep hold of them.

"He was angry about what your brother did out there in the fields, but I told him that I knew how he could make it up to me. Aren't you happy? This is what we've been wanting! You're going to be my wife."

"I'm thrilled." She smiled at him, blinking in an effort to hold back tears. "This wonderful news has made me a little emotional, that's all."

"I love you, Pip. We don't need anyone else. Not my mother, not Tate, not anybody. Just you and me, okay? You and me."

"You and me," she repeated.

He let go of her hand to push some hair out of her eyes. "You're so beautiful."

But even these words that he'd first used to steal her heart, weren't enough.

His mother had so much to answer for. She was ruining everything. It was time to add her to his list of people he was going to ruin in return.

PIP

THE NOW

*P*ip lay down on her bed and shuddered. Thankfully she'd managed to avoid having Edison come into her room by convincing him that the wonderful news of their marriage had made her tired.

Pip knew that sometimes in relationships people fell out of love, but that was usually after the wedding, not before. Or in her parents' case, she wondered if they'd ever been in love at all. But how many people could pinpoint the exact moment they fell out of love? And how many of those people fell out of love due to the realization that their future husband wanted them dead.

She picked up Prin and held her soft woolen body to her chest.

"I've been foolish," she said.

Prin stared back at her, unblinking as always, forever the patient listener.

"You knew he was using me, didn't you?" asked Pip. "You saw it all."

She put Prin down on the bed and went to her windowsill. She really had been a fool. She'd fallen for Edison's charms. She should've known better than that. He hadn't liked her when they were kids and he didn't like her now. Nothing had changed.

Actually, that wasn't right. Everything apart from his feelings had changed. Tate was locked in the dungeon and Edison was destroying the lives of the Guardians, treating them like he owned them. And his poor mother! Ariel had been so kind to Pip, teaching her all about the different foods and how she used them to make her tonics, including the special one she'd made for Pip, to build up her body with lean muscle and make her strong. Not only that, but Ariel had been the one to open Pip's eyes and see clearly what she'd become. A skeleton. A waif. A walking corpse.

It was hard to think of herself like that. She was so used to thinking of herself as fat. She pushed at her middle, watching as the tip of her finger made an indent in her stomach. She was going to try to do her best to build up her strength with Ariel's tonics, but it wasn't going to be easy to see her girth expand. Especially if Edison insisted on calling her fat. Her problem was that she still wasn't convinced she deserved the food she was being given.

A knock at her door disturbed her thoughts. She went to it and held it closed, not bothering with her spy hole when she knew who it was. She'd had enough of her future husband's face for one day.

"Please, let me be, Edison," she called through the door. "I need to rest."

"It's me," came a voice that wasn't Edison's. "It's River. Can I come in, please? It's important."

Pip opened the door immediately. Perhaps this new sister of hers had some news about Tate.

"We need to talk," said River. "I went to the herbalist to find you, but she said you'd gone. Your father has had Tate thrown in the dungeon! We need to get him out of there."

"I know," said Pip.

"You know?" River's mouth fell open. "Then what are you doing here? Why aren't you trying to get him out?"

Pip sat down on her bed, the familiar feeling of shame washing over her. Was there nobody in her family she was able to save?

"This is all because of Edison," said Pip, determined not to take the blame this time. Ariel had assured her she wasn't responsible for her mother's death. It wasn't her fault Tate was in the dungeon either. "It's always all because of Edison."

River went to speak and seemed to stop herself.

"It's okay," said Pip. "I've seen him for who he is. I've been so stupid. So, very stupid. How could I have fallen for his charms so easily?"

"Oh, Pip. You're not stupid." River sat down next to her on the bed. "He's a master manipulator. He caught you when you were vulnerable, that's all."

"What do I do? He told me just now that our marriage has been agreed upon. I begged Father to give us his support until he did, and I now want to run as far away from Edison as I possibly can."

"You can talk to your Father," said River. "When you ask him to release Tate, you can tell him you no longer wish to be betrothed to that monster."

"You want me to ask Father to release Tate?" Pip picked up Prin, no longer caring what River thought. "I'm afraid you think I have a lot more influence over him than I actually do."

"You stopped him from taking Edison's head, didn't you? That was so brave. You can do it, Pip. I know you can."

"That was when I loved him." Pip pulled at Prin's dress, then worried she was going to tear it, she set down the doll. "My love for him gave me strength."

"What opened your eyes to him?" asked River, placing a hand on her back.

"Ariel," said Pip. "She opened my eyes to so many things. I walked into her kitchen as one person, and I left as another."

"Pip, what happened to you?" River removed her hand and turned to her. "Why were you locked in your room wasting away? Tate said as a girl you used to run all over the palace. He said you were happy. Where did that girl go?"

"She died with my mother." Pip got up from the bed and took a seat at her table. As much as she was beginning to like River, she needed her space.

"Broken hearts can mend," said River, picking up Pip's Guardian doll and turning her over in her hands.

"You don't understand." The urge to lift the burden on Pip's shoulders grew. "I killed her."

"How could you have killed her?" River put down the doll and stared at her. "Tate said she was very ill. That there was nothing anybody could do to heal her."

Pip sighed. Was it really that hard to understand? "I made her ill. Edison had me swap my mother's tonic. He said it would make her better, and it did for a while. But then she fell even more ill, so I stopped giving it to her. And... well, and then she died and it's all my fault. I thought it was because I stopped the tonic, but now I wonder if that's what was killing her all along."

"Oh, Pip! You were only a child," said River. "It's not your fault."

"It is," said Pip. "That's why I can't bring myself to eat now. Or leave my room. I don't deserve it. How can I run through the garden with food in my stomach when my mother is buried in the ground?"

"Because it wasn't your fault," said River, going to Pip and crouching down in front of her. "It sounds to me like it was Edison's fault."

"But why? Why, River?" This was the question that had been haunting her. "He had no reason to want her dead."

"He must've had a reason. We just don't know what his reason was. All I can tell you is that it wasn't your fault. You were only a child and you thought you were helping her. You'd never have done anything to hurt her on purpose. You must forgive yourself. It's time to move on."

"But he was only a child, too. Just a few years older than me."

"Edison was never only a child." River screwed up her face as if she'd just swallowed a bitter tonic. "And besides, look how nicely he's moved on."

Pip nodded, wondering if it was possible to let go of her past. If only it were as easy as River seemed to think.

"My mother used to tell me a story," said Pip. "About a girl called Snow whose jealous stepmother tried to kill her with a poison apple. Do you think maybe Edison was jealous of my mother? Because she was more powerful than his. Would someone really kill for jealousy?"

"I don't know." River stood up. "Maybe. But what I do know is that right at this moment Tate is locked in a dungeon and we need to get him out. Let's go and talk to your father."

"I'll probably only make things worse," said Pip. "The best thing I can do for Tate is stay right away."

"That's rubbish," said River. "You already tried that for almost a decade and look what's happened. Tate was there for you when you needed him. It's time for you to do the same for him."

Pip nodded slowly and River's face lit with hope.

There was no way her father was going to listen to her.

He never had.

RIVER

THE NOW

*R*iver followed Pip into the throne room, hoping the King would listen to their request to have Tate released. Surely, he didn't intend to keep him down in the dungeon for too long? He was his son! His heir!

The King smiled at them as if nothing was wrong. For once, he didn't have any food in his hands, although the chicken carcass beside him explained why.

"We've come to request that you release Tate from the dungeon," said River, surprising herself that she hadn't been able to wait for Pip to speak first. "We're attempting to produce you an heir, and that's quite impossible with him down there and me up here."

The King's eyebrows shot up to greet his hairline. "I can arrange a double cell for you both, if you like?"

River watched as the King tipped back his head and laughed.

Both Pip and River fixed stony gazes on him as they waited for him to finish.

"Father," said Pip. "Please, Tate's your son. You can't lock him up like this."

"Why not?" he asked. "You locked yourself up for the best part of ten years and look at you now. You've never been better. It'll be good for him. Give him some time to think."

"Think about what?" asked River. "About how Edison is destroying this kingdom?"

"Watch yourself!" The King held a long, crooked finger up at her. "You're overstepping the mark here. Do I need to remind you who your King is?"

"No, Your Majesty." River bowed her head.

"Better," he said, nodding his approval. "My son needs some time to think about his behavior. If I hadn't arrived when I did, he'd have had Edison killed."

"I thought you wanted him to prove his worth as future King," said Pip, pulling her shoulders back. "You asked him to take charge."

"Well, Phillipa, this is a development I didn't see coming," said the King. "Have you hardened your heart to your future husband? I only just agreed to your marriage earlier today."

River held her tongue and waited. Pip had finally found her voice and her courage. It was important she learned to answer for herself.

"The wedding is off," said Pip.

River could see a strong resemblance between father and daughter as they stared each other down.

"The wedding is not off," said the King. "I've given Edison my word. You're to be married in the morning."

"But you said he could marry me if he restored the Guardians to health," said Pip. "All he's done so far is strip them of their rights and turn them into pawns in his game. They're worse than ever, not better at all."

"Sometimes things have to get worse before they can get better." The King seemed happy with this statement, and River wondered if Edison had put these words into his mouth.

"It was only days ago that you wanted his head," said Pip. "How can you change your mind like this?"

The King laughed. "Look who's talking, Philippa. I've decided Edison talks a lot of sense. While your brother has been busy skipping through cornfields in the morning and failing to impregnate his wife, Edison has been making plans to control an army and bring strength and power to our Kingdom. It saddens me to say that Edison would make a far better King than my own son."

"Edison can't be King!" cried River. "Tate is going to be King. A wonderful King. And our children after him."

"What children?" The King glared at her.

River's hand flew to her stomach, wondering if the seed of a child had begun to grow in her belly after the last passionate nights she'd spent with Tate.

"We need more time," she said. They hadn't been married for long at all. How quickly did he expect this baby to be conceived? "You must release Tate!"

"Relax. I will. After Phillipa's wedding."

"Why not now?" asked River. Every day it took to release him was another day too long.

"We can't have him interfering with the wedding," said the King. "I'm happy with the husband Philippa chose for herself."

"I choose him no longer," said Pip, holding her voice level.

"Your choice remains," said the King. "It cannot be undone. I've given my word. Go now and prepare for your wedding. I'm granting you your greatest wish. Edison shall be your husband. Whether you choose him no longer or not."

"No, Father," said Pip. "Please! He's a cruel man. He killed Mother."

The King's head snapped to attention. "Your mother died of a weak constitution. That's some claim to blame Edison for that. He was merely a child."

"Edison was never merely a child," said Pip, repeating River's words from earlier. "He gave me tonics to give Mother that made her sick."

"So, you killed her?" he asked, sitting forward.

"No! I just told you what happened."

"And I just told you I don't believe you. Now, leave me be. Both your requests are denied. Tate will remain in the dungeon for now and you, my daughter, will be married in the morning."

"But Father!"

"Go now. Pretty yourself up in the way you women do. Curl your hair and try on your dresses. And be here in the morning for your wedding or I'll see to it that far worse happens to your brother than being locked safely in a cell. Do you understand me?"

Pip nodded, leaving River to wonder if the King would really take the life of his heir. But Pip knew her father far better than River did and the frightened look on her face seemed to indicate that she believed him.

If only the Guardians knew what kind of King they'd spent their lives training and fighting to protect. It was like protecting the devil himself.

TATE

THE NOW

*T*ate sat up with a start.

"What the hell?" He brushed his hands across his face. Was that a rat? It was hard to tell in the dark.

He hadn't been inside one of these cells before. Only seen them from the passageways that wound between them on the rare occasion he'd ventured down here. It'd always given him the shivers with the dank walls that seemed to close in the more steps he'd taken. He'd never imagined that one day he'd be locked inside one of these terrifying cells. He felt just like one of his rabbits caught in a trap. He could wriggle and squirm all he liked, but there was no way he was getting out of here unless someone took pity on him and turned the key in his lock.

A dim light flickered into life in the passageway and Tate rose from the hard bench he'd been lying on and went to the iron bars to peer out.

"Hello?" he called, hoping that whoever it was had brought him some water. He was going to have to start licking the walls soon in search of moisture.

"Tate?"

"River!" She'd come for him! It seemed too good to be true.

"Where are you?" she called.

"Over here." He waved his hand furiously between the bars, hoping to attract his wife's attention.

The light came closer and brighter as a familiar figure approached.

"River," he cried again.

"Oh, Tate." River held up a lantern. He'd forgotten how beautiful she was with the soft angles of her face illuminated by the light and framed by her golden hair.

"How did you get down here?" he asked.

"You forget who guards this place," she said. "And that I was once a Guardian. I only wish I could convince them to let you go free, but that would be taking things too far. They've granted me a few minutes to see you and that's all."

She rested the lantern on the stone floor and reached into a sack handing him a cup full of almonds and a flask of water. He lifted the flask to his cracked lips and drank deeply, the water tasting like liquid magic as it swirled in his mouth.

"Have you talked to my father?" he asked.

River nodded. "He says he's teaching you a lesson while he keeps you out of the way."

"Out of the way of what?" Tate put a handful of almonds in his mouth and chewed, enjoying the feeling of the way they crunched under his teeth. His stomach groaned in response to the nourishment.

"Pip and Edison are getting married in the morning," said River.

Tate swallowed and spluttered. "That was fast. I suppose Pip is happy about this."

But River shook her head. "Not at all. She's seen him for who he is. She's frightened of him. This marriage is the last thing she wants."

Tate set down both the empty flask and the almonds and reached through the bars for River's hands, clasping them tightly. "You have to help her."

She shook her head. "I can't. I can be there for her, but there's nothing I can do. Your father's made up his mind. Says he's made a promise and he can't break it."

"That's never bothered him in the past," said Tate.

The jingling of keys came from down the hallway. It seemed their time was up.

"I have to go, Tate. But I'll come again just as soon as I can. And I'll find a way to get you out of here. I don't care what it is that I have to do. You're going to be set free."

River pressed her face to the bars and Tate found her sweet lips with his own, enjoying the softness and love in her kiss.

"Princess," the Guardian called, growing impatient. "Your time is up."

"I love you," said Tate, realizing he'd never said this before, even though it was true.

"I love you, too."

And with those precious words, River picked up her lantern and vanished down the passageway.

He took two steps backward and sat back down on the bench.

River loved him. Together, they'd find a way out of this. They were lucky. They had each other. But poor Pip was about to be married to a man who was as evil as River was good. She'd seen the truth in him, but she'd seen it too late.

How could their father do this to her? His only daughter! But what could he do to help her from here? Nothing.

He'd forgiven his father for so many things over the years. But there was no way he was ever going to be able to forgive this.

Although, as evil as his father could be, he was far from stupid. He'd have known when he'd sent him here that there was no chance of their relationship ever being repaired. Which meant he never intended to release him. He planned to make Edison his son and heir instead.

ARIEL

THE NOW

*A*riel pressed her ear against the door and listened to Edison work in the kitchen. *Her* kitchen. What could he possibly be making in the middle of the night? The night before his wedding, no less.

The cooks in the palace would be working furiously through the night, having had a wedding feast foisted upon them at short notice, but Edison was the groom. There was nothing he needed to do, except make himself look nice and turn up.

She heard him chopping furiously as the fire crackled under the pot he'd brought to the boil. The undeniable smell of mushrooms leached under the door.

Ariel's nose twitched. Years of making tonics had trained her nose to differentiate between scents. That wasn't a regular mushroom that could enhance a person's immune system and improve the health of the heart. This was slightly different. Had he mixed it with sometime else? Or...

A cold sweat raced down Ariel's spine as another thought swept through her. What if...

She crept out the back door of her small home and out into the garden, pausing briefly to thank the full moon for giving her light as it cast its shadows across the earth. Picking up her shovel, she pressed on desperate to know if her suspicions were correct. Please, let her be wrong.

It was cold in the garden, with a light sprinkling of rain that was sticking her hair to her face. She slipped her shawl from her shoulders and knotted it over her head as she made her way to the parsley patch.

Squinting as her eyes adjusted to the dark, Ariel forced her shovel into the soil and pressed down with her foot. The earth was soft and pliable, used to being turned over to plant a fresh harvest. Lifting away the dirt, she pressed down again and dug the hole deeper. This wasn't going to be an easy task.

She'd planted the chest deep in the earth, hoping it would remain undiscovered until she could one day pass it onto the right person. Nobody knew it was here. Not even Edison. Especially not Edison. For this chest contained the recipes to the most dangerous of her ancestors' tonics. Recipes that would be deadly in the wrong person's hands, a category that her son sadly belonged in. It was so long ago that she'd buried it, but she'd known as soon as she'd seen the interest Edison had shown in it what she'd had to do.

Once, she'd caught Edison digging in the garden and she'd managed to steer him away. Had she done this with too much urgency and alerted him to the potential of digging up more than just seeds?

She lifted away more soil, continuing until she heard the clunk of metal on metal. Bending to her knees, she scooped at the earth with her fingers, clawing the chest until it came free. It was still here! And it was heavy. Too heavy to be empty.

Setting the chest down on the ground she worked on it, prizing off the lid and running her hand over the black velvet cloth that encased the book.

Very carefully, she peeled back the velvet, bracing herself to set eyes on the book once more.

She stared at the leather cover for a few moments, knowing something was wrong but it was like her brain had stalled and she couldn't work out what it was.

The book was black when it had once been brown. The embossing was in gold when it'd once been silver. And the name of the book was not the one she'd been expecting. She ran her finger over the words, trying to understand how this book had ended up in here.

Princess Snow and the Magic Mirror.

"Edison!" she breathed. "What have you done?"

He had to have taken her recipe book, replacing it with this storybook she'd seen kept by the Queen's bed when she'd cared for Tate and Edison in the early days of their life.

But why had he chosen this specific book and not left the chest empty?

She turned the cover of the book and there pressed in the pages was a dried valerian root—an ingredient in a recipe she knew far too well.

That was when it hit her. This was a sick joke. The storybook had belonged to the Queen, who had no doubt died as a result of that very recipe. Edison was telling her that he was responsible. Her son's heart was not just gray, it was as black as the velvet this book had been wrapped in.

She leaned to her side and heaved, her stomach expelling its contents, making her wish it was her memory that could do that instead. Edison had given her a message and it was one that she didn't want.

And if he'd killed the Queen, then no doubt the Guardians who'd fallen ill had to have been his work, too. Burying the recipe book in the garden hadn't been enough. She should've burnt it. How many people would still be alive if only she'd done that?

He must've thought he was so clever finding it and replacing it with a book of the Queen's. Well, she'd show him what clever was. He may be cunning, but he wasn't as clever as he thought he was. She may be too late to save the lives he'd already taken, but she could put a stop to any further evil he had planned.

Placing the book back in the chest, she lowered it into the earth, picked up her shovel and re-filled the hole, arranging the parsley to cover the recently disturbed earth.

Going to the kitchen window, she very carefully went to the shutters, moving slowly so as not to catch Edison's attention. She peered in, having to put her hand over her mouth when she saw two mushrooms on the workbench. Innocent and white, they may look like any kind of mushroom to the uneducated, but Ariel knew what they were.

Death cap mushrooms. Just as fatal as their name implied.

Edison had been taught how to identify these mushrooms from an early age, despite them having been eradicated from the palace gardens. Where had he gotten such a thing?

The Bay.

It all became clear now. He'd been so keen to help her by fetching her supplies of kelp from the Bay. No doubt he'd sought out other ingredients while he was there. There was a whole black market going on in the grounds of what had once been the King's palace. A person could buy anything they wanted for the right price. She'd once considered procuring her own supply of valerian root to help her sleep when her worries about her son had first begun to grow roots of their own. But knowing how deadly it was when mixed with skullcap, a common ingredient in the Guardians' tonics, she'd disposed of it, not wanting to risk an accident.

The Queen had been one of the palace's biggest consumers of skullcap. Was it possible that somehow Edison had gotten some valerian root into her tonics? Or the Guardians' tonics? That would fit with the slow and painful deaths they'd experienced.

But it seemed there was a more pressing problem in front of her, in the form of the death cap mushroom. There was nothing slow about a death by this fungus. It would be as fast as it was effective.

There was only one reason Edison could be cooking with them. Her son, who she'd raised to be the best person he was capable of being, was planning to murder someone else. And adding valerian root to their tonics wasn't fast enough. Whoever he wanted to kill this time, he wanted them gone. Fast.

But who?

She watched as Edison sliced the mushrooms into fine slivers and added them to the pot. His face was impassive. Not the face of someone who was about to commit the worst sin imaginable.

Ariel stepped away from the window and made her way back into her home, wiping her filthy hands clean on a rag. There was no point going to her bed. Sleep wasn't going to come to her. She had to figure out what she was going to do.

Was Edison planning to poison Pip after the wedding had taken place and he had the title of Prince? Although, surely, he'd want to have an heir before this happened to firm up his position in the palace.

Was the poison for the King? But this didn't make sense either. Edison had the King right where he wanted him. He'd be a fool to kill him now.

Perhaps it was for one of the other Guardians? Everyone knew how much he despised them. Could it be for River?

Ariel gasped as the obvious answer came to her. It was for Tate! It had to be. With Tate gone, Pip would be the heir. And when Edison was her husband, this made him exponentially more powerful.

Ariel had to find a way to warn Tate. To make sure he didn't accept any food or drink from anybody he didn't completely trust. No doubt in the dungeon he wasn't being too fussy right now.

She'd honestly thought that if she raised Edison right and put enough time and love into him, that she could make him a better person than the one he was born to be. It seemed his father's genes were too strong. But she didn't want to think about him now. She had to figure this out alone, just like she had to do everything else alone.

Maybe things would be different moving forward. She had Pip back in her life now. And she had Tate, once she figured out how to get him out of the dungeon. She wasn't going to let Edison poison him.

She'd die stopping him if she had to.

PIP

THE NOW

*P*ip walked down the aisle, wondering if she looked as miserable and uncomfortable as she felt. Surely, she did. Although, River had told her she looked beautiful when Elise had helped her into her dress.

She wasn't sure she wanted to look beautiful. Not for Edison, anyway. Perhaps it would've been better if she looked a wreck. But her mother had wanted her to wear her wedding dress one day and this would be the only wedding she'd ever have. It would be an insult to her mother's memory not to wear all these yards of the kingdom's finest woven thread.

The dress was so heavy, but Pip liked the way it pressed down on her. The constriction made her feel safe and the veil over her face was doing a great job at helping her pretend she was anywhere except where she was. But still, her heart beat wildly knowing how many people had gathered at short notice for the privilege of attending a royal wedding. She'd wanted to slowly immerse herself back into society, not plunge in with rocks tied to her ankles. For that was how she felt right now. Each step was an effort beyond what she was certain she was capable of. But the only way to get this over and return to the safety of her bedchamber was to keep moving forward. One painful step at a time.

The throne room had been set up with seating on either side of a wide aisle and through her veil, she could see Edison and her father waiting for her on the platform in front of the throne. As complicated as her feelings were for these two men, it was easier to focus on them than the crowd of strange faces staring at her. Judging her. Comparing her to how her beautiful mother had looked in this dress.

Her steps were slow and measured and she wondered how long she could stretch this out. Each step took her closer to marrying a man she didn't trust. A man she was certain was going to kill her one day.

If only Tate were here. He'd be standing there in the front row, his smiling eyes urging her forward, reassuring her that he'd look after her as he'd always done. Either that or he'd step in and put a stop to this sham of a marriage. If it hadn't been for Tate, she'd have wasted away in her bedchamber years ago. He'd given her love and attention and made sure she kept going no matter how hard or lonely life had felt.

As she got closer, she could see River at the front of the room standing beside Ariel, so she focused on them trying to draw strength from the two people who understood her.

Her footsteps pushed forward and far too soon she reached the end of the aisle where Edison reached out his hands for her, greedily snatching at her veil and dragging it up, leaving her face bare and her soul exposed.

She smiled at him, aware that her pretense at joy was failing to reach her eyes. Instead, her chest grew tighter and each breath became harder to draw into her lungs.

"You look lovely, my dear," said Edison, the genuine joy more than prominent in his eyes. This was the day he became a Prince. A day he'd manipulated her into giving him, by pretending that he loved her.

He wore a dark suit with a deep blue robe over the top and she could see a hint of his leather cord around his neck. The one he'd let her wear as a symbol of his love, until he'd asked for it back so he could wear it to their wedding. She'd happily given it to him, not wanting to have anything of his around her neck. His presence alone was enough to choke her.

"Thank you," she said, curious to know if any part of him had ever loved her. Or did he hate her? Perhaps he felt indifferent. She was just a pawn in his sick game to rise to power in the kingdom. He really didn't care about her either way and for that, she hated him even more.

Her father cleared his throat and began to say the words that would bind them together for the rest of their lives, however long that may be, and she found herself retreating within herself. She wasn't really here. She was back in her bedchamber with the blankets pulled up to her chin and Prin on the pillow beside her.

But the racing of her heart and the droning of her father's voice told her that wasn't true, so instead, she focused on the window over Edison's head and imagined she could see the spirit of her mother in the sunlight instead.

Protect me, Mother, she urged the light. *Don't let him kill me.*

She listened as Edison promised to love and care for her for the rest of their lives and she said the same to him, the hollowness of her words echoing around this soulless room.

When the deed was done and they were proclaimed to be husband and wife, Pip obediently tilted her head to receive Edison's kiss. A kiss that would once have set her heart on fire, but now did nothing but turn it to ice. How could she have thought she wasn't worthy of this man? He wasn't worthy of her! He wasn't even worthy of the air in his lungs.

He broke the kiss and stood tall, smoothing down his blond hair with a satisfied smirk.

The crowd of people cheered and Edison took her hand in his raised them in the air in triumph, a gesture that elicited more cheers as the people stood and threw petals at them.

If only she was marrying a good man with a good heart, it would be the most beautiful and romantic moment of her life.

They walked back down the aisle, hand in hand as they accepted the good wishes of the people. Pip's fingers itched to pull the veil back over her face.

"She's just like her mother," a woman said to the person beside her.

Pip knew this wasn't true. Well, not on the outside anyway. But perhaps she was like her mother on the inside? Had her mother felt like this on her wedding day? Pip couldn't remember any affection between her parents and her father certainly didn't seem to be mourning his wife's loss too greatly. Was that why she'd been sure to tell Tate and Pip to marry for love? Not because she wanted them to have what she had, but because she wanted something different for them. Something better.

It felt like history was repeating itself. No wonder her mother had taken to her bed so often over the years. Sometimes it was easier to hide under a blanket than face your reality. After all, that's exactly what Pip had been doing all these years.

They walked from the throne room into the palace courtyard where a feast had been set up. The combined aroma of all the ingredients hit her nose and her mouth watered in response.

She could see plates of corn dripping with butter, roasted capsicums stuffed with rice and spices, bread loaded with tomatoes and basil, and small pies made from barley and tarragon. An enormous roast boar turned over a fire. The sight of all this food made Pip's stomach turn in much the same way as that poor boar.

Could she allow herself to eat any of this without purging it later? Ariel said she deserved to eat. And she trusted Ariel. But her relationship with food was still complicated at best. She both loved and hated it at the same time.

Edison let go of her hand to go to the table with the pots of soup, leaning over each of them and sniffing deeply. Pip's brow wrinkled at the sight of his nostrils twitching. How could she possibly have ever been in love with this man?

People were streaming into the courtyard now and some musicians had started to play a festive tune. She fought the urge to run. This was all too much, too soon. It was even worse than walking down the aisle. So many people, so much noise and so much movement!

She went to the wedding table and took her seat before her legs crumpled underneath herself. Her breath was coming fast now as if in competition with the beating of her heart and she did her best to try to slow her body down before her dress completely stuck to her with the cold sweat she'd broken out in.

River patted her gently on her back as she walked past her to take her seat two places to her left, leaving a space where the King was to sit at the very center of the table. Pip caught the scent of the oils that Edison had brought back from Wintergreen. It was no wonder River had taken to wearing it so often. It had a way of calming the nerves. She really did need to try to get a bottle for herself.

A steaming bowl of mushroom soup was placed in front of her and Pip focused on it, hoping she'd be able to keep it down.

Ariel was seated two places to her right and she smiled at Pip with nothing but sadness in her eyes. But before she could talk to her, Edison sat between them and edged Pip's bowl closer.

"Eat up," he said.

"The King hasn't eaten yet." She raised her eyebrows at him. Nobody ate before the King. Surely, he knew something as simple as that?

"Of course," he said. "It smells so delicious I just got carried away."

A loud clatter sounded somewhere near the musicians and Pip turned her head to see what it was.

"Clumsy fool," said Edison, craning his neck for a better look.

The crowd hushed for a few moments, but when they saw the noise had only been a cook dropping her ladle, they went back to what they'd been doing only moments earlier.

The King approached the table and Pip and Edison stood and bowed their heads.

"Are you happy?" the King asked Pip, as he took his seat.

She looked at him without answering. Did he really think she was happy? She'd begged him not to let today happen. He knew she'd no longer wanted to marry Edison.

"You know exactly how happy I am." She patted her father's cold hand.

"Then let the feast begin," he said, bending his head forward and spooning a large gulp of soup into his mouth.

"You can eat now." Edison pressed his elbow into her side to get her attention, as he tucked into his own bowl.

He sounded like Tate, always trying to get her to eat, afraid that if she didn't, she'd waste away.

She dipped her spoon into the soup and watched the hot liquid pool in the hollow. It did smell good.

But just as she was about to lift it to her lips, she paused. Why was Edison so keen for her to eat? He certainly wasn't worried about her health. Had he poisoned her soup? Were his murderous plans coming into play so soon? Surely not.

"Eat," her father said, draining the last of the liquid in his bowl directly into his mouth, his eyes locking on hers as liquid dribbled down the bristles on his chin.

The thought of the soup being poisoned added another even more complicated layer to her relationship with food. She needed food to live, but... was this particular food going to do the opposite?

The thumping of her heart resumed and she lifted the spoon to her lips.

"I said eat it, Phillipa!" Her father shook his head, his disgust for her even more apparent than usual.

She drew in the soup and swallowed, just as she was told, accepting that it was delicious, even if it was most likely going to kill her.

Edison smiled as she ate, eating from his own bowl, and making appreciative noises.

When she'd scooped the last of the soup into her mouth, Edison turned to her with a smile that made her skin crawl.

"Did you like that?" he asked.

Now certain she'd been poisoned, she contemplated how long she had to throw up before it took effect.

"It was lovely, thanks, but I need to freshen up now if you can excuse me?"

She stood, but Edison grabbed her wrist and pulled her back down in her seat.

"You're not going anywhere," he said.

She winced as his grip on her tightened.

"Edison, I need to go."

Sweat beaded on her forehead and her stomach pulled into a tight knot. She may only have minutes left. Nausea raced up her throat and a bead of sweat ran down the side of her face. Perhaps if she threw up at the table right now, she could be saved?

She looked at her father, who was motioning for a servant to bring him another serve of soup. Would he care? Would he try to save her?

"Why?" she asked.

"Why, what, my love?" He raised his eyebrows at her and smirked.

"Why would you poison me?"

Edison tipped back his head and let out a loud roar of laughter.

"It's not funny." Her hand clasped over her mouth and her stomach began to heave.

"Oh, but it is. Because, you see, I didn't poison you, you foolish girl. I just wanted to see the panicked look on your face." His laughter came out as more of a shriek now. "You really thought you were dead, didn't you"?

Pip's hand fell to her lap. "So, I'm not going to die?"

"Of course not! You haven't given me my heir yet." He patted his stomach as his laughter died down, shaking his head at her apparent stupidity.

And she never would give him an heir if she had any power over that decision.

A noise behind her stole her attention and she spun around to see what the commotion was about, shocked to see her father was spluttering as he tipped back a goblet of wine, trying to dislodge something in his throat.

A crowd of people huddled around the table trying to offer assistance and advice as their King's face turned red and he spluttered some more.

"I'm okay!" He held up the palm of his hand and shooed everyone back.

But it was clear to Pip that he was very much not okay.

His spluttering worsened and he rose from his chair, doubling over as he clutched his middle, then fell to the ground, his large belly rising and falling rapidly as he took what were sure to be his last breaths.

People crowded around him, blocking Pip's view of him as they screamed and wept.

Pip turned to Edison, certain he'd had something to do with this, only to find him smiling as he watched on.

"You think this is funny?" Pip wasn't sure if her heart could take any more of this. It felt like it'd beaten more times in this one day than it had in the past ten years.

Edison leaned forward to whisper in her ear. "I think it's hilarious."

She pulled back from him, realizing this man was even more evil than she'd thought. "You did this to him. I know you did."

"It was time he cleared the path for the next generation, my love," whispered Edison.

"Tate is his heir, not me. You've gained nothing from this!"

"Funny you mention Tate right now." He placed a hand on her back and she cringed. "I wonder if he's enjoying the soup I had sent down to him."

"What did you just say?" This couldn't be happening. Not Tate, too! "What have you done to my brother?"

Edison smiled once more, even more broadly than he had all day.

"Let's just say that Tate's presently enjoying a little bit of wedding soup in his cell right now. A special bowl of it, made up just for him."

Pip stepped back from the table, almost tripping on the long hem of her dress.

Edison had poisoned her father and now Tate. She had to get to him before it was too late.

But just as she went to turn around, Edison's face turned purple and he started to cough.

He stood, making a hacking noise as he gasped for air. Clutching at his throat now as he tried to breathe, Pip was reminded of her earlier thought that he didn't deserve the air in his lungs. Had she somehow caused this to happen?

"Do something!" someone called from the crowd that was gathering. "It's happening to our new Prince, too."

A man grabbed Edison and thumped him on the back, but Pip already knew that wouldn't work. Edison was going to die, just like her father was sure to. He'd poisoned the King and somehow ended up poisoning himself.

People were bending over and vomiting now, trying to expel any food they'd eaten as they realized the food had been tampered with. Women were screaming and men were shouting and pumping their fists in the air like that was going to solve anything.

"The King is dead!" someone cried over the noise.

Pip's head spun and she bent over trying to get enough air, but it only seemed to want to come to her in short gasps.

Glancing up, she saw Edison fall to his knees, then collapse on the ground and roll to his back in the same way her father had only moments before.

Ariel crouched down beside her son, the howl escaping from her lips sounding like a wild animal. As much as Pip had grown to despise Edison, the sight of a mother so wrapped up in grief, pierced Pip's heart. Ariel was a good person. She didn't deserve to suffer the loss of her only child.

The hacking noise silenced and very slowly all color drained from Edison's face.

Pip went to him and squatted beside Ariel, who locked eyes on her, seeming to want to tell her a hundred things, yet saying nothing.

Then Ariel stood and raked her hands through her hair, looking around the crowd as if she didn't know where she was.

"Edison." Pip gently shook her new husband.

"You…did…this." His voice was shaky and she had to lean forward to make out the words. "You…did…this."

"I didn't," she said, not sure why it mattered to her what he thought when soon he was not going to be capable of thinking anything.

"Your fault," he said, his lungs rattling now as he drew in what was sure to be his final breath. "You… did this."

Pip glanced up at Ariel, and deciding she was out of earshot, she leaned in, her lips hovering at Edison's ear.

"I didn't do it," she hissed. "But I wish I did."

She pulled back to see Edison's eyes open wide as his lip curled. It seemed he hated her, almost as much as she hated him. Then, the life drained from his eyes like the last drops of water in an overturned bucket and his disgust turned to… nothingness.

He was gone from this world, taking his evil plans with him. At last, his lungs held no air. The man who'd tricked her and betrayed her and killed her father, was dead.

Unsure who to thank, Pip looked to the sky, overwhelmed with a sense of pure gratitude.

She was free. Free of her bedchamber. Free of her guilt in the part she'd played in killing her mother. Free of her father and his relentless judgment. And now she was free of the man who'd said he loved her when the only person he'd ever loved was himself.

"He's gone," she said to Ariel, tugging at her skirt.

Ariel crouched down and pressed her fingertips to Edison's neck, checking for a pulse.

"He killed my father," said Pip, still unable to see her father's body with all the people gathered around.

"He did some horrible things." Ariel removed her hand from his face.

"And possibly my brother," said Pip, remembering what else Edison had told her before he'd died.

Ariel reached for Pip and shook her head. "No, Tate is safe."

Pip stood, not sure how Ariel could possibly know such a thing. She hadn't heard what Edison had said. He'd specifically told her that he'd poisoned Tate's soup. His only hope was that he hadn't eaten it yet.

Leaving Ariel, she hoisted her dress and ran in the direction of the dungeons. Her brother needed her. The last time she'd seen him, she'd looked at him with such anger. He couldn't die thinking that she hated him! He couldn't die at all. He'd only been trying to protect her. And he'd been right in everything he'd said.

Please, let her get to him in time.

TATE

THE NOW

*T*ate sat on the stone floor of his cell and listened to his stomach groan. Food did that to him now. Like his body no longer knew what to do with it. Maybe he should just throw it up, like he knew Pip did. He'd never seen a sign of her having vomited before, but there was no other reasonable explanation. She couldn't possibly have eaten all the food he'd brought her over the years and still be as thin as she was. Unless she hadn't eaten any of it at all. Was that why she always waited until he left the room?

He could feel himself losing weight now and resisted the urge to bring up the breakfast a Guardian had brought him earlier in the day. He needed all the sustenance he could get and today's soup had been an unexpected treat. It was far tastier than anything else he'd been brought down here. Perhaps River had something to do with it.

"Tate!"

He scrambled to his feet at the sound of his sister's voice.

"Tate!"

He went to the bars of his cell and pressed his face against them, trying to peer down the passageway.

"Over here, Pip!" He waved his hand through the bars.

"The soup!" she said, running toward him, wearing what was unmistakably their mother's wedding dress, even in this dim light.

"What about it?" They had more important things to talk about than his soup. "Did you send it? I thought it was River."

Pip was panting now, and holding her up dress, revealing her boney ankles.

"No," she said. "Did you eat it? Hurry, Tate. Talk to me."

"Did you just get married?" he asked, unable to get past what she was wearing. "Is that Mother's dress?"

She waved her hands at him. "The soup, Tate. Did you eat it?"

"Of course I did," he said. "I was starving."

"Vomit!" She was screaming at him, her eyes wide and filled with fear. "Quickly! Throw it up. Now!"

"Why?" He stepped back from the bars, feeling a little uncertain about what was going on.

"Poison. It's poisoned. I'll explain later. Just vomit it. Now! Hurry."

So, that was why he'd been provided such a delicious meal. Was it also why his stomach felt rock hard and kept groaning?

He put his fingers in the back of his throat and tried to heave, but nothing happened, except a shakiness that spread to his limbs. He couldn't die! Not now. He was too young with too many things left that he wanted to do. And he couldn't leave River. What would become of her if he wasn't there to protect her?

He tried to heave again but it was as if his body was fighting him to keep hold of the only sustenance he'd provided it with in recent time.

"Do it, Tate!" cried Pip.

Feeling his pulse rate increase as his panic took hold, he removed his fingers from his mouth and went back to the bars of his cell. "It's too late, Pip. It's already gone down."

Pip reached through the bars trying to take hold of him and he stepped closer, letting her run her fingers down his face as he tried to accept what was happening with some kind of grace.

"My brother," she said. "You were always the best brother. I'm so sorry that I didn't listen to you. You were right about Edison. He told me he poisoned your soup. He was a very evil man."

"Was?" asked Tate, wondering if he'd heard correctly.

"Edison's dead," said Pip. "And so is father. And I'm pretty sure that soon you will be, too."

"Pip. Slow down. You're making absolutely no sense. What's going on out there?"

He knew life had been going on while he was trapped down here, but this was out of control. What she was saying couldn't possibly be true. She must be confused.

He watched his sister take in a deep breath.

"Try to vomit again," she said. "Please. Father and Edison died so quickly and so horribly after eating their soup. I can't bear for that to happen to you."

"Hold on. Father is really dead?" He stepped away from the bars and sat down on a wooden bench as he tried to process this. His father had been indestructible. He couldn't possibly be dead.

"He's dead, Tate. I saw him with my own eyes. He ate the soup, choked and spluttered and dropped to the ground. Dead. Then Edison followed. The same thing, only before he died, he told me he'd poisoned your soup and had it sent down here."

"How soon after eating it did they die?" Tate shook his head, still unable to make sense of what was going on here.

"Straight away. That's why you have to hurry! You don't have much time!"

"But Pip, I ate the soup a while ago." Relief crashed through his body in a wave. "Wouldn't it have killed me already if it was the same thing?"

"Oh." Pip's hands slid down the bars she was clutching until she crumpled to the ground, her dress pooling around her like a dirty cloud.

"Why are you wearing that dress, Pip?" Tate tried to breathe the stress from his lungs. He was going to live. Probably.

"Father made me marry Edison today. That's what the soup was for. It was part of our wedding feast."

"And Edison poisoned Father's soup? Is that what you're saying?"

She nodded. "Yes. And he told me that he also poisoned yours. He thought that would make me Queen and as my husband, he'd be able to gain control of the kingdom."

A headache gripped Tate around the temples. This was all too much to take in. He'd gone from staring at the stone walls in total boredom to having all this information to process.

"So, who poisoned Edison's soup then?" he asked.

"I don't know!" she wailed. "Anybody could have. I wish I had the courage to do something like that. But it wasn't me."

"I'm glad it wasn't you," he said. It'd been hard enough watching her blame herself for their mother's death all these years. He didn't want her carrying any more guilt on her shoulders.

"It wasn't River, was it?" Pip asked. "She was there. She could somehow have switched your soup for Edison's."

"No!" He surprised himself with the force he used to push this word from his chest. "River's a gentle soul. She didn't like Edison, but she wouldn't kill him. It wasn't her. Someone else must have done it. Or he got confused and poisoned himself by mistake."

"Are you sad that Father's dead?" Pip asked.

"I'm not sure." This was the most honest answer he could give her right now. His father had never treated him with love, making it clear what a disappointment he was to him. Sometimes it was hard to believe they shared the same genes. They were so different. Edison would probably have made him a better son. They were a lot more alike, even in looks. How ironic that they'd died together.

"I've just realized something," said Pip, standing up. "If Father's dead, then that makes you King. You can get out of here! They can't hold the King prisoner."

Tate leaped to his feet, too. Pip was right. And as much as he didn't want to be King, he really did want to get out of this cell.

"Guard!" Pip called. "Release my brother immediately. He's our King."

Tate blinked in the dim light, wondering if perhaps he'd been too fast to dismiss the possibility that River had something to do with these deaths. The last thing she'd said to him was that she was going to find a way to get him out of here. She'd said she didn't care what it was that she had to do. But was murder included on that list?

What exactly had his beautiful wife done, and did he really know her at all?

RIVER

THE NOW

*R*iver stood perfectly still, watching the chaos around her.

The King was dead. Edison was dead. And that made Tate not only a free man, but it made him the King. And it also made her the Queen.

She pulled back her shoulders and tried to take that in.

Queen of The Bay of Laurel.

It really did feel strange.

The King had deserved his death and as she'd watched him choke down his last breath of air, she hadn't been able to find a single part of herself that was sorry.

Although, she didn't really understand what had happened. Because no matter how much she stood to gain from the King's death, she wasn't responsible for it. She wouldn't know how to poison some-one, even if she wanted to.

There were only two people who would know how to do that and one of them had died a horrible death only moments after the King, so it couldn't have been him. That left one.

Ariel.

It had to be Ariel. She knew what foods healed and she knew what foods harmed. And she'd been sitting right by Edison's side as he'd eaten his soup.

But Ariel had been devastated when Edison had fallen to the ground. Her grief was obvious to all. But was it really grief? Or was it something else? Was it guilt?

Why would Ariel murder her own son? She was the only person in the world who loved him, even if deep down she knew the color of his soul. Surely mothers didn't kill their children, not even mothers of children who grew up to be like Edison.

River's eyes went to Ariel now. She was standing beside her son's body. Her tears had stopped and she was staring at him in silence, perhaps contemplating where she'd gone wrong.

The thing that didn't make sense to River, was why Ariel would poison the King? What could she possibly have to gain from that?

But there'd be time for questions later. Right now she needed to get to Tate. Her husband. Her King.

She turned around to go to the palace, but before she could get far, someone grabbed her on the arm. She gasped to see it was Ariel.

"I have to go," said River, trying to pry her fingers from her arm.

"Are you going to see Tate?" Ariel's eyes were wild and her dark hair flew in all directions, reminding River of Tate when he'd come back from the cornfields.

River nodded. "I need to make sure he's okay."

"He's okay," said Ariel. "He's better than okay. He's going to be a wonderful King."

"Keep your voice down." River glanced around. Now wasn't a time for public celebration with their King's body still warm on the ground. It could be considered treason.

Ariel nodded, seeming to be gathering her senses.

"Did you kill the King?" asked River.

Ariel shook her head in such a way that River was certain she was telling the truth.

"Then who did?"

"You know who did," said Ariel, plainly.

"Edison?"

Ariel nodded. "I couldn't save him."

"Nobody could. Whatever that poison was, it was strong."

"I don't mean the King," said Ariel. "Although, I couldn't save him either, as I didn't realize he was being poisoned. I mean Edison. I couldn't save him from himself. I tried so hard to raise him to be a good person. But he was determined to rule the kingdom and he was in such a hurry to remove anyone in his path. That's why he poisoned the King's soup. And Tate's."

River's breath caught in her throat as she stepped away from Ariel. "I need to check on Tate."

"I told you he's okay," said Ariel. "I swapped the soup headed for his cell."

"You swapped it?"

Ariel nodded. "With Edison's bowl. I had a cook make a distraction and I made the switch. I figured that if whatever soup he made was good enough for Tate, then it was good enough for him to eat himself."

"Why are you telling me this?" asked River. Didn't murderers normally die with their secrets? Why would she confess so easily to having killed her son?

"Secrets can eat a person alive. I can't carry another one." Ariel was openly crying now with silent tears sliding down her face. "My entire life has been a lie."

"But why me?" she asked. Surely Ariel had other people she could confide in.

"Because your soul is light. I trust you. And you're carrying a very important child in your belly. I can feel the goodness of his young soul from here."

River blinked as her hands flew to her belly. Could this possibly be true? Was she really pregnant with Tate's child?

"The King had Edison fetch you a fertility elixir from Winter-green," said Ariel. "Only as soon as I smelled it, I knew the Alchemist had been playing games. Fertility elixirs should smell strongly of clary sage, but the one you were given smelled more like lavender. He gave Edison a calming elixir instead. I imagine he wasn't behaving too calmly when he asked for it. But it seemed it didn't matter. For you're carrying my grandchild regardless of the elixir you breathed in."

"Your grandchild?" asked River. "But Edison isn't the father."

"That's right," said Ariel. "Edison wasn't my son. Tate is."

ARIEL

THE BEFORE

*A*riel looked at baby Edison asleep in his basket and marveled at his perfection. His sweet little nose, the faint shadow of his budding eyebrows, his dark eyelashes… she absorbed every detail of him, letting the bliss of his arrival sink in.

He'd only been part of this world for a matter of hours and already she couldn't imagine her life without him. He was perfect and his soul was good. That part was a relief. She'd wondered what she was going to do if her own child had a dark soul. But even when he'd been in her belly, she'd known this wouldn't be possible. His goodness had seeped into her core and she'd loved being pregnant with him.

Her husband, Jacob, had gone to the palace to share the news. She'd practically had to push him out the door away from his son, to go. But rules were rules. Every baby born on royal land had to be recorded. Besides, the Queen would want to know when Ariel would be able to resume her duties as the herbalist. Jacob had been doing a good job in the past few days when Ariel had taken to her bed, but it wasn't the same. His heart wasn't in the tonics, it was with her. And now with Edison.

She looked to the window, wondering how long it would be before he returned. She'd enjoyed watching him cradle his newborn son in his strong arms.

Hearing the sound of a baby cry, Ariel blinked, and looked at Edison who remained fast asleep. Did babies cry in their sleep? She hoped he wasn't having some kind of newborn nightmare. Her breasts ached to feed him and the sound of his cry had only made this worse.

But when Jacob appeared at the door, she realized it wasn't Edison who'd made the sound. Jacob was standing there with another baby clutched in his arms and a Guardian standing beside him.

"Jacob?" His name became a question, as she searched his face for answers. What was going on? This baby was wrapped in a blue silk blanket, and even from her bed, she could see the anger in its scrunched up red face.

"This is the Queen's baby," said Jacob, bringing the child to her. "Birthed at almost the same time as Edison, only the Queen isn't well. She lost blood and is confined to her bed. She's... unconscious and unable to feed her son."

Ariel adjusted herself in her bed, fearing the words her husband would say next. There was only one reason he'd bring a baby to her in these circumstances.

"When the King heard of Edison's birth, he commanded you to come to the palace, although I explained that you were unable to leave your bed. So, he had me bring the Prince to you. He's hungry and his mother can't feed him."

"Nor can I," she said, raising her voice above the sound of the baby's cries.

"His name's Prince Tate." Jacob perched on the side of Ariel's bed and held him out to her. "He'll perish without milk and the King will hold you responsible. He said to tell you that Edison will suffer the same fate as the Prince. He has to live. Please, Ariel, you have to do this. We don't have a choice."

Ariel glanced at the Guardian, wishing to speak her mind freely. "Please, will you leave us?" she asked him. "This is a private matter."

"My instructions are to not let the Prince out of my sight," said the Guardian, shifting his feet.

"A woman needs her privacy." Ariel unbuttoned her nightdress and looked directly at the Guardian who flushed a color similar to the baby Prince's angry face.

Jacob handed her the hungry bundle and went to the Guardian. "She can't harm the Prince. That would be no different to her harming her own child. You heard what the King said. They suffer the same fate."

"I suppose so," the Guardian muttered, stepping out the door. "I'll be right out here though, so don't try anything or we'll all be dead."

With the Guardian gone, Ariel dropped her voice and locked eyes with her husband.

"I can't do this," she hissed. "It's not right."

"This is our future King," Jacob said. "The King's only child. And he's put his life—and our son's life—in your hands."

She could see the fear in Jacob's eyes. Surely the King wouldn't harm Edison. He was an innocent baby. But she also knew the King's heart was dark.

"Hand him to me," she said. "And comfort Edison. He's starting to wake with all this noise. We don't need two hungry babies. I'm not sure I have enough milk for that."

Jacob placed Prince Tate in her arms and Ariel studied him, noticing the opposite feeling rushing through her to the one she'd felt when she held her own child.

Edison drew her in. Prince Tate repelled her.

She knew this Prince was innocent, not having had enough time to commit an evil thought, let alone an evil deed. But she couldn't ignore the feeling that his soul was dark. Was that just because he was crying? Was it because it was the first child she'd held since falling in love with Edison? No, this child had a soul that was a darker version of the man who'd sired him. As evil as their current King was, this Prince surpassed him.

"What if I don't have enough milk left over for Edison?" she asked, desperate for an excuse not to feed the Prince.

"You will." Having lifted Edison from his basket, Jacob pressed his lips to their child's sweet forehead. "Please, Ariel, just do it."

"We could run away," said Ariel. "If we climb out the window and head west to Wintergreen, we could be safely across the border before anybody notices we're missing."

"Ariel." Jacob's voice was firm now. "We won't make it even a mile before we're noticed. There's no choice here. Besides, you can't just leave this baby to die."

Ariel cradled the Prince with one hand and finished unbuttoning her nightdress with the other. Could they leave him to die? She couldn't help but feel their kingdom would be far better off if they did exactly that.

Barely able to look at what she was doing, she pressed the Queen's child to her breast.

He slurped and gurgled, suckling from her and drawing out goodness that her body had made for her own son. A child whose heart was filled with light, not the blackness in this Prince's soul. But it was her son she was doing this for. She had to keep him safe. And if this was the only way she could do it, then so be it.

Edison was awake in his father's arms now and crying softly, wanting what she was giving to someone else.

This wasn't right. None of this was right.

Forcing her eyes to the child on her breast, she looked at the tiny silk gown he wore, another contrast to the rough woolen vest keeping Edison's chest warm. There was nothing about these two babies that was the same, apart from their age and size. Their lives were going to take two very different trajectories. One would be King and the other his servant. For that was what the herbalist was. A servant, if not in title, but in reality. Ariel worked for the King. What he was forcing her to do now was proof that he owned her body and he owned her soul. And one day this small child would own the souls of their entire kingdom, able to do with them as he pleased.

Ice gripped Ariel's spine. The reign of this child would spell the end of peaceful life in The Bay of Laurel. He'd be their downfall. The single worst thing to happen to this kingdom. And here she was keeping him alive with the milk her body had made for a child whose heart was pure. It wasn't right. Edison would make a wonderful King if their roles were reversed. How could the universe be so stupid and cruel?

But what could she do? Stop feeding this child and let him perish, sacrificing the life of her own child for the good of the kingdom? But the King would only go on to have more children, and their souls could be even darker than the child she currently held in her arms. That solved nothing. And besides, she could never sacrifice Edison's life. She'd sacrifice her own life before she did that. She'd give up everything.

The ice down her spine turned glacial as she realized that perhaps that was exactly what she needed to do.

Ariel needed to give up everything to save the kingdom. Including her child.

JACOB

THE BEFORE

*J*acob stirred the large pot and drew in the aroma. He'd gotten pretty good at making tonics, while Ariel had been busy with the two babies. It made a nice change from how he usually spent his days, braiding belts and ribbons from hemp for the Guardians, a skill he'd learned from his own father. It was a skill he hoped to pass to Edison one day, even if he was going to have to give most of his attention to learning to make tonics. Because one day Edison would be the herbalist for the kingdom. A huge honor that'd been passed down the generations. Jacob had known when he'd married Ariel that this would be the future for his children and he was fine with that. Making the tonics was vital for the survival of the kingdom. One look at the Guardians told him that. Nobody would invade them with an army so strong.

But still, the idea of passing on the skill of braiding warmed his heart. Edison might be Ariel's son, but he was his son, too.

He hadn't thought it possible to love another person as much as he loved Edison. He'd already braided him a cord identical to the one he wore himself for Edison to wear when he was older. A symbol to the world that they were bonded by blood. He'd also made him a set of woolen dolls for while he was still young. There was a King and a Queen, a Prince and a Princess and two Guardian dolls. They'd turned out beautifully and he looked forward to seeing Edison play with them one day.

As soon as Ariel had been well enough, she'd been taken to the palace to continue to care for the Prince while the Queen recovered. It'd been days now and he missed her terribly, but he'd finally received news that the Queen was waking and there was hope she'd be able to feed her own child. Soon, his wife and son would return home and they could be a family once more.

He added some rosemary to the tonic, thinking about how proud he was of Ariel for the part she'd played in keeping the Guardians strong. Her tonics were even more powerful than those her ancestors had made. Her abilities surpassed them because she didn't just follow her recipes when she made them, she followed her intuition. And nobody's intuition was sharper than his wife's.

Dipping a spoon into the tonic, he tasted it to make sure he had the balance of ingredients right. Satisfied he had the recipe perfected, he lifted the pot from the flames and set it aside to cool.

He'd done a good job. Ariel would be happy with him.

He looked up to see his wife standing in the doorway, a gurgling bundle of blankets in her arms. His beautiful son.

"You're back," he said, wiping his hands on a cloth and smiling.

She looked pale with dark circles under her eyes. Was she crying? Had she become attached to Prince Tate and leaving him was more difficult than she'd expected?

"Ariel, what's wrong?"

He went to her and took Edison from her arms so she could sit down.

"Please forgive me," she said, collapsing into a chair and burying her head in her hands.

"I don't understand." He shook his head just as Edison let out an almighty cry and he looked down to see what was troubling his son.

Only, it wasn't his son.

The baby he held in his arms, who was wearing a woolen vest and wrapped in a simple brown blanket, wasn't Edison. It was unmistakably the baby Prince.

"I don't understand," he said again, jiggling the Prince to quieten him down. "Where's Edison?"

Ariel lifted her tear-stained face from her hands and looked at him.

"You're holding Edison," she said. "This is your son."

He shook his head and looked down at the baby. "This isn't Edison."

"It is now." Her voice was a whisper. "And your son is a Prince. He'll make the best ruler the kingdom has ever seen."

"Ariel, what have you done?" He could feel the panic rising in his voice as well as his chest. This couldn't be happening.

"You can't tell anybody." She grabbed for him, but he stepped back. "I knew as soon as I saw the Prince that he had a dark soul. He was destined to destroy the kingdom and everyone in it. The more I cared for him, the more convinced I became of it. I couldn't let him be King. Too many lives depended on it."

"You swapped the Prince for our son?" Jacob kicked the table leg, wishing he had free hands to flip it over. "How could you do that? How?"

"Nobody knew those babies except me. Nobody took the time to look at them, not even the King himself. The Queen would have, but she was asleep. So, I swapped their clothes and laid them in each other's cribs and nobody noticed. When the Queen woke, I placed our child in her arms and she cried tears of love and joy. She'll take good care of him, I know she will. He'll have a much better life in the palace than we can give him here."

Jacob couldn't believe what he was hearing. This wasn't happening. This was a nightmare he was having while he was awake.

"You have to swap them back," he said, trying to hand her the baby, no longer interested in holding him.

"I can't." She took the baby and soothed him. "The Queen knows Edison now as her own. If she finds out what I've done, that she's fed a commoner from her breast, then all our lives will be at risk. It's too late. What's done is done."

"Ariel. You gave away our child!" Tears of his own pricked at his eyes now and he took a few steps back. "Our child!"

"I had no choice." She lifted her head in a determined way he hadn't seen before. "We'll raise this child as our son. If we give him enough love and attention, we can make him good. We can fill his heart with light. This is Edison now."

"And what of our son? Our real son? What will become of him?" Jacob combed his fingers through his dark hair.

"He's Prince Tate and one day he'll be King," said Ariel. "The best King, for he'll rule with kindness."

"I cannot raise another man's son, while I watch another man raise mine," he said, with yet more realization dawning on him.

Ariel had done a terrible thing. She'd made a horrible mistake that couldn't be undone and it had the very worst consequences. There was no way he was going to stick around to watch it. When he looked at that child in his wife's arms, he knew he couldn't raise him with love. He hated him.

He turned and left the kitchen. He left the tavern. And before long, he left the palace grounds.

Turning to look at the palace looming in the distance, he said a silent goodbye to his son. A boy who'd grow to know himself as Tate. A boy who'd one day be King.

A boy who'd never wear the necklace he made him or know how much his father loved him.

EDISON

THE BEFORE

*E*dison straightened his back, lifting his head, wishing he was taller. He was only a young boy, with plenty of years left to grow, but it wasn't happening fast enough for his liking. He regularly downed a cup of the Guardians' tonic when his mother wasn't looking, but it didn't seem to be helping. He needed the right genetics to go with it, and sadly he'd been born to a short and somewhat dim-witted woman and a father who took off the moment he was born, leaving him with nothing but a hemp necklace to remember him by. He hadn't gotten off to a good start.

He walked toward the palace, spotting Pip who was waiting under the plum tree for him, clutching that princess doll she seemed to like so much.

"You came!" she said, shuffling her feet and smiling at the ground.

"Of course I came." He tried not to roll his eyes. "I meet you here every day."

"It's still a surprise," said Pip, wringing her doll's hair in a way that didn't look good for it.

Edison reached into his pocket and removed the small glass jar of tonic he'd made when his mother had been out in the field picking rosemary to dry out for her supplies. At least she wasn't hovering over the parsley patch today. She must think he was stupid not to have realized she had something hidden in there. Little did she know the joke was on her.

"Make sure you give her the whole tonic," he told Pip. "And don't let her see."

"I know, Edison!" Pip giggled, as she tucked the bottle into her doll's skirt. "You've told me that a hundred times. But do you really think Mother's going to get better? She's gone back to her bed and her skin is looking a bit yellow. Are you sure it's still working?"

Edison smiled to cover his nerves. He hadn't thought Pip would notice when he switched over to the new tonic. "You're doing a great job. Trust me. She's getting better. Sometimes getting better can be tiring, that's all."

"And why can't I tell anybody?"

Now, this he had told her a hundred times. But he'd tell her once more as it was important she understood she needed to keep her big mouth closed. "Because it's going to be a surprise. Imagine how happy she'll be when she's all better and you tell her it was you who helped her."

Pip smiled and he tried not to notice that her teeth were crooked.

He felt a sharp tap on his shoulder and turned to see Tate run past him.

"Catch me if you can!" Tate called out, not pausing his steps, his long mess of dark hair trailing behind him as he ran.

"See you tomorrow," Edison said to Pip as he took off after Tate, doing his best to make chase, but knowing he'd never be able to catch up. Tate was faster than him.

Tate was also taller than him. And more handsome. And he definitely had more gold than he did. Tate was happier than him. And a nicer person. And he had a father. A father who was a King, no less.

And a sister who loved him. Even his mother was prettier than Edison's.

Just like Tate was beating Edison in this running race, he was also beating him in every competition life had to offer. Every. Single. One.

"You can't catch me!" Tate called back to him, fanning the fire of determination in the pit of Edison's stomach as he continued his chase.

Tate was right. He couldn't catch him. Not now. Not yet. But one day he would. He was going to take down everything that Tate had, piece by piece.

He watched as Tate threw himself on the ground. Lying on his stomach, he reached out and picked up a stick. Edison puffed as he caught up to him, already knowing what Tate was doing.

Sitting down, cross-legged in front of Tate, he waited for him to draw a large square in the dirt, then divide it into eight columns and eight rows. Then Tate sat up to reach in his pocket for two bags of counters, throwing one at Edison.

As Edison caught it, he noticed how filthy Tate's clothing was, with smears of dust on his white silk shirt and a tear in his mud-stained trousers. Those clothes were worth more than Edison's entire wardrobe, yet Tate didn't seem to care. If Edison had clothes like that, he'd take far better care of them.

They positioned their counters on the dirt in lines. In the back row was a King and a Queen with two warriors, two palace towers and two holy men. In front of them was a row of smaller pieces that Tate said were supposed to be called pawns, but they always called them Guardians.

Just like in real life, the job of these pieces was to protect the King. But it wasn't the King that Edison was fascinated with. It was the Queen. She was the most powerful piece in the game, able to move in any direction. Without the Queen, you had no hope of winning and she could be taken easily if Edison didn't concentrate, so he kept his eye on her at all times. He didn't worry so much about the King, as at least with that piece Tate would have to warn him when he was in danger and he could move him out of the way.

"You want to start?" asked Tate, being annoyingly polite.

"No, you go," said Edison. There were advantages in letting your enemy make the first move. It gave him time to think about how he'd react.

Besides, who went first wouldn't make much difference. Tate would win today as he usually did. Edison had only managed to beat him three times and in every one of those times it was when he'd been able to take Tate's Queen. It was only a matter of time after the Queen was gone, that the King would fall.

It was from playing this game, that Edison had first come up with his idea as to how he could beat Tate in real life. He was going to take Tate's Queen. And once she was gone, all the other pieces would be left vulnerable, ready for Edison to win.

Tate's hand hovered over the Guardians as he decided which one to use first. He always took forever to make his move, but Edison was patient.

The game he was playing in real life was a long one. Far longer than this game he played in the dirt. But this one was a game he had every intention of winning.

All he needed to make was a series of clever moves, taking one of Tate's pieces at a time and ultimately he'd sweep the board.

One day he was going to wear that crown. One day he was going to be King.

Tate moved one of his Guardians forward and Edison responded quickly.

"I'm watching you," said Tate, laughing.

Edison laughed in response at his foolish friend who wasn't watching him nearly close enough.

TATE

THE BEFORE

ate heard Pip scream and his feet started to run to her before he'd even had time to think about it. His sister needed him.

Pip's screams were soon replaced by loud sobs and he followed the noise to their mother's bedchamber. Pip had been spending a lot of time in there lately, sitting at the end of her bed watching her sleep. It wasn't healthy. If only Edison had a younger sister for her to play with. But that was a bit hard given he no longer had a father.

Tate threw open the door to find Pip sitting beside their mother on her bed, shaking her by the shoulders.

"Wake up, Mother," Pip cried. "Wake up!"

Tate paused as he took in what he was seeing. Was she... dead? No, she was just asleep. Like always. Pip was young. She couldn't be expected to know the difference between a deep sleep and the deepest sleep of all. Although, now that he thought about it, he was still a boy himself. Did he know the difference?

"Move out of the way," he said to Pip, scooping her up from the bed and placing her bare feet on the floor.

Taking her place on the bed, he sat down and studied his mother. She was very still. And pale. She had an odd smell about her, too. Normally she smelled like flowers. But not now. She was still beautiful, though, with her smooth blonde hair combed around her shoulders and her blue eyes closed to the world. Her white nightgown was buttoned right up to her chin and Tate listened hard, trying to detect some breathing. When he couldn't, he reached up a quivering hand to touch his mother's face.

When skin touched skin, he withdrew his hand as quickly as if he'd put it in the fire. Except his mother's face hadn't burned him. It'd been the opposite, for her face had turned to ice.

"Is she dead?" Pip asked.

"I... I don't know." Tate stood up and placed an arm around his sister, noticing her soft warmth in a way he hadn't before.

They stood, side by side, and watched their mother, half expecting her to sit up and call to them so she could wrap them in her arms.

"I think she's dead," said Pip, breaking the silence.

"I think so, too." His words felt like a betrayal, but it was true. She couldn't possibly be alive.

They continued to watch her, trying to draw comfort from each other when the only person who could offer such a thing was lying there in front of them like a block of ice.

"I killed her," said Pip.

"You didn't." Tate squeezed her shoulder. "She's been dead for a while, I think."

"I've been switching her tonics," said Pip, her voice little more than a whisper.

Tate let his arm fall as he crouched down in front of Pip.

"Quiet," he said. "Don't say another word. Not here. Not now."

His caution came just in time as their father swept into the room.

"What's all the howling about?" he asked, searching the wrong faces for an answer.

Tate pointed to the bed. "Mother's dead."

His father jolted at these words and rushed to his Queen, repeating much the same process Tate had used as he checked for a sign of life.

"Who found her?" A purple rash spread up his neck and his eyes darted around the room.

Pip shrank into Tate's side and whimpered.

"We both did," said Tate, determined to protect his sister. "Just now."

"I'll kill whoever did this!" their father boomed with such anger that Tate wondered if perhaps some love had existed between his parents.

Four Guardians appeared at the door, rushing to the King's side when they saw what was happening.

Tate took this opportunity to drag his sobbing sister from the room. She didn't need to see their father's anger. More importantly, she didn't need to hear it. She couldn't possibly have been switching their mother's tonics. Where would she even get a tonic to switch it with?

Then he remembered Edison's sudden interest in his sister. An interest he'd put down to an awakening of feelings as they were getting older. He knew that he himself had begun to look at girls differently and just assumed Edison was the same. But what if his interest in Pip had been something different? Something that had more to do with his mother and less to do with his sister. But why would he want to hurt her, let alone kill her?

"Where are we going?" Pip squirmed under the grasp he had on her.

He loosened his grip and led her from the palace out into the strawberry patch, and down the path that led to the Guardians' village.

"We're going to talk to Edison," he said.

"It wasn't him!" said Pip. "I made the tonics myself."

"I'm going to help you." He stopped to look at her so she understood. "But not if you lie to me. Tell me now. Has Edison been giving you tonics to give to Mother?"

Pip nodded, as a flood of tears burst from her eyes. "He told me not to tell anybody!"

"I bet he did." Tate took Pip's hand and walked as quickly as he could to find Edison. He had no idea what his friend had been up to, but he was certain it hadn't been anything good. If their father found out, he'd kill Edison. He might even kill Pip. Then who would Tate have left?

Now that his mother had gone, Pip was all he had left in the world.

PIP

THE BEFORE

*P*ip allowed Tate to drag her toward Edison's house. It wasn't fair! He was behaving all angry with her and all she'd done is what she'd been told. Edison had said the tonics would help her mother. He never said anything about them making her go dead. And she didn't want her mother to go dead! She wanted her to play with her and tell her stories about princesses called Snow.

She was trying not to cry but it was hard not to. Her tears were coming out all by themselves.

"Hush," said Tate. "People are looking at us."

"People always look at us." If Pip hadn't been walking so fast, she'd have stamped her foot. Stamping her feet always made her feel better.

It was true, though. People did look at them all the time. That was why she'd been so proud of herself for sneaking the tonics into her mother each day. It wasn't easy to do something like that when you were being stared at.

"There he is." Tate pointed at the field beyond the village where the Guardians were training.

Pip kept her eyes on the ground. She didn't want to see Edison. Not now and not ever. He'd tricked her! He'd made her kill her mother. He should be the one in trouble, not her. Although, the way Tate was looking at him, maybe he was.

Tate led her across the field, not listening to Pip's complaints, until they were right in front of the person she didn't want to see.

"We need to talk," said Tate.

Pip dared to look up at Edison, only to look back down when she saw him scowling at her.

They walked into the trees and Pip held back as Tate jabbed his finger into Edison's chest in a way that looked like it would hurt.

"What tonics have you been giving Pip for our mother?" he asked.

Edison held up the palms of his hands and took a step back. "Just something to make her strong. They've been working, too. Pip said she's been better than ever."

"She was." Pip crossed her arms and gave her foot a stamp. "But then she got worse than ever."

"I was only trying to help," said Edison. "I swear it. Why else would she have felt better to begin with? She must have something else wrong with her. You know, on the inside. I can fix it! I'll make her something new."

"She's dead, Edison," said Tate. "Dead. And Pip here seems to think she killed her. Only, she didn't. It was you! You killed our mother."

"Dead?" The color drained from Edison's face and just for the tiniest second Pip thought she saw him smile before he rearranged his face to look almost as sad as Pip felt.

"Dead," said Tate, locking eyes on him. "And my father wants to kill whoever's responsible."

"But I didn't!" Edison looked panicked now. "I didn't do it. Tate, please, you're the only friend I've ever had. Don't tell your father about this. It wasn't me! I swear it."

Tate stepped away from Edison and let out a big sigh.

Pip watched with wide eyes, waiting to see what her brother

decided. Had Edison meant to make their mother go dead? Or had he really been trying to help?

"Come on, Pip." Tate took her by the hand and led her back out onto the field.

They retraced their steps of earlier and Pip wondered what the point of that conversation had been. Tate was making even less sense than a grown-up.

When they reached the strawberry patch, Tate stopped and bent over to make them the same height.

"Are you going to tell Father?" she asked.

He shook his head. "I'm not going to tell anybody. And neither are you."

"Why? Is Father going to kill me?" She'd never really felt like her father loved her, but surely he wouldn't kill her dead.

"I don't know." Tate's dark eyes were serious and she threw her arms around him, wanting to go back to yesterday.

"Did Edison mean for me to kill Mother?" she asked.

"I don't know that either," he said. "I don't think so. I can't see why he would. It must have been an accident."

She bit down on her lip, wanting to ask one last question. "Did I kill Mother?"

"We need to go back inside," he said. "Father will be looking for us."

Pip followed her brother inside and went to her bedchamber and threw herself on her bed. Tate hadn't answered her question. Which meant he was protecting her.

She'd killed her mother. She was an awful person. She didn't deserve to be happy ever again in her whole life. She didn't deserve to live.

RIVER

THE NOW

"Tate is your son?" asked River. "I'm sorry, Ariel, but I don't understand. Edison was your son, not Tate."

Ariel shook her head. "Technically, you're right. In that Tate's real name is Edison, which makes Edison my son. But that man lying dead in the dirt right there... that's Tate. The real Tate. The true Prince of The Bay of Laurel. My son, Edison, is your husband."

"You're not making sense." River took Ariel by the arm and walked a few further paces away from the commotion. Ariel either wasn't thinking straight or she was confessing things that nobody must overhear. She wasn't even sure Ariel should be trusting her with such secrets. If they were true, of course. This seemed like something she was better off keeping to herself.

Ariel's hands raked at her hair as her chin visibly trembled. "I swapped them when they were babies."

"You what?" River took a step back, her hands cupping her mouth almost as if she'd been the one to do something so unthinkable.

"I knew Tate would make a terrible King," said Ariel, speaking quickly as if the words themselves were desperate to be released. "The real Tate, that is. The man you know as Edison. I also knew my son would make a wonderful King. It almost killed me, it certainly killed my marriage, but it had to be done. It was the only way to save our kingdom from disaster."

River pushed down the rush of cold that raced down her spine, wishing she had a chair to sit on. What Ariel was saying had to be true. Nobody would make up something as outrageous as this!

"You know I'm right," said Ariel, clutching at her arm. "Can you imagine what would've happened to the kingdom with the man you know as Edison on the throne."

River had to admit Ariel was right about this. Edison would be a terrible King. Dangerous. Whereas Tate would rule with compassion and thoughtfulness.

"How can any of this be true?" asked River, shaking free of Ariel's grasp. Princes weren't left in their cribs, able to be swapped by passing herbalists without anybody noticing.

"Just look at what's right in front of you and you'll see that it's true," said Ariel, avoiding her question. "Look at the color of my hair, the darkness of my eyes and you'll see your husband reflected back. Sometimes I worry we look too much alike."

"The King had blue eyes," said River, her own eyes widening at the memory as her legs began to tremble. "And so did the Queen. And Pip."

It had never occurred to her if it was possible for Tate to be born with brown eyes, as the product of two blue-eyed parents, but she knew that all the Guardians had blue eyes and none of them had ever produced a brown eyed child. And it was true about Ariel's eyes. She saw Tate in the shape of them. In the kindness that seeped from them. Was Ariel really Tate's mother? This would mean her husband wasn't a Prince at all. Nor was he the King.

"If you're speaking the truth, then Pip is the true ruler now." River leaned against a tree for support and swallowed hard. Everything she thought she knew was a lie! She wasn't a Princess. She was the wife of the herbalist's son.

Ariel went to grab her arm once more but stopped herself when River held up her hands. She needed space to try to process this shocking news.

"Nobody can tell Pip," said Ariel. "She's fair of heart, but she'd make a weak Queen."

This was true. As much as Pip had proven she had courage deep inside her, she wouldn't make a very good Queen. She had no idea about how the kingdom worked having missed the past ten years of her life. She couldn't possibly understand the needs of her people when she barely understood who she was herself.

"It has to be Tate," said Ariel, the wild expression on her face making her look more like a mad woman than the calm herbalist River had known all her life. "Followed by the child you carry now. It's the way it's meant to be. If you tell Pip, then your child will never be King. And as great a King as Tate will make, your child will be even more powerful."

"Then why did you tell me?" asked River, shaking her head. "Why risk undoing everything you've sacrificed?"

"Because you're a good person," said Ariel, with deep furrows forming on her brow. "And I can no longer carry this alone. I made a decision all those years ago that changed the direction of the kingdom and it's been a huge burden to carry."

This explanation still made no sense. Deciding that she trusted River wasn't a strong enough reason for her to want to tell her such a dangerous secret. There was something else going on that River couldn't quite put her finger on just yet.

"I'm trusting you now to make a decision to take us forward once more," said Ariel.

"And what decision is that?" It seemed to River that all the decisions had already been made. They were simply dealing with the consequences now.

"It's up to you if you think Tate should know. He'll want to be an honest King." River saw a flash of Tate in Ariel's anguished face. Now that she knew their connection, it was impossible to miss. How had she not seen this before? How had anyone not seen what was right in front of them? Ariel had been right to fear that they looked far too alike. But who would possibly believe this incredible story? If River hadn't witnessed the pain in Ariel's face, she doubted she'd have believed it herself.

"You could always tell Tate yourself," said River.

"I can't be the one to tell him," said Ariel, a flood of tears breaking free and running down her face. "It's been torture to watch him grow into such a wonderful man and not have been the one to raise him. I understand now why my husband couldn't stay around. Perhaps I should've left with him. But someone had to stay and watch over our son. He would've died today without me here to protect him."

This was true. If she hadn't swapped the soups, Tate would certainly be dead.

"Thank you for saving Tate's life," said River, standing up from the tree and doing her best to gather her wits. "And for giving him life. But I'm not sure this is a secret he should know. I wish I didn't even know, nor do I understand why you told me."

"I had to tell you," said Ariel.

"No, you didn't." River brushed down her dress and straightened her back. This wasn't going to be an easy secret to carry. Perhaps this was the real reason for Ariel unburdening herself just now. She'd held this secret for almost two decades and could hold it no longer.

Ariel's shoulders slumped, seeming to lose control just as River had managed to gain some. This was clearly not the decision she wanted River to make. She wanted Tate to know.

"If Tate knows, he'll step down," said River. "I know he will. You said yourself that he wants to be an honest King and there's nothing honest about any of this."

"You think it's right to keep it from him?" Ariel crossed her arms and shook her head.

"And you think what you did is right?" This time it was River to take Ariel by the arms. "None of this is right. Anyway, I thought you said it was my decision?"

"It is," said Ariel, locking eyes with her. "But are you certain?"

"Of course not! How could I possibly be certain about such a thing? Look, even if I'm not sure why you've told me this, I understand why you did what you did. Or at least I think I do. But Tate can't know. It's too much. He has enough to get used to right now. We can't risk him stepping down and handing the throne to Pip."

"That's right." Ariel nodded. "Pip would be a better ruler than Edison, but..."

"So, you didn't really kill your own son when you swapped the soup," said River, another piece of the puzzle falling into place.

"I was protecting my son, not killing him," said Ariel. "If Edison tried to kill him once and failed, then of course, he'd try again. And next time I might not have been there to protect him. That was a risk I couldn't take."

"But you seemed so upset," said River, confusion still clouding her mind no matter how much she tried to clear it. "I saw you cradling his head in your hands."

"I was upset," said Ariel. "I still am. I raised that man, fed him, clothed him and taught him everything I know. I tried to turn him into a good man, a kind one, but I failed. Badly. It was never more obvious than today and that's broken my heart. I feel like a terrible person."

"Ariel, you're not a terrible person. You did an extraordinary and selfless thing and I can see what pain it's caused you. I, for one, am grateful for the sacrifice you made. I can't bear to think what Edison would've done to our kingdom. Just look at what he did to the Guardians the moment power came his way. Tate would never do that."

Ariel nodded and River saw something else in her face and finally it all made sense.

"I know why you told me," said River. "Oh, Ariel."

She stepped forward and wrapped an arm around this broken woman's shoulders. The broken woman who had the unmistakable look of yearning buried deep into every feature of her face. "You want him to know what you did so you can be free to love him as his mother once more."

Ariel sniffed and placed her own arm around River's waist. "I'd rather die today than live another without Tate knowing I'm his mother."

"But you're going to have to," said River, letting go, so she could look directly at her. "One day, we'll tell him. I promise you. But not yet. It's not the right time."

"When?" asked Ariel, her heart breaking before River's eyes.

"You said you trusted me," River reminded her. "When Tate becomes a father himself, he'll understand so much more than he does now. Do you think you can wait? If you're right about the child in my belly, then it won't be too much longer. You've already waited so long."

Ariel nodded and straightened out her clothes, looking more like the sensible herbalist River knew.

"Things will get better now," said Ariel. "You'll see. Edison was messing with my tonics to weaken the Guardians. He was adding valerian root to some of the Guardians' tonics to make them sick. He thought if he could make me look incompetent, he could take over from me and make the Guardians well to prove his worth to the King. But all he had to do was stop poisoning them in the first place."

River felt the well of anger she had stored in her gut at the death of her sister explode and she kicked at the dirt, ruining her pale blue slipper.

"It was more than that," said River, shaking her head. "He was targeting specific Guardians. Ones who he thought wronged him. It wasn't just to make you look bad. He was getting revenge."

Ariel wailed. "I feel so responsible!"

"How can you be responsible for any of this?" River clenched her fists, wishing there was an iron ball she could throw into the orchard right now to expel some of this anger. She'd never properly grieved Daphne. Her beautiful sister whose life Edison thought he had a right to take.

"I'm so sorry about your sister," said Ariel. "This is all my fault."

River pushed back her tears, deciding her grieving was going to need to wait just a little bit longer. "It's not your fault. What you did saved the kingdom from Edison. If he'd ever found his way to the throne, he'd have killed us all."

"I messed with his life," said Ariel. "I took him from the life he was born to live and forced him into another. I thought he'd never know. But he did, River. He did know! Maybe he didn't know exactly what happened, but he felt the royal blood flowing through his veins. He wanted Tate's life, not just because he was jealous, but because somehow he knew that was supposed to be his life. And so he looked for ways to get back there."

"By marrying his sister," said River, another horrifying thought occurring to her. "Not that he knew that, of course."

Ariel nodded. "Just another reason things have worked out for the best."

"And the Queen?" asked River, pushing down the sick feeling in her stomach. "Was that Edison, too?"

The sadness in Ariel's eyes answered for her. "What he didn't know, was that when he killed the Queen, he actually killed his own mother."

River let out a long sigh, wishing she could push the stress from her body with it. If Ariel had made the right decision, then why did it feel so very wrong?

There was a shout and a cheer, and River looked toward the palace to see Tate and Pip walking toward them.

Tate was blinking in the sunlight, his clothes clean but his face drawn. He must've freshened himself up before he faced his people. Pip held her head high, her admiration for the man she thought was her brother clear for all to see.

"All hail, King Tate!" cried a man in the crowd.

"King Tate! King Tate!" A chant began as the wedding guests dropped to a bow, their respect for their new leader written on their faces.

River looked at Ariel and saw such unmistakable pride on her face.

Everything she'd sacrificed had been for this moment. And the reaction of the crowd was evidence that she'd done the right thing. Many of the Guardians had come up from their village to see what the commotion had been about and they stood with tears in their eyes to see that there was now a brighter hope for their future.

Tate stood beside River and placed an arm around her shoulders, holding up a hand to hush the crowd.

"You're free," River said to him.

"We all are," said Tate. "Including your family."

Then turning to the crowd, he cleared his throat and projected his voice. "Please don't cheer for me while my father's body lies still warm on the ground."

A humbled murmur rippled through the crowd.

"Times have been difficult recently," he said.

River noticed some of the wedding guests looking confused. But the Guardians didn't. They knew exactly what their King spoke of. Their lives had been torn apart by Edison.

"It will take me some time to speak to you all and understand the best way forward," said Tate. "But to begin with, I'd like to announce two changes immediately."

River looked across at him, wondering what this could be.

"I may be your new King, but I'm supported by two very strong and equally as capable women. My sister and my wife. I've spoken with my sister just now to ask her if she'll take the place of Edison as our future herbalist and she's gladly agreed. But the tonics she makes won't just be for the Guardians. We'd like to open our tavern to all the people of the kingdom. Every one of us has the right to be healthy and strong."

Pip was nodding and smiling broadly. Ariel was smiling, too. Her life was about to have a whole lot more meaning to it than it already did.

"And my wife," said Tate. "I haven't had a chance to speak to her privately about this yet, but I'm certain that she'll agree to what I'm about to propose."

River tilted her head, hoping he was right. Because whatever it was that he was about to suggest, she was going to need to agree to. He wasn't just her husband now. He was her King. But she trusted him.

"River, I'd like to appoint you as Master of the Guardians. Someone who can lead them back to health and greatness. Most importantly, someone who can lead them back to happiness. Do you accept?"

River's heart swelled as she nodded. "I accept. Although, I'd like to change the title if I may. I'll be Protector of the Guardians instead. Nobody will harm them under my watch."

The Guardians let out a cheer and River looked across at Ariel, who had tears pouring down her cheeks now, her hands held to her heart. The woman who'd spent her life feeding the Guardians with strength and courage was perhaps the strongest and most courageous woman of all. One day she'd hold her son again in her arms. And when she did, he was going to know exactly who she was.

TATE

THE EVERNOW

*I*t was tradition in The Bay of Laurel that when a new King or Queen was crowned, they'd ride in an open carriage through the streets of the main village. People would come from all over the kingdom to line the streets and cheer on their new monarch.

This tradition was what brought Tate to this exact moment, as he sat in a carriage with River beside him, wearing their crowns of gold as two white horses pulled them slowly through the streets. He could walk faster than they were traveling right now, but that was okay with him. It gave him time to connect with individual faces rather than be overwhelmed by the sea of color.

Although he was smiling, Tate wasn't too sure how he felt about this tradition. It seemed pompous and superior. He wanted to be the kind of King who walked with his people, not the sort who waved at them from a carriage.

"I've got an idea." He turned to River and she raised her eyebrows at him.

He removed his heavy crown and handed it to her. "Will you look after this for me?"

"Why?" She seemed more confused than ever as she put it on her lap, close to the baby that was growing rapidly in her belly. One day that baby would wear the crown for himself... or herself. A baby who'd be half Guardian and half royal. But more to the point, a baby who'd be half River and half of him. He loved that idea because more than anything, he loved his wife.

Without further explanation, he leaped from the carriage and landed on the dirt road. Several Guardians came running forward to protect him, but he waved them away.

"Tate!" River called after him. "This isn't a good idea."

"It's okay," he called back, smiling at her.

"No, really, Tate. I don't think you should do this."

He blew her a kiss and let the carriage move forward, walking a few paces behind it, stopping every now and then to shake hands with someone or pat a small child on the head.

This was the kind of King he wanted to be. It was time the people saw that things were going to be different from now on. He wasn't going to be like any King they'd experienced before.

A woman approached him and handed him a soft but tiny woolen hat.

"For your baby," she said, proudly. "I knitted it myself."

The last thing Tate wanted to do was take from these people who had far less than he had, but it would be an insult to this woman to refuse. So, he smiled and touched her gently on her shoulder.

"Thank you," he said, tucking the hat into his pocket. "You're very kind. This will keep the baby nice and warm."

Before the woman could respond, she was pushed out of the way by a younger woman, desperate to get his attention.

"King Tate!" she called over the growing roar of the crowd. "Marry me!"

He furrowed his brow as the crowd roared laughing. He was already married. The people knew that. Did they not recognize the marriage because their nuptials had been kept private?

Another man pushed in front of the woman.

"Ouch!" she complained.

"What are you going to do about the locust on our crops?" the man asked, his face more of a sneer than a smile. "It's come back this season."

The woman pushed back, trying to get in front again, but was shoved aside as a woman with a gaunt face tried to get Tate's attention. "My daughter has gone missing!" she cried.

"And my son!" cried another woman, from behind her.

Then it was all on.

People were tussling and scuffling, grabbing Tate by the arms and trying to get in front of him to have their say.

He couldn't hear what any of them were asking of him, so desperate were their shouts and cries.

The people at the back of the crowd pushed forward and Tate felt his heart rate pick up. He was in genuine danger now of being crushed, as were the people at the front of the crowd.

He looked up at the Guardians who were also pushing through the crowd toward him. River was standing up in the carriage now as it rocked with people jostling it from the sides.

He should have listened to her. He'd been foolish to break tradition and leap to the ground. If anything happened to River or their baby, he'd never forgive himself. This was a lesson to him. Some traditions existed for a reason. He could still be a different kind of King, but he needed to tread carefully, learn from others, and not make such rash errors.

The Guardians reached him and pushed the crowd back with the threat of their swords.

Slowly, so slowly, the crowd moved back, and the frenzy was stilled.

The Guardians led Tate back to the carriage. But as he walked, a man in the crowd caught Tate's eye. A man with wild, dark hair and an unkempt beard. Tate noticed tears staining the man's eyes and he mouthed words to Tate that he couldn't hear.

As the Guardians led him further away, something around the

man's neck caught Tate's attention. Edison's necklace. There was no doubt about it. The same colors, the same distinctive pattern to the weave. How odd? Could this man be Edison's father who ran away the moment he was born? He didn't look anything like Edison.

Tate held his gaze all the way back to the carriage before the crowd pushed the man back and he could no longer be seen.

"You look like you just saw a ghost," River said, clutching at his hand.

"I think I did." He shook away his thoughts deciding to talk to River about it later when there wasn't a crowd of people watching him.

River handed him his crown and he placed it back on his head and concentrated on the woman before him. The woman he loved with all his heart who he saw as his wife, yet it didn't seem to be a union accepted by his people.

"Will you marry me?" he asked, sliding into his seat and draping an arm around River and squeezing her tightly.

"We're already married," laughed River as the carriage took off once more. "Did you bump your head out there?"

"You deserve a real wedding," he said. "After our baby is born. I want the palace filled with people. I want everyone to see what a beautiful bride I have. When my father married us, it was a marriage of two strangers. I want a wedding between two people in love. Will you marry me properly this time, River?"

"No, Tate." River smiled widely at him, her expression not matching her words. "I won't marry you again because I don't need to tell you that I love you in front of the world, for our love to be real. When your father married us, we were bound legally to each other. But when you kissed me for the first time in the garden, we were bound by our hearts. Our love is a private one. I don't need to share it with the world, just as long as we can share it with each other."

Her words joy filled him with a kind of joy he'd never felt before. This must be the Evernow his mother had told him about. Because it didn't matter what challenges were in his future or what hardships he'd suffered in his past. Right here, right now, he was the happiest he'd ever been.

"Why are you always right?" he asked. He knew River was his wife and she knew he was her husband. It didn't matter what anyone else thought. They'd come to accept their union in time. Especially once their baby was born.

"I'm not always right," said River, her face turning dark. Just another thing he'd need to talk to her about later. Was she hiding something from him?

The carriage hit a bump in the road and he pulled River closer to him, placing a kiss on her cheek, a gesture that sent a roar of approval rising from the crowd.

Looking back at the people, he searched for the face of the man with the beard once more.

But he was gone, leaving Tate wondering who he was and if he'd ever see him again.

RIVER

THE EVERNOW

*R*iver held Tate's hand as she walked across the hot desert sand. She was glad they'd made the decision to leave little Jacob at home. The desert was no place for an infant.

It'd been River's idea to call their son Jacob, telling Tate it was a name she'd liked since she was a girl. Tate had readily agreed, unaware this was the name of his father. His true father. A man who'd loved him so much he'd chosen to run away rather than sit by and watch another man raise him. It was only right that this baby had the name of the grandfather he'd likely never meet.

Jacob was a beautiful baby, with Tate's dark soulful eyes and River's fair hair. It pained River to have left him in the care of her parents, even though he was no doubt being doted on. Ariel would be checking on him regularly too, although nobody really understood why she was so enamored with the baby Prince. They just thought she was lonely after the death of her son.

Not forgetting Aunt Pip who shared most of her days between

spending time with Ariel in the kitchen and fussing over her beloved nephew. Pip may not have the blood of a herbalist, but she had the passion and it seemed that was enough, for she was learning fast. She was a wonderful aunt as well and had even given Jacob her set of woolen dolls, saying she no longer needed them now that she had her herbs. And despite Jacob being so young, Pip often read to him from a storybook she had about a Princess called Snow. The book had been lost for many years but had turned up in the bottom of Pip's wardrobe even though she said she'd searched there a thousand times before.

As much as River hated leaving Jacob behind, it was important she go with Tate to the desert. The daughter of the Emperor of The Sands of Naar was marrying the son of a man they called the Colonel, and the royal families of the other four kingdoms had been invited to witness the union between these future leaders. The Bay of Laurel's presence here today showed they stood in peace and unity for the first time in history.

In years gone by, Tate's father had received other royal wedding invitations and had torn them into pieces. But not Tate. He was keen to join the alliance The Sands of Naar had formed with Forte Cadence and Wintergreen. River agreed. They'd be unstoppable if they worked together.

The only kingdom not here was Feldspar, a strange island where the people kept themselves in isolation. Nobody knew a lot about them or what kind of life they had behind the thick band of dead trees that lined their western shore. All they knew was that it had something to do with mining minerals. Apparently, they hadn't even bothered to reply to their wedding invitation. Perhaps they didn't even know what a wedding was.

As River and Tate approached the top of the sand dune, they saw a large crowd of people gathered. The desert seemed a strange place to get married, but the choice spoke to River about the kind of people the future Empress and Colonel were. People who embraced the harsh environment of their kingdom, rather than cursed it. Apparently, it was out here that the bride and groom had first met and fallen in love. River sensed there was a lot more to the story, but nobody seemed to want to talk about it, which of course only made River all the more keen to find out.

A gust of hot wind sent sand flying into River's eyes and she adjusted the veil she wore so that it covered more of her face. All the women out here wore veils, and she could see why. The men wore scarves for the same purpose and she looked across at Tate now in his loose fitting shirt and trousers, his scarf draped over his head covering his neatly tied hair. His face was freshly shaven and he looked every bit the King he now was.

"What's the matter?" he asked, aware of her gaze.

"Just admiring my King." She squeezed his hand a little tighter.

"I'd admire you right back, if only I could see you."

She lifted her veil to give him a grin, but there was no way she was going to leave her skin exposed out here, and she quickly covered her face once more.

How must it be for the people in this kingdom to grow up in such an unforgiving climate? Not that the whole kingdom was like this. The people spent most of their lives underground in a place called the Colony. This was where River and Tate had been taken on their arrival and two healers named Freya and Azrael had put their hands on them to restore their energy after the long journey. It had felt like a miracle. There was so much they could learn from this kingdom.

After their healing, an endearing but odd man had led them through a tunnel to the kingdom's Capital. The palace was in the Capital, which was where all the visiting royalty were staying. As they'd walked, the man had proudly explained that it had been his idea to connect this kingdom's two cities like this. River had given Tate secret smiles as they'd watched the man flap his arms as if he'd prefer to be flying than using his feet.

And as impressive as the Colony had been, when they emerged in the Capital, it'd taken River's breath away. Tall buildings ringed a circle of perfectly manicured lawn, with two giant glass orbs sitting in the middle that kept time as red sand slipped from one to the other. It was incredible to think that something like this was right here in the middle of the desert.

"At last," said Tate, as they joined the people on the top of the dune and River lowered her veil so she could nod and smile politely at the other guests who were mingling on the outskirts. A windbreak had been erected and a giant sail hung above the guests to shelter them from the direct heat of the sun. A series of tiny glass orbs dangled from the edges of the sail catching the light and splintering the rays into thousands of tiny rainbows that reflected across the sweeping dunes. It was no wonder the wedding was taking place out here. It was like all the angels in heaven were with them as honored guests.

"It's so beautiful," said River, accepting a cool glass of water from a man holding a tray.

"I've never seen anything like it." Tate let his scarf fall to his shoulders, as several strands of his impossible-to-tame hair flew free.

"It must be inspired by their Shining," said River. They'd been told that once a year the sun would reflect through the giant orbs in the city circle at exactly the right angle to produce a miraculous show of lights. Watching it was supposed to be like witnessing a miracle. It was hard to imagine it could be any more spectacular than what they were seeing now.

"Thanks for coming with me," said Tate. "I know it wasn't easy for you to leave Jacob for so long, but this wouldn't have been the same without you."

"He's in good hands," she said. "It was important for us to both be here."

At first, when Tate had been crowned, River hadn't felt the acceptance from her people as Queen. But the more they were seen as a united front, the more people had stopped questioning her role and instead embraced her. The birth of Jacob had, of course, sealed that.

They made their way through the crowd and stood beside Queen Rose and Prince Jeremiah of Forte Cadence. They'd brought their daughter, Lily, with them, a spirited young girl with a shock of orange hair, who liked to ride on her father's back and pretend he was a dragon.

King Ari and Queen Jasmine of Wintergreen approached and

River gasped to see the way the rainbow light made patterns on Queen Jasmine's lavender dress.

"You look wonderful," said River.

"As do you," said Jasmine, kissing her cheek. The two of them had spent many hours talking since their arrival and River hoped to spend a lot more time with her in the future. Queen Rose had been harder to sit down and talk to, as she was always so busy chasing after Lily, who didn't seem to be able to keep still for more than a moment at a time. Even now she was winding her way through the guests touching all the long dresses and kicking at the sand.

"That girl of mine is a handful," laughed Rose. "Worse than my three younger sisters put together."

"She looks more like a Marigold than a Lily, with all that beautiful red hair," said Jasmine, touching her own dark locks.

"She's named after my sister," said Rose. "Although, somehow she looks and behaves exactly like my husband's sister, Micah."

River smiled politely, finding it hard to imagine a grown woman with that much spirit.

It felt good to be able to stand with the female rulers of her neighboring kingdoms and speak like friends. They were fortunate this new generation of rulers were aligning so successfully, going against the pattern set by their ancestors. But there was an unlikeliness about this that nagged at River. Why were all the kingdoms finding peace at almost exactly the same time, when they'd had generations of war and turmoil? It was like there was a greater force at play. Something they hadn't yet discovered. Perhaps if they all got together one day, they could uncover the mysterious reason why peace was spreading across the land like a wonderful plague. A plague that for some reason hadn't yet reached the remaining kingdom of Feldspar.

"That must be Aarow," whispered Tate, pointing to the groom. "I wonder where Princess Rani is?"

They looked around, but there was no sign of the bride just yet.

River and Tate had met Princess Rani briefly at the palace, but Aarow had been busy in the Colony and their paths hadn't been able to cross.

"Told you he was handsome," Jasmine whispered in River's ear, making her giggle.

It was true. This man with his sleek black hair and copper-colored skin exuded strength. He wasn't layered with muscles like the Guardians, but his lean body had obvious power with his strong forearms protruding from the loose fitting shirt he wore.

Tate nudged River playfully, laughing at the look on her face.

"Not a patch on my handsome King," she said, meaning it. She hadn't just fallen in love with Tate's face, she'd fallen for his heart.

Tate grinned, clearly approving of her answer.

A series of bells tinkled and as the assembly of guests parted to form an aisle, River saw Princess Rani on the arm of her father, the Emperor.

She was tiny in stature, quite the opposite to River, almost lost in the large volume of the crimson fabric of her expertly cut dress that trailed behind her as she walked, making patterns in the red sand. Her black hair had been scooped up and pinned on top of her head, revealing a slender neck underneath her delicate veil.

She looked like a young girl, too young to get married, even though she was older than River. Surely growing up in the sun would have the opposite effect on her skin of spun gold? Although, maybe the Princess hadn't ventured outside all that much. River knew very little about her life, hoping to get to know her better after these formalities were over.

When Princess Rani's eyes locked on Aarow's, something passed between them that was almost visible in the heat of the air. It was like they were alone on this dune and all the people who'd come to watch them exchange their vows simply didn't exist.

But then the Princess returned her gaze to the people as she passed them and she smiled so warmly that River was certain that not only did she know they existed, but she cared very deeply about each and every one of them. These were her people and after her marriage to the Colonel's son, the Princess was to become the Empress.

This had never happened in The Bay of Laurel before. The crown was only ever passed over after the death of the King or

Queen. River looked at the Emperor now and wondered what it was that'd made him agree to hand his crown to his daughter so long before his death. But it wasn't really like he was the true ruler anyway. In what she'd observed in this kingdom, the Colonel was the one who made all the decisions. It was a most unusual relationship.

The Colonel was standing beside his son now, ready to conduct the marriage. He stood with a straight proud spine, his smile passing between both his son and the bride. This day was important to so many people, not just the two who were being married today.

The proud way the Colonel looked at Aarow reminded River of how Ariel looked at Tate. As soon as this wedding was over, she'd decided to tell Tate the truth about his parentage. They'd have plenty of time to talk on the journey home. He was a father now and had been King long enough to accept he had no choice but to continue on in his position. It would be too complicated to step down. She just hoped he forgave her for taking so long to tell him.

Tate looked at her now and gave her that dark-eyed smile of his, punching guilt into her stomach. Was he better off not knowing? Was telling him simply passing her own burden to him? Like Ariel had done to her. Because she really wished she didn't know, even if she could understand why Ariel had needed to unburden herself.

She sighed, not wanting to have this debate in her mind again. She'd tell him after the wedding and that was that. It was decided.

Her thoughts were dragged back to the desert as Princess Rani took Aarow's hands and promised to love him until the last grain of sand was blown from the desert.

And despite the red sand of the desert not running through River's veins, she knew without question that she felt the same way about Tate. A man who she was forced to marry, and a man who she'd now have to be forced to ever leave his side.

The ceremony came to a close, and Aarow placed a kiss upon his bride's lips. Then much to the surprise of the crowd, an extremely large man, in both height and width, placed an animal hide on the sand dangerously close to the edge of the dune.

"What's he up to?" River asked Tate, who shrugged in response as he tilted his head.

Rani and Aarow grinned at each other, and began running to the hide, although Rani tripped in the length of her dress and Aarow had to catch her before she tumbled to the sand and carry her the rest of the way. They sat down and Aarow tucked Rani safely between his legs.

"Long live the Empress!" cried Aarow.

"Long live the Colonel!" she replied.

"They're not going to..." Before River could finish her question, she saw Aarow push off the edge of the dune and disappear from sight, taking his bride with him.

The crowd surged forward to the edge of the dune to see where they'd gone.

"I specifically asked them not to do this," said Aarow's father, shaking his head. "Toran, I hold you responsible!"

"It was Jinn's idea!" said the large man as he attempted to hide behind his much smaller friend, who punched him on the arm and howled laughing.

River stepped as close to the edge of the dune as she dared and saw the bride and groom disappearing rapidly down the sand, their cries of joy echoing back up to their guests.

"What a spectacular way to begin married life," said River. "We should try that later, Tate!"

"Is she serious?" asked King Ari, overhearing.

"One of the perils of marrying a Guardian," laughed Tate. "She's deadly serious."

"Lily!" cried Queen Rose from behind them. "Lily! Where are you?"

Prince Jeremiah broke from the crowd to run to his wife's side.

"Where is she?" asked Rose. "Has anybody seen my daughter?"

"Lily!" Jeremiah called. "Lily!"

River's eyes scanned the crowd. Surely Lily couldn't be far away. She was probably seeing what happened if she tipped a glass of water into the sand or admiring the fabric of the tablecloths.

"Where's my daughter?" Rose's voice had an edge of panic now and soon the entire crowd was searching for the girl with the hair of fire, who should have stood out amongst them, but was nowhere to be found.

River and Tate joined in the search, unable to understand how a small girl could go missing when there were so many people here to look out for her.

"Lily!" River cried, her heart twisting and breaking when still the girl didn't appear. They didn't have long to find her. If she'd wandered off into the heat of the desert, she'd perish in no time.

"But we whispered for her safety," River heard Rose say to Jeremiah, her knees buckling as he put a steadying arm around her.

"We're searching the palace," said the Colonel, rushing to their side. "All our best men are looking for her."

"I hope Jacob's okay," River said to Tate, sudden concern for her own son washing over her. She'd like nothing better right now than to hold her child in her arms and know he was safe.

Tate grimaced. "He's fine. You know that."

"Do you think somebody took Lily?" she asked, keeping her voice low.

"How could they have?" He swept his arms across the crowd. "She has to be here somewhere."

The Colonel was gathering people now and dividing them into groups, each assigned to search in a different direction.

"I'm going to help," said Tate. "You head back to the palace with Jasmine."

She shook her head. "I'm going to help, too. Just one of the perils of marrying a Guardian..."

He didn't seem amused at what he thought was her attempt at a joke. But yet again, she was deadly serious. There was no way she could stand by and wait while that beautiful child was somewhere out there in trouble. She'd spent her whole life training for situations like this.

Tate nodded, knowing her well enough to know when it was useless to enter into a debate.

"Which team do you want us on?" Tate asked the Colonel.

The Colonel raised his eyebrows momentarily, then deciding this was too important to argue over, he assigned them the team led by the large man, Toran.

"And us," said Ari, standing behind them with Jasmine's hand in his. "You have our support, too."

"We'll find her," said Tate, directing his words to Prince Jeremiah.

It was then that River noticed the fire burning behind Prince Jeremiah's eyes. This man had a strength and determination like River had never seen before. If anyone was going to get their beloved daughter back, it was going to be him. Queen Rose had composed herself, too. And if the stories were true of how they'd escaped the misery of their former lives under the brutal control of Rose's father, then this wasn't a couple to be underestimated.

It seemed that River's earlier thought was about to either be torn to shreds or proved correct. Were they unstoppable when they worked together? Could they find a Princess when she seemed to have turned to sand and blown away in the hot desert wind?

ARIEL

THE EVERNOW

*A*riel cradled Jacob in her arms, watching him sleep. Babies knew how to sleep in a peaceful way that was unattainable to any grown human. Was that because they lacked the burden of troubles weighing them down? Or because their tiny bodies were exhausted from all the growing they were doing?

She ran the tip of her index finger down the length of his tiny nose, reveling in the delicious innocence of him. His soul was good, filled with the same light and goodness as his father's. This small sweet baby was going to be King one day and he was going to be the greatest King the world had ever seen.

And she was his grandmother.

Her heart swelled with love and pride. The moments since Jacob's birth had been some of the happiest of her life, almost equal to the moments she'd spent with Tate when he was first born, back in the time when she'd called him Edison.

River and Tate were wonderful parents. She could see the pain that leaving Jacob behind while they traveled to the desert had caused them. But the desert was no place for a baby. He was safer here and River's parents were doing an exceptional job taking care of him. If they were perplexed by River's request to give Ariel time with Jacob, they didn't show it. Perhaps they suspected the truth. Or perhaps they were just grateful for Jacob to be loved by as many people as possible.

Jacob screwed up his tiny face and Ariel rocked him, humming a soothing tune until his features smoothed out once more and he drifted back into his dreams. It was strange to have a Jacob back in her life. Each time she said his name out loud, she missed her husband that little bit more. But it was such a lovely gesture for River to want to call him this that she couldn't object.

She was seated in her kitchen and the air was heavy with the aroma of the tonic she and Pip had made for the Guardians that morning. Pip was a fast learner and for the first time, she felt confident that her craft would be able to be passed on and survive beyond her years. Pip had started to put on a little weight and was looking more like the healthy child who'd grown up beside Ariel's son. The Guardians were regaining their strength, too. Not one of them had fallen ill since Edison's death.

She winced at the guilt she felt at Edison's death. He may have been evil, but still, she'd raised him as her son. Had she done the right thing placing a bowl of soup in front of him that she'd known would kill him? But what was the alternative? Let him make another attempt on Tate's life and next time succeeding? She couldn't have let that happen. Jacob needed a father. And she needed her son. Even if Tate didn't know that was what he was to her.

The door to her kitchen opened and she looked up to see Tate smiling at her. Or rather, smiling at Jacob. A warm wave of joy spread through Ariel's body. He was back!

"Oh, he's sleeping," said Tate, rushing to Ariel's side and reaching out his arms.

"Never mind," said Ariel, handing the person she loved second most in the world to the person she loved most.

"He's okay," said Tate, sighing deeply as he sat down. "Thank goodness. We were so worried."

"Of course he is," said Ariel, surprised at his concern. Didn't he know Jacob had been in good hands?

Jacob stirred, opening his eyes and staring up at his father like he'd seen some kind of ghost.

Tate looked at Ariel and smiled. "He's in shock to see me."

"So am I," said Ariel, reaching across to touch Tate on the arm. "I didn't expect you back so soon."

"Something happened." Tate's face filled with anguish. "Something awful. I'll explain everything in a moment."

"Is River okay?" Ariel was aware of her heartbeat picking up pace. "Where is she?"

"She's okay," he said. "She went to her parents' hut. We weren't sure where Jacob would be, so we both went to see our mothers."

His words hung in the air like shining stars in a cloudless sky and Ariel held her breath as she waited for him to say more.

"River told me," he said, shuffling his seat closer to her.

Ariel swallowed, her words washed away by the stream of tears that were running down her cheeks.

Cradling Jacob with one arm, Tate reached out with his other and wiped her tears with the back of his fingers.

"Thank you," he said.

She shook her head, unable to decipher what he was thanking her for.

"Thank you for being so brave."

"You're not angry?" Her voice was weak like the rapid beating of her heart was taking all her energy.

"At first I was," he said. "Or perhaps angry isn't the right word. I felt... betrayed. Rejected. Like you hadn't wanted me. But then River made me see that you did it because you wanted the best for our kingdom, putting the needs of our people above what was best for you."

Ariel leaned forward and took Tate's hand in hers. "You'll never know how much I love you."

"That's where you're wrong," he said, squeezing her hand. "Because

I feel the same about my son. I wouldn't have understood before Jacob was born. But now... as hard as it would be to imagine giving Jacob up, I can see why you did it."

"Tate, I never gave you up. I want you to know that. I may have let another family raise you, but never did I give you up. You've been right here in my heart every moment of every day since I first held you in my arms."

"But how did you know?" he asked, his own eyes sparkling with tears now. "How did you know what light or shade was in our hearts?"

"That, I can't tell you," she said. "I just know these things about people. I always have."

"Do you think my mother—the Queen—knew I wasn't her son?" he asked. "Was that why she took to her bed so often?"

Ariel shook her head. "No, her sadness ran deep, long before you were born. I think it had more to do with her husband than her children. Just like you, she was forced to marry a stranger, only love didn't blossom in their union like it did in yours."

"I need to tell Pip," he said. "She has a right to know. It's her throne, not mine."

"That's not a good idea," said Ariel.

He shook his head. "River said the same thing. But this kingdom needs an honest ruler."

"Just moments ago you told me you understood my actions. That you'd do the same for your son if you had to. Well, Tate, that moment is here. If you tell Pip, then Jacob will never be King and he must. Please, Tate. These are hard decisions, but they need to be made, not for our own good, but the good of the kingdom. Pip won't want to be Queen, you know that."

"I do know that. She was always grateful to be the younger child without the responsibility of the throne. But shouldn't she know that I'm not her brother?"

"But you are her brother! Brothers aren't just made from blood. Sometimes brothers are made from love. And you love your sister. You've taken such good care of her always."

Jacob started to grizzle now, his lips puckering and his face turning red.

Tate stood up and rocked him, until his cries were stilled, kissing the top of his head making soothing noises.

"Do it for Jacob," said Ariel. "Just like I did it for you."

"Come here," said Tate, motioning with his free hand. "It's time you gave your son a hug."

Ariel rose and went to Tate, wrapping her arms around him, sandwiching Jacob gently between them.

"I'm sorry," she said again.

"There's nothing to be sorry for." He held her just that little bit more tightly.

Was he right? Because part of her was sorry for everything, but another part was sorry for nothing. She'd done what she had to do. And now it was Tate's turn to do the same.

River burst into the room and without so much as glancing at Ariel, she raced to her child's side and took him from Tate's arms. "Oh, here he is. He's okay. My sweet baby, we were worried about you."

"What's wrong with you two?" Ariel directed her question at Tate. "What happened out there?"

"The wedding. It was amazing," said Tate, running his hands through his hair. "But then… something terrible happened. Princess Lily of Forte Cadence went missing. She vanished."

"What do you mean?" asked Ariel, her heart sinking. "How can a Princess vanish?"

"We don't know," said River. "We searched everywhere for her. Thousands of people looked for her, but she was nowhere to be found."

"Oh, her poor parents." Ariel tried to process how such a thing could happen. What if it'd been Jacob? No wonder River and Tate had been so keen to see him!

"They're devastated," said Tate.

"It was hard enough losing you," said Ariel. "And you remained right in front of my eyes."

River's head snapped up at this and she put her hand on Tate's arm. "You told her?"

"I did," he said.

Ariel smiled at River. "Thank you. I'm glad I trusted in you."

"You finally have your son back," said River.

"I do." Ariel felt her eyes prick with tears again, to look at this little family unit of three that filled her heart with love.

"And we have our son back now, too," said Tate, putting an arm around his wife and running his fingers over his son's cheek.

River leaned over and kissed Tate gently on the lips, and Jacob gurgled contentedly.

"I'll give you a moment," said Ariel, standing up and walking to the door, needing a moment of her own as well. "I'll be back."

She walked from the kitchen to the tavern and into her garden, brushing the leaves of the rosemary bushes as she passed, releasing their scent into the air.

"Ariel!"

She looked up to see a familiar shape ambling his way across her garden. She blinked in the sunlight, watching the man approach, unsure if her heart could take anything more today. She'd come out here for space to clear her head, not for it to be crowded with even more surprises.

Her hands fell to her side, and she took a step toward the man.

"Jacob," she breathed, as her husband approached and stood before her, studying her face. How she must look to him after two decades of life lived without him?

"Ariel," he said again, the familiarity of his voice tearing at her from the inside.

He'd aged well. His hair had streaks of gray, and a beard covered the lower half of his face, but his eyes were still kind, surrounded by a series of fine lines that hadn't been there before. He still wore the necklace woven from hemp around his neck. This was her husband and it wasn't until right at this moment that she realized how much she'd missed him. Her heart had been so full of missing Tate she hadn't stopped to mourn him properly. But there was a time when once she'd thought this man was her whole world.

"What are you doing here?" she asked.

"I thought it was time I came home." He wrapped her in his arms and pulled her close.

Her heart may have been filled by the small family sitting inside her kitchen, but now it was overflowing, the joy spilling into every inch of her body.

"My Evernow," she said, her words muffled by his chest. "I've found you at last."

And she had. For right at this moment, everything was perfect. Her Evernow was here, and this time, she was determined not to let it go.

TATE

THE EVERNOW

Tate watched River hold their son and felt his heart melt.

"I'm so glad he's okay," he said.

"I thought you said you weren't worried!" River raised her eyebrows.

He smiled. "Of course I was worried. I just didn't want to make you worry more."

"We shouldn't have left Rose and Jeremiah like that." She held Jacob just that little bit closer to her chest.

"There was nothing more we could do." He pressed his hand to Jacob's cheek, wanting to lift him from River's arms, but knowing that wasn't possible. "We searched everywhere."

They had, too. They'd searched the desert and the Capital and every corner of the Colony. They'd searched until there was nowhere else left to look. Even Princess Rani and Aarow had joined the search, after they'd made their way back up the dune and realized something had gone horribly wrong. Their wedded bliss had quickly turned to wedded distress to think that something so awful could have happened while they'd been sliding down the sand.

"How could Lily just disappear like that?" River bent forward and kissed Jacob's forehead. "She was right there with us one moment and gone the next."

"I don't know." He didn't, not any more now than he had the other hundred times River had asked him this.

"What if it happens to Jacob?" Her voice rose to a worried pitch.

"It won't." He wished this was something he could promise. "We'll watch him every second."

"It's impossible to watch someone every second of their life," she said. "What kind of King will Jacob make if we don't give him the space to grow? Besides, we were watching Lily! She was hardly left alone and look what happened! There must've been something else we could've done."

"We did everything we could." He shook his head, the image of that sweet girl with the orange hair filling his mind. "And we've pledged our support if Rose and Jeremiah need anything else."

"The only thing they need is their daughter back." River stared at him blankly. "It's like when Daphne died. My parents have never been the same. Why do you think they dote on Jacob so much?"

"They would always have doted on him, you know that. But yes, losing a child is the worst possible thing that could happen to a person. And we may not be able to get Daphne back, but I'm still hopeful that one day Lily will be found."

"The only way she'll be found is if someone took her," said River. "And I don't know what's worse. She could be anywhere by now."

Jacob woke properly now and started to howl. It was perfect timing as Tate really didn't know how to answer River's questions that so perfectly mirrored his own.

"Let me take him." Tate held out his arms and River reluctantly passed Jacob across.

Jacob looked up at him and cried even louder, forcing Tate to hand him directly back. Babies knew their mothers, even at this age. Had he cried like this for his mother when he'd been taken from her arms? He imagined he would have. Although, his new mother, the Queen, had loved him and he'd loved her. But had it been the same? This was just one of those things he'd never know. And perhaps it didn't matter. Both he and Edison had been raised with love. And they'd both grown into the men they'd been born to be—perhaps not with their station in life, but with the qualities they possessed.

"We won't give up on Lily," he said, as River rose from her chair and jiggled Jacob, until his eyes began to close. "We'll find out what happened to her."

"How can you be so sure?" she asked.

"You've met my mother." He winked at her, although it was true. His intuition did seem more finely tuned than most people's, as if some of Ariel's talents had been passed down to him. Maybe if he listened to his instincts a little more, he could hone these skills and grow to be the kind of King his mother believed he was.

"Who's that man?" asked River, looking out the window as she rocked Jacob side-to-side.

"What man?"

Tate joined River at the window and peered out.

"The one talking to Ariel." She pointed and Tate's heart skipped a beat.

"I know him," he said. "That's the man I told you about. The one I saw in the streets who was staring at me. The one who was wearing Edison's necklace..."

"Oh, Tate..."

There was no need for River to finish her sentence. The necklace explained it all.

The man looked across at the window as if he'd felt the gaze of his son. He held up a hand to Tate, and unlike the last time he'd seen him, he broke into a smile that was filled with pride.

His father. A man who was proud of him, instead of ashamed. A man who saw the good in him, instead of his faults. A man who knew how to open up his heart to let in love, even if that meant exposing it to the possibility of pain. A man who was so different from the man who'd raised him.

Tate had the same feeling as when he'd been a boy and had slid that last piece into place in the squares in the dirt and declared his win. Everything was where it was meant to be. They hadn't been able to save Princess Lily just yet, but hopefully one day they could help put that right. She deserved her Evernow, just like he'd found his.

He had the most wonderful wife, a healthy son, a mother who'd proven she loved him more than herself, and now his father had returned. On top of this, his Guardians were healthy and his sister was growing into the woman she was meant to be.

If Edison had had his way, none of this would've happened. Tate would be dead and everyone he loved would be in danger.

He glanced at the sky, wondering if Edison was watching him now.

"Checkmate," he said, nodding his head to the clouds.

AFTER THE EVERNOW

"*Next! Step up. Next! Next! Next! Step up.*"

The children shuffled forward, their pace slow and measured, their heads kept bowed. The overalls they wore were filthy and their hair was hidden under scarves, making them look like mirror-images of each other. As each child reached the front of the line, they paused and waited for the King to make his assessment, aware he was selecting which of them would be given a new life.

It would be such a relief to be asked to step up. A joy to make his shortlist. This group had been chosen for their size and age, but only a handful would make it to the next stage. And only one would make it to freedom. But they were all grateful to have been given the chance.

For these were no ordinary children. These children were Fossickers, mining the kingdom of Feldspar for treasures to please their King. Their bodies were made of bones, born to dig and trained to work. The Fossickers' duty was to their King. There could be no greater purpose than serving him. All the generations of Fossickers before them felt the same, male and female alike.

However, they'd never been asked to step up in this way before.

There was one Fossicker waiting patiently in line who was different from the others. She wasn't different on the outside, though.

She walked in step with the rest, doing what they did, dressing as they dressed and saying what they said. She was the same malnourished height as the others, had the same skeletal build, and the same filth on her skin. Just like every one of these Fossickers, she spent her life underground, mining for shiny treasures to please her King.

In fact, so similar was this Fossicker on the outside that she'd almost forgotten she was different. But there was no question about it. For this Fossicker was destined to alter the course of the Kingdom. This Fossicker was no ordinary Fossicker at all.

"Next! Next! Next!" The King shuffled some gemstones in his hand as he shouted. This was a leader who liked to dig up treasures in his kingdom and was rarely seen not covered in gemstones, almost like his clothes were made from stars.

The Fossicker reached the front of the line, keeping her gaze low so as not to make eye contact with the King unless asked to do so.

"Step up."

Her heart swelled to have made the shortlist.

"Ne—" The King set down the gemstones he'd been holding to concentrate on the potential treasure before him. "No, wait. The last one. Step back."

She stepped back, disappointed at being returned to the pack of Fossickers, but determined not to show it.

"No, not back to the pack," the King said. "Back here."

She stood in front of her master and waited.

"Look at me," he instructed.

Trying not to focus on the King's ostentatious show of wealth, she locked eyes with him, feeling her life change with each moment that passed.

"Remove your scarf," the King instructed.

She untied her scarf and let her hair fall to her shoulders, the orange strands sparkling like sunbeams.

"Yes! This one. Send the rest away."

She steadied her breathing and waited. Others may not be able to see that she was different, but the King had.

"Send for my Queen immediately," the King said, leaning back and strumming his fingers on the arms of his throne. "Tell her I've found her a daughter."

THE END

Ready to discover the next kingdom?

Check out Book 5, The Angels of Evernow!

http://mybook.to/hcangels

THE ANGELS OF EVERNOW

BOOK 5 THE KINGDOMS OF EVERNOW

Will the Evernow be united at last

Or will the wicked queen blind them all?

Taken far from her home, Lily has been forced to mine for treasures alongside an army of starving children. Until the Queen decides she'd like the King to present her with the greatest treasure of all—a daughter.

Lily is brought to the Queen's bejewelled palace in the middle of the angry sea, only to discover the Queen is as mad as she is selfish. She demands Lily tell her bedtime stories, polish her crystals, and dive into the freezing ocean to search for the magic treasure she lost when she threw it from her tower in a fit of rage.

As Lily fights the madness that surrounds her, she attempts to unlock the power of the crystals to call on the four Angels she dreams of each night. Unless this is a sign she's going mad herself…

Raphael has been having dreams of his own. Blessed with inexplicable visions of the future, he sees Lily trapped in a faraway kingdom, feeling her cries for help deep in his heart. Could Lily be the missing piece of his life that nothing else has been able to fill?

With only one way to find out, Raphael gathers an ambassador from each of the Kingdoms of Evernow and together they set out to defeat the Queen, release the children from her greedy rule, and bring Lily home. But will the Evernow be united in peace at last, or will the mad Queen use her power of sight to capture them all?

With a story that will light your soul, this stunning conclusion of the spellbinding *The Kingdoms of Evernow* series is a must-read by award-winning author, Heidi Catherine.

Grab your copy now!

http://mybook.to/hcangels

ALSO BY HEIDI CATHERINE

The Kingdoms of Evernow
Five kingdoms. Five senses.
One secret that will change them all.
The Kingdoms of Evernow (Prequel)
The Whisperers of Evernow
The Alchemists of Evernow
The Empress of Evernow
The Guardians of Evernow
The Angels of Evernow

The Soulweaver series
Two girls. Two lives. One soul.
The Soulweaver
The Truthseeker
The Shadowmaker

The Sovereign Code
Humans saved bees from extinction...
and created the deadliest threat we've seen yet
Harvest Day
Hive Mind
Queen Hunt
Venom Rising
Sting Wars

Elemental Games

Elemental powers. Deadly games. No escape.

Elemental Games

Elemental Uprising

Elemental Wars

Elemental Solution

The Thaw Chronicles

Four tests. Seven days. Nine teens.

Only the chosen shall breed.

Burning (Prequel)

Rising

Breaking

Falling

Reckoning

Extant

Exist

Exile

Expose

Tournaments of Thaw

Conquer the Thaw

The Oasis Trials

The Oasis Deception

The Last Oasis

WANT TO STAY IN TOUCH?

Heidi loves to connect with readers, so please say hello on social media, leave a review on Amazon or Goodreads, or visit her at www. heidicatherine.com

facebook.com/HeidiCatherineAuthor
instagram.com/HeidiCatherine
tiktok.com/@heidicatherineauthor
amazon.com/author/heidicatherine

ABOUT THE AUTHOR

Heidi writes fantasy and dystopian novels, which gives her a chance to escape into worlds vastly different to her own life in the burbs. While she quite enjoys killing her characters (especially the awful ones), she promises she's far better behaved in real life. Other than writing and reading, Heidi's current obsessions include watching far too much reality TV with the excuse that it's research for her books.